GEORGE MACKAY BROWN is remembered for his poetry, novels, plays and short stories. Much of his fiction and verse was based on his life in Orkney, especially his childhood. He was born in Stromness, Orkney, in 1921. He was at Newbattle Abbey College when Edwin Muir was Warden. He read English at Edinburgh University and did postgraduate work on Gerard Manley Hopkins.

He was awarded an Arts Council grant for poetry in 1965, The Society of Authors' Travel Award in 1968, The Scottish Arts Council Literature Prize in 1969 for *A Time to Keep*, and the Katherine Mansfield Menton Short Story Prize in 1971. He was awarded the OBE in January 1974.

He received honorary degrees from the Open University (MA), Dundee University (LLD), Glasgow University (DLitt) and he was a fellow of the Royal Society of Literature. In 1987 his novel *The Golden Bird* won the James Tait Black prize. George Mackay Brown died in 1996.

Under Brinkie's Brae

George Mackay Brown

Steve Savage
LONDON AND EDINBURGH

Steve Savage Publishers Ltd
The Old Truman Brewery
91 Brick Lane
LONDON
E1 6QL

www.savagepublishers.com

Published in Great Britain by Steve Savage Publishers Ltd 2003

First published in hardback by Gordon Wright Publishing Ltd 1979
Copyright © George Mackay Brown 1979

ISBN 1-904246-07-9

British Library Cataloguing in Publication Data
A catalogue entry for this book is available from the British Library

Cover photographs: Gordon Wright

Typeset by Steve Savage Publishers Ltd
Printed and bound by The Cromwell Press Ltd

Contents

Introduction

No one who grows up in Orkney can get away from childhood and memories of childhood.

Edwin Muir's childhood in Wyre was the fountainhead of all his poetry. His literary criticism was the work of a citizen of the world.

Reading over these *Orcadian* articles, the pleasant by-product of three years at the writing of verse and tales, I was disconcerted to see how often the words 'enchanted', 'marvellous', 'magical', appear. Words like those should exist only in the intensity of poetry; not in small scraps of journalism.

I might be content to call the best of these little essays 'prose-poems', and leave the matter there. The hybrid does not flourish well in English, but I have a weakness for overlaying plain prose with a wash of lyricism.

Prose-poems lie bedded like ore in the work of another Orkney writer, Eric Linklater. Think of the opening of *The Man on My Back*, and from the same book the description of an Orkney regatta, or the harvest ritual. In modern poetry such pure lyricism is hard to find.

Perhaps in the cold grey air of the north the hybrid is most at home.

*

I will not go into the question of whether poetry can only exist in verse-forms, or whether it can live, an honoured guest, in the austere House of Prose. Hundreds of passages of the Authorised Version of The Bible would seem to prove that it can. Also, I'm sure, there might be one line of 'poetry' in every 10,000 lines of published verse.

I claim for only a few of these jottings the grandiose title of prose-poems; and that for only the reminiscences of childhood.

*

Those of us who were born and grew up under Brinkie's Brae, in the nineteen-twenties and thirties, lived in a time that was bleak politically and economically. But the poverty of country people and island people is altogether different from urban poverty. Poor, we lived among the immense inexhaustible treasures of sea and earth and sky. In childhood, it was those enduring things that meant everything to us. Little princes, we lived between the hard acres and the perilous sea.

So, I justify to myself the too frequent use here of 'enchanted' and 'marvellous'. They are the crude shorthand for states of mind that only such pure poets as Vaughan, Dylan Thomas, Blake, Muir, Traherne and Wordsworth could celebrate.

George Mackay Brown

A Tribute to the Men of Kirkwall

5.2.1976

Through the kitchen window, where I write most mornings after breakfast, a sky of dove-grey clouds, silver-edged, and blue chasms.

January is going out—this is the last day of the month—in a cold serene beauty; not at all in keeping with her moods earlier on. On the whole January 1976 has been a trull, a termagant, a virago. And we have come not to expect this—the three previous Januaries were mild and sweet. But they—we ought to have known this—were exceptions. Traditionally, January is perhaps the fiercest month of the year. February comes in tomorrow; we will welcome her with gratitude— the month that dies younger than the others and comes with shy offerings of snowdrops and crocuses, and with promises of springtime.

How sentimental can you get? February can be a ranter and a raver too, flaunting blizzard and gale... Yes, but she screws the wick of the sun that much higher. One late afternoon, you discover to your joy that you are having tea by daylight.

* * *

I usually think, some time during the course of January the first, about the strength and endurance of the men of Kirkwall. One assumes that, like the men of Stromness and every other town in Scotland, they have brought in the New Year with revelry, and carried on with the first-footing till four or five or six in the morning.

For all the other townsmen of Scotland, the rest of the day is spent in sleep and heavy eating and a kind of muted visiting and welcoming. Not for the men of Kirkwall. Under the Market Cross 'the ba'' is thrown up and Uppies and Doonies, Earl's men and Bishop's men, meet in a furious onset. Compared with it, rugby is as correct and mannered as croquet. I have, only once, seen the pall of steam hanging over the motionless scrum at the top of Tankerness Lane. How, the men of the other towns must ask themselves, can the Kirkwallians do it, on the day after Hogmanay? What fire is in them—what iron—compared to other men? If it was all over in an hour, the heroism would still be there—but I read that the 1976 Ba' went on for eight punishing hours!... Supposing the ba' goes 'doon', there is an extra element of bravado, for the sweating steaming weary (probably 'hungover') players plunge into the winter waters of the harbour.

As a Stromnessian, born under Brinkie's Brae, I forget ancient rivalry for two days a year and waft a tribute over the Orphir Hills to those brave warriors.

Clapshot

12.2.1976

It seems that the most famous of Orkney foods is clapshot. The man who talks about food prices on the radio one morning each week[1] was talking the other day—and I in bed half-asleep—about potatoes, and the very high price of them nowadays. Then he said something like—'Why don't you try that splendid Orcadian recipe, clapshot; potatoes and turnips mashed together?'... That woke me up completely. A good way to start a day.

The BBC food-adviser was right—clapshot is one of the best things to come out of Orkney, together with Highland Park and Orkney fudge and Atlantic crabs. I have it at least once a week, sometimes more. It goes with nearly everything—sausages, corned beef, bacon, mealie puddings.

The other day, by way of a treat, I bought a piece of steak for grilling. Would clapshot go with grilled steak? No harm in trying. I peeled carefully the precious 'golden wonders'—and thought, what a shame, in a way, 'golden wonders' being so delicious boiled in their thick dark jackets. And while the tatties and neeps were ramping away on

1 John Lease

10

top of the electric grill, it came into my mind that somewhere, a while back, I had read a recipe for clapshot that advised an onion to be added. (It may be in one of the books of F. Marian McNeill, the Orkney-born connoisseur of food and ancient Scottish lore.)

In no time at all I had an onion stripped and chopped and delivered (my eyes weeping) among the neeps and tatties in the rampaging pot... Fifteen minutes later the probing fork told me that all was ready. Decant the water into the sink, set the pot on the kitchen floor on top of last week's *Radio Times*, add a golden chunk of butter and a dash of milk, then salt and plenty of pepper, and begin to mash...

Everything about clapshot is good, including the smell and the colour. I think this particular clapshot, with the onion in it, was about the best I've ever made. And it blended magnificently on the palate with the grilled steak. And it made a glow in the wintry stomach.

Everything good about clapshot? I have a certain reservation about the name. It sounds more like some kind of missile used in the Thirty Years' War than the name of a toothsome dish. And yet I've no doubt the roots of the word are ancient, worthy and venerable. As soon as I've finished writing this I must dip into *The Orkney Norn*.

Pentland Firth Crossing

19.2.1976

The wind blew from the westward, the windows rattled on the Monday and Tuesday. Some time on Monday the weatherman on the wireless mentioned an 'imminent gale' in the Hebrides sea-area, rising to 90mph. And in the evening the isobars on the weather chart were thickly compressed, a rapid west-to-east stream.

I was more than usually concerned because I was going south on the *St Ola* on Wednesday morning. Absolute necessities, therefore: buy sea-sickness tablets, and eat a good breakfast before sailing.

How capricious our weather is! I woke early on Wednesday morning. Outside, hardly a breath stirred in the twilight of 7am. Still, though I wasn't hungry, I had a good breakfast of an orange, poached egg, sausages, toast, marmalade, coffee. And didn't forget to swallow, with the dregs of the coffee, the 'Avomine' tablet.

Only a few passengers lingered in the huge spaces of the new boat as she drifted through the harbour. She didn't turn into Hoy Sound, and we could see why—the Kame of Hoy was indistinct with the fury of the recent storm—the lingering roar and spindrift of sea against crag.

All through Scapa Flow the sea was as calm as a millpond, almost. The 'oil island', Flotta, brought a few passengers to the port side as it hove in sight. But there's nothing to be seen: a barren moor. The great on-goings are at the other, hidden end of the island.

'After Cantick,' I said, 'we'll come into rough seas'... And with Hoy behind us the ship indeed took a new rhythm. Through the wide windows the horizon rose and fell, the ship trembled and plunged, and threw stinging arcs of spindrift from her bows... One or two of the passengers began, all at once, to look preoccupied—occasionally one would slip away for ten minutes or so. But the Pentland Firth that day wasn't unpleasant at all—enjoyable, even, if you were fortified with breakfast and a tablet.

Soon we were in calmer water again. Scrabster was white with a new snowfall. For some reason we couldn't get down the gangplank—we had to disembark via the ramp, after all the cars and carriers and huge transport vehicles had preceded us. Then we discovered, with a throb of panic, that the bus had gone! We might have to wait till the afternoon train. But no, the bus returned; the few passengers climbed aboard; and presently I found myself at the railway office in Thurso asking for a return ticket to Pitlochry.

Northwards by Train

26.2.1976

It last happened so long ago that I had almost forgotten—I mean the train journey from Edinburgh to Thurso. I had done it often as a student; occasionally, in summer, by bus.

Ten past eleven at night the train leaves from Waverley. One hopes for an empty compartment where one can drowse in peace—even stretch oneself the full width of the train. But the train was fairly full—I found myself in a compartment with an elderly Edinburgh couple. And the compartment was hot! First I took off my duffle, and an hour later my jacket, but I was still clung about by a light sweat. I am one of those people who are all for peace at any price, so I didn't like to ask for the window to be opened, especially when the lady said she was feeling the cold. Later I was glad of that closed window.

Not being used to travel, I am one of those 'anxious' travellers. A cluster of lights—a town—swarmed out of the darkness. I asked my fellow-travellers the name of the place, and the man said, 'Linlithgow.' I felt a stab of panic; surely Linlithgow was south of Edinburgh! Were we perhaps headed for Newcastle and London?... But when the next town threw its web of light about us, and he said, 'Grangemouth,' I felt more reassured.

First, after a few hours in a train, a dull ache begins to locate itself in the lower back. Outside, there is nothing but night, with a few occasional lights here and there. The rhythm of the engine puts a vague hypnosis on you. You find yourself nodding into a light drowse, full of queer dreams and images, and then emerging into wakefulness with a jolt—time after time.

At Perth there was a long wait—it seemed, my friend in the compartment said, for Glasgow northbound travellers to join our train. In those intervals, when absolutely nothing happens, it is best not to fret or feel indignant. Make the mind a blank. Consider how very fortunate you are in comparison to the Russian poet Mandelstam I have just been reading about, sent east on an endless train journey into exile for writing a few words that Stalin did not like.

The early morning passed in shallow drowses and sudden awakenings, during which you are part of the enormous urgent rhythm of the train... Somewhere about 5am I had to change trains at Inverness, and there of course the old 'travel anxiety' reasserted itself. Even though, at last. I got ensconced in the Thurso section of the new train, I wasn't entirely certain that I wouldn't find myself, at daybreak, going towards Oban or Mallaig. In fact, morning came slowly and delicately, a seepage of light in the east, through low-lying swathes of fog. We hurtled north from station to station.

The sky assumed the faintest of tints—pink, eggshell blue, primrose. In the growing light I saw that the Highlands had been sheathed overnight in a huge armour of frost. Every blade of grass was salted, and it was difficult to know sometimes, in the universal greyness, what was countryside and what was sea.

A Flu-infested City

4.3.1976

In Edinburgh everybody I met was coughing his or her head off. They had either had the flu, or were in the throes of it, or were on the verge of a relapse. The kind house where I stayed was suddenly stricken for the second time.

I had left behind an Orkney that had borne the winter wonderfully well. The usual twinge of rheumatism, of course, and bits of snivels: but who in Orkney has ever escaped them?

I wandered around in flu-infested Edinburgh and nothing afflicted me worse than a mild hangover one morning. How wonderful to meet, unexpectedly, old friends! That's really the best part of a holiday for me. In one hotel I was sipping a pint of beer when a voice hailed me from the corner—no other than a Stromness man, Mr John Gibson, retired teacher. And we spoke for half an hour or so, with kindling enthusiasm, about such old-time characters as James Leask (Puffer) and many another.

Another afternoon I had just emerged from Marks & Spencer's in Princes Street, and was making for a bus, when a voice hailed me from the pavement. It was one of the best friends from my student days, John Durkin—a deep thinker and a mighty laugher. We rifled for hours the treasures of a common memory.

On the night of my departure I had supper with Dr Mary Peace and her husband, Dr More, and Orkney and Edinburgh mingled streams again. (She owns that beautiful house at the foot of Hellihole, which still bears the sign 'The Arctic Whaler' on the outhouse.) They finished their kindness by driving me to the train.

The thought struck me, somewhere in the vastness of the Highlands, as the train thundered North, that maybe I was taking the Edinburgh flu to Orkney. They say there are such people. Unscathed themselves, they bear the nasty germ among virgin populaces; and then the decimation begins.

The crew of the *Ola* weren't grey-faced and weak and shaken with coughs. Nor were the few lingerers at the Pier Head that mild Friday afternoon after I disembarked. Nor were the shopgirls when I bought a few errands—bread and bacon and cheese—to tide me over till the morrow.

I opened the door to find a vast scattering of mail in the lobby, a matter for delight and alarm. (But more of that again.)

Stromness was enjoying very good health.

Three mornings later I was shopping along the street when a friend told me that folk were suddenly going over like ninepins! I comforted myself that the incubation must have started long before I left Waverley Station. I depressed myself by thinking that I might be the next of the ninepins.

Letters

11.3.1976

I must have said somewhere before that two of the highlights of each day are when the postman delivers the mail, round about 10am, and 3pm. These winter mornings I usually lie late abed—nothing gets me up so fast as the rattle of the letterbox and the soft swish of falling letters on the lobby floor. Sometimes of course it turns out to be only the Hydro-Electric bill, or a lavish advertisement for one of those lavish Time-Life books. Sometimes a little cheque, or a commission, comes singing out of the ripped envelope. But best of all is to hear from old friends.

Again in the afternoon, I rarely go out shopping before the postman calls. How disappointing it is, when from the window you see him rounding the corner at the South End, having for once given Mayburn Court a miss!

The debit side of this account is, of course, that all those letters have to be answered. At 6½p and 8½p a time, it mounts up: but still, what is eightpence-ha'penny to be in touch with a friend?

I usually keep all my mail for answering at the weekend. A busman's holiday, in a way, after bashing away with the pen from Monday to Friday. But letter-writing is a different kind of writing, relaxed and easy as conversation. You don't have to worry about structure and style; you don't have to plan to please an unseen anonymous audience. When I got home from Edinburgh two weeks ago, and inserted the key and flung open the door, it was as if a snowdrift was lying there— a strewment and scattering and profusion of mail—letters of all shapes and sizes, familiar scripts, half-forgotten scripts, utterly strange scripts... What a pleasant way to arrive home!

The next hour or so was pure joy, going through letter after letter. Then when the last one is folded again into its envelope, comes the sobering thought that all twenty of them must be answered. (And some of them required difficult and intricate composition.)

It was more than one Saturday morning's work. It was more than five or six mornings' work. I am still hacking away, a bit wearily, on the backlog. And even as you moisten the gum and stick down another flap, the letterbox rattles and a new shower whispers on to the floor of the lobby.

A Painter and a Poet

18.3.1976

We watched a film on TV the other night about the painter Van Gogh, called *Lust for Life*. With a painter like Van Gogh especially it HAD to be in colour—black-and-white would have drained half the excitement from those radiant sunflowers and cornfields. It seemed to me to be extraordinarily well done: even the American accents of Kirk Douglas (Van Gogh) and Anthony Quinn (Gauguin) didn't sound too phoney. It was remarkable how they achieved the facial resemblances too.

* * *

The poet who seems to me to be closest in spirit to Van Gogh is Gerard Manley Hopkins. They have the same 'lust for life', an endless thirst for the sensuous beauty swarming everywhere in nature, an urge to discover and praise the Creator of it all, an impatience with the old stale ways of painting and writing. There are one or two statistical resemblances—the Dutchman and the Englishman lived almost contemporaneously; they died before they were middle-aged, even, and each in a strange country. Each in his own way was a preaching man—Van Gogh to begin with was an evangelical pastor, and Hopkins was the other extreme, a Jesuit priest and teacher. Both of them endured periods of blacker depression than most of us can imagine—the whirl of rooks over the ripe cornfields, the dark sonnets ('I wake and feel the fell of dark, not day... ').

When I was in Edinburgh I was fortunate enough to be able to devote two years' study to the poet Hopkins; and it used to strike me then how close in spirit and outlook and technique these two artists were. They brought a startling new vision into the world; and each in his own way suffered for the presumption or the sheer daring of the attempt.

How tired Hopkins must have been of the smooth perfect versification of Tennyson! The language of poets was tired and over-pretty. Hopkins deliberately broke it up, and remoulded it so that it resembled man's first language, charged with energy and purity. A tremendous primal labour, like a blacksmith at forge and anvil, with the elements of fire and water and the magic of changing metal:

> 'Thou at the random grim forge, powerful amid peers
> Didst fettle for the great grey dray-horse his bright
> and battering sandal.'

These are the last magnificent lines of his elegiac sonnet for the farrier Felix Randal.

Polite society rejects such revolutionaries. Hopkins published only one major poem in his lifetime, 'The Wreck of the Deutschland'. The rest were kept in a locked drawer till thirty years after his death... And in the film *Lust for Life* Van Gogh sold only one of his masterpieces.

I am sorry to have missed the Hopkins Exhibition that was in Aberdeen last autumn; some anonymous person kindly sent me a poster and a catalogue which I treasure.

Easterlies

25.3.1976

Wearing on for the equinox, it is so cold that you have to huddle over the electric fire. All month, with short interludes of peace, Orkney has been scourged by this south-east gale. When the wind sits in the east in March it is loth to shift, the old folk used to say.

It is the very worst wind for Stromness. It comes raging up the seaward closes; to walk 'north' along the street for messages becomes a hilarious adventure. Tall houses shelter you, you trip along douce and canny until the gale takes you by cuff and sleeve at the next close-mouth and fairly hurls you across the street. Very erratic its behaviour can be, perhaps only to be explained by some meteorologist or mathematician. For why, I would like to know, does the easterly give you a helping hand—rough and over-boisterous to be sure—at some close-heads, propelling you on the way you want to go? But at the very next opening it behaves like a ruffian, stopping the breath in your throat, forcing you back by the shoulders, cracking scarf and trouser-end like whips.

Even inside a Stromness house, in such weather, you have to take steps to avoid the hundred grey daggers of draught that stab and slice everywhere. When all the doors and windows are shut, that merciless wind still sifts and sieves through every crack. Several nights last week I had to sit reading with my jacket on, a thing that never happened before. (But it may be only old age—the marrow shrinking, the blood coursing more slowly...)

Equinoctial gales—but it's still two days to the equinox as I write this, and that young outlaw of a wind has gone berserking over Orkney for weeks. Surely the equinox can have nothing worse in store for us (and half the populace creeping around, post-flu spectres). No—after the equinox spring has really returned to us, and soon she will drift every ditch under with daffodils. (Or so we hope, with not much conviction.)

Stromnessians don't mind westerly gales. That kind old mothering hill guards us from the worst the west can do. We only know that spectacular things are happening by the stampede of clouds in the upper air, and the broken thunder of sea from Breckness and Yesnaby.

But easterlies—there's nothing we can do about them, except be patient and take the scourging, and think about April. That cruel wind is not utterly evil: when the tide is nearing its height I can see from my seaward facing window the grey waves charging against the piers below, and suddenly becoming sheets of torn lace, thousands of flung drops of bitter thrilling salt: time after time, until the waters withdraw again. I could watch it for hours, except that the window is a cold post to stand at for long.

Money Language

1.4.1976

'One pence'... I must have heard that a hundred times since decimal money came in. It should, of course, be 'one penny'—or simply 'a penny', as we said in the old days. Even on TV the other night a man who should have known better said 'one pence'... People say, too, 'a half-pence'. Strange the way we use language in a new situation.

For one thing, we alter the stress. 'Six PENCE,' we say awkwardly, instead of the old cheery SIXpence, running both words together. If you were talking to a pal, it wasn't sixpence, it was 'a tanner'. A lot of music has gone out of money-language. Shilling, florin, half-crown have vanished; and guinea too, which was always a posher way of dealing with sizeable sums of money, as between gentlemen. Editors used to pay writers in guineas rather than pounds; wherefore writers nowadays feel slightly cheated.

'Bob' was the colloquial word for shilling. Two-and-sixpence was referred to often as a 'half-dollar' by the smart boys who knew what was what. (Since then the actual dollar has become more majestic, measured against our tottering scale of values.)

Of course the £p scale is much easier and handier compared with the £sd; but the fact that it took twelve pennies to make a shilling, but twenty shillings to make a pound, held an element of mystery and fascination.

We're having none of that nonsense nowadays—metrication and decimalisation is all—so we close down forever mines of history and lore and ancient venerable values.

I like to think that in the Stromness of old, in the merchants' stores and in the taverns, there would be heard a rich monetary European music, as the firkins of rum changed hands, chickens and fresh cheese and fragrant new bread. 'Marks', 'kroner', 'doubloons', 'escudos', 'francs', 'cents'—the men who built Stromness would have been as familiar with those words as with 'shillings' and 'guineas'. And no doubt, being the men they were, they would have been able to do the work of value-translation swiftly and accurately and with well disguised excitement; allowing the scales always to tilt slightly in their favour...

These days have vanished forever. A penny was a treasure on a Saturday morning when I was a boy; now you look at the inflation-shrunken thing—which hasn't even got a right name, 'one pence'—and you wonder how soon it will vanish into nothingness, like the smile on the face of the Cheshire cat.

Old Yew

8.4.1976

One afternoon about six weeks ago, five of us had lunch in a small country inn in the heart of Perthshire. Then we went for a long circuitous drive through some of the most spectacular scenery in Scotland. Last time we had come that way, in late autumn, much of the landscape had been hidden by the year's last foliage—yellow and orange leaves drifted across the windscreen and hit the road lightly but with audible tinkles.

But now through bare winter branches we had an uninterrupted view of those magnificent mountains. Wherever we went—however the road turned and twisted—we were surrounded by a circle of mighty snowcapped presences. It was as different as could be from the small green hills of Orkney.

Once we stopped beside a country church. We wandered, in cold sunlight, through the cemetery with Highland names carved on the stones. And there, massive and black beside the church, gloomed a yew tree. I remembered Tennyson's lines that I first read thirty years ago, so lovely in spite of the fact that then I had never seen a yew tree:

> Old yew, that graspest at the stones
> That name the under-lying dead,
> Thy fibres net the dreamless head,
> Thy roots are wrapped about the bones...

These living symbols of mortality are of course in many churchyards in England and southern Scotland; they are so old, and the generations carved on the stones are mere stirrings of the dust in comparison.

Then we read a notice in a glass frame fixed to a gate; the words were faded by ancient streaks of rain. But it proclaimed that this particular yew tree was three thousand years old; it was, in fact, the oldest yew in Europe! We looked at it for a long time—all black gnarls and knots and cleavages—and knew the briefness of man's seventy years...

But there was a legend attached to this village even more remarkable than the actuality of the yew tree. It said that Pontius Pilate had been born there. (His father must have been a Roman soldier on the far frontier of the Empire.)

And that, if it is true, was two thousand years ago. The conclusion came inevitably: this tree was already multi-rooted, earth-sunken, a huge twist of black flame against the sky, when Pontius Pilate was a boy. It is almost certain that he climbed among its branches when he was a boy (assuming of course that the legend is true). Did he then have intimations of another tree, and a fiercer sun, and a different death?

Three Channels

15.4.1976

All of a sudden, a goodly number of us Orcadians have taken another step into the twentieth century and the marvels thereof.

Because a tall metal structure has been erected on one of our hills, we have three sources of entertainment to draw on instead of only one. I'm referring of course to old one-eye in the corner of the living room, the TV set, and how he can now give us a choice of BBC1, BBC2 or ITV.

All I had to do, once that mysterious potent mast on Keelylang was working, was to buy an aerial for £5 or so. Two kind friends arrived one afternoon with a stepladder, and they fixed the aerial in the attic. Then the threefold magic began. (There were certain teething troubles later, I admit, but they are all sorted out now; or at least I hope so.)

For years I and hundreds like me had been shackled to BBC1. We had to take the fare offered—there were no alternatives—everybody must have found it a mingling of good and indifferent. Many a day I scanned the *Radio Times* and saw things on BBC2 that made the mouth water—*Horizon*, *The Book Programme*, the Sunday evening nature programme, the 'Close Down' poem, etc.

Now they're all available—plus the amazing things on offer from Grampian. You never realise, till you see those gooey luscious advertisements, every half-hour or so, what a wonderful consumer universe we live in! We're not half thankful enough. How would we ever know the inner truth about that chocolate, beer, mashed potato, dog-food, cat-food, toothpaste, unless we saw their virtues bodied forth endlessly by all that melting rapture of voice and image?

Of course, black-and-white is old-fashioned now. We are meant to experience programmes in colour. We old-fashioned ones are living in a drab workaday world—greyly we spend our evenings. The next thing is to buy, or rent, a colour set. (Always, of course, the great snag is that the more complex the piece of machinery, the more liable it is to break down: and that needs thinking about.)

My lifetime has known this fantastic movement in piped domestic entertainment—first the wireless set with earphones; then the loudspeaker, with its complication of batteries wet, dry, and grid-bias; then the plug-in radio; then the first one-channel TV with snow falling diagonally across it; and now the threefold programmes, and colour. It is hard to imagine what may come next.

It's perhaps best not to ask if we might not have a penalty to pay for all the luxury, in terms of weakened speech and colder social relations.

Ballpoint Pens

22.4.1976

One thing I've noticed about ballpoint pens and transistor batteries, you can't entirely depend on them—they're like friends who can be delightful but are not to be relied on in a crisis.

Some batteries last for months—a splendid performance day after day, until they suddenly wilt and die of old age. The next one you buy, after a boisterous childhood, turns sickly in its youth, and never sees age at all... I admit to being baffled.

But pens are the tools of my trade—my whole livelihood and well-being depend on them. How pleasant it is when after a page or two, the new ballpoint goes easily and fluently across the page, line after line; and no clotting; and no spidery faintness, so that you have to grit your teeth and dig into the page.

It happens sometimes—you get a dud ballpoint. There it lies in its box with a half-dozen brothers, identical in every respect: the long slim yellow hexagonal barrel, the sleek black hood. But underneath, it is a lazy good-for-nothing; or else it doesn't like you, and will not perform, no matter what you do... Be patient with it, coax it across a half-dozen white pages or so, forgive time after time its pale performance—it's no go—in the end, exasperated, you throw the miserable thing in the wastepaper basket! And you eye once more, with hope and dread, the half-dozen virgin ballpoints in the box. Which one to choose? It's a gamble.

Sometimes I think those pens have wills of their own, to the extent that they can thwart or facilitate your literary designs. You get one pen that is a wretched speller, and perpetrates hideous bits of grammar, and can make a fine fankle of a sentence. His identical twin, on the other hand, is a friend of yours; he's delighted to help you in every way possible, even to the extent of delivering an unborn thought and setting it down on the paper with precision and fluency. That pen you want to have on your desk for ever, to help you when you are writing to the Income Tax man, or contemplating a poem, or idly wondering what's going on this week 'Under Brinkie's Brae'... Alas, pens like all created things are mortal. One fine morning, in the midst of a sentence, it dies in your hand, without any pain or trouble. Then, with reverence, you lay it in the wastepaper basket and say a silent farewell, and cover it with a crumpled envelope.

Leaves on a Winter Tree

29.4.1976

I dropped into the Reading Room of our Library the other day; which I often do when it's raining or when I'm tired after carrying a heavy bag of messages along the street.

In that peaceful oasis you can spend a pleasant hour, with the large variety of newspapers and magazines on display—all tastes catered for, from *Weekend* to *The Guardian* and *The Spectator*.

The racks, on the day I looked in, had been swept bare as if by a hurricane! Of daily newspapers two had survived, frail leaves on a wintry tree—*The Scotsman* and *The Press and Journal*. (*The Orcadian* was there still, and without disrespect to *The Orcadian* I wondered why, since presumably every household in Stromness and environs gets *The Orcadian*, until it was pointed out that *The Orcadian* file must be kept up to date. And apart from that, there are visitors and tourists who, presumably, will go for *The Orcadian* before anything else.)

The slaughter among the magazines had been equally frightful. If you want to know what the intelligentsia of the world is saying and thinking, from now on you will have to buy your own *Spectator* and *New Statesman*.

One sits in the Reading Room now with a feeling of desolation—a few dry bones in a desert place. It is no longer an oasis where you can spend a pleasant afternoon.

And this cactus of austerity has blossomed from one of the best-off communities in Britain.

The Reading Room, since the Library building was completely reconstructed inside, is a pleasant little place. If you get tired of reading, you can rest your eyes on the street outside, that goes past Melvin Place and Gray's Noust, and then surges up, a stone wave, to the top of Hutchison's Brae.

Before that, the Reading Room was a vast dark chamber—far too big for its purposes. On the shelf mouldered an ancient set of Harmsworths Encyclopedia; and a box for donations with knife-marks on it. There was the strangest collection of magazines—that, I imagine, was not a reflection of Stromnessians' tastes, but they were simply there because they cost nothing. I remember *The Vegetarian News*; and one article in particular from the thirties—the author wrote scornfully about those who advocated meat-eating and instanced the ox (that powerful animal) that ate only grass... And there were *The Anti-Vivisectionist*, *The Elim Evangel*, and many another...

Even so, the tree of knowledge in that other era of austerity—the 1930s—had richer foliage than today.

An Ailing Couch

6.5.1976

Something will have to be done some time soon, otherwise my friends will have nowhere to sit when they visit. It began about six years ago, when a friend bought on my behalf a couch at a sale. The couch I had taken from Well Park, though deep and commodious, had lost the power of its springs. So another friend came one day with a hand-cart and wheeled it round the west shore and there cremated it—a good way for a well-worn piece of furniture to go.

The couch bought at the sale was an altogether more austere article: long and narrow and covered with a kind of grey cloth. But it fitted well with the general austerity of the living-room. Besides, I sit on the rocking-chair given to me by a cousin when she went to live in London nearly twenty years ago. (A separate article could be written about that rocking-chair, which must be very ancient—the arm ends have been polished bright and thin by a multitude of thumbs.)

So there, in the middle of the room, facing the electric fire and side-on to the TV, sits this couch. I only use it for after-dinner naps, or to let a TV programme flow over me, or to hold a surplus of books and papers.

If a visitor, or visitors, come, the couch is instantly cleared for them to sit down.

About four months ago one of the rubber supports snapped—I saw it trailing forlornly on the floor, a long black strap, one morning.

Well, these things happen. In spite of that wound, the couch seemed as robust as ever. Three people could huddle together on it; it took their weight serenely. Apart from a little fraying of the cloth, it seemed set for a good decade of useful life.

The other day I was expecting three rather important visitors. While I was knocking some shape into the cushions that adorn the couch, I discovered to my horror that a second rubber strap had gone. It was time then to examine the couch's understructure. Of the ten or so black rubber supports, every single one showed signs of perishing. The couch's days are almost over.

It will soon be time to go to another sale, or visit a furniture shop.

In the meantime, I hope none of my visitors will be very fat, or have a weak heart (in case the thing collapses under him).

The rocking chair continues to swing calmly, at right angles to the doomed couch. It is powered by a spring manufactured in the days when things were made to last. That chair could still be swaying reposefully, back and fore, at the turn of the century.

The Green Bench

13.5.1976

One of the signs that summer is on the way is when they put out the public benches here and there along the street—Graham Place, Bank of Scotland, Commercial Hotel, etc. There they suddenly appeared a few days ago, all smart and shining in their new green paint. Many a visitor will sit on them in the months to come, and watch the life of Stromness flowing past. Many an old body, too, is glad of the benches, struggling homewards with a bag of messages. Even children seem to love the long green seats—running, balancing, performing all kinds of acrobatics on them...

Now, for the first time, Mayburn Court has its two benches. I sat on one of them yesterday, on a beautiful spring afternoon. Between the Museum and the tall building south of it, there is a noust with a white fishing boat hauled up. A little stream—the 'Mayburn'—tinkles over the stones into the harbour. Beyond the noust can be seen a segment of blue harbour, and the Outer Holm; and beyond that the tranquil brown and green flow of the Orphir hills.

I can foresee that the Mayburn seats will be well occupied from now to September.

The single snag is that only the morning light shines there. About 2pm the sun went behind the steep roofs. About the same time yesterday, a sudden breeze flawed the mirror of the harbour. The wind freshened rapidly, and presently I had to put my jacket on.

* * *

It has been a beautiful week, altogether. I've been fortunate to get car-drives every afternoon. Afresh each spring, driving through the West Mainland, you appreciate how beautiful Orkney can be. The fields were burgeoning with lambs and new grass. Ditch after ditch was edged with a lace of daffodils—loveliest of flowers. Nor will anybody deny a shaggy comeliness to the millions of dandelions that constellate the grass verges. Some flowers are undervalued, I suppose, because they are so common. But there's nothing to despise in the dandelion, especially when you taste the delicious wine that is its ghost and essence. I have a friend who makes the delicious stuff. Any evening now he'll be taking his basket to the teeming fields behind the town.

What Might Have Been

20.5.1976

I sometimes wonder what would have happened if those 18th-century wars between Britain and France had continued into the 19th and 20th centuries; and if the charming race of scientists had not been already hotfoot on the scent of steamships and oil-powered ships—if, in fact, the world's traffic and warfare had been contained forever in the billowing of sails and the clumsy thunder of cannons.

The English Channel, in such a case, might have been permanently blocked to peaceful traffic. The great tobacco ships, rice ships, iron ore ships would have had to keep taking the northern route through the Pentland Firth. And when they wanted fresh water, a few more sailors, shelter from an easterly gale, they would have slipped into the harbour of Stromness. Year after year, decade after decade, generation after generation.

'So,' as some hypothetical local historian might have written, 'Stromness continued to grow and flourish. In the 1830s it was already bigger than the Orkney capital, Kirkwall. By the middle of the century it was the largest town north of Aberdeen. Terraces of houses were built into Brinkie's Brae, and over Brinkie's Brae; and the Loons became a populous and rowdy part of the town. Soon the harbour proved to be too small for the volume of traffic. The harbour front was extended eastwards, in the direction of the Bu and Congesquoy and Waithe and Clestrain. Ancient farms like Carson and Feaval were swallowed up in the frenzy of new urban building. The rich merchants built their houses as far as possible from the noise and stink and tumults of the town, at Outertown and Breckness; even the barren moor between the Black Crag and Yesnaby became, in a decade, a large suburb of elegant stylish villas.

'In the huge warren of new buildings, a few charming little closes and corners were preserved. How delightful, to emerge suddenly from the noise and squalor of dock-side Cairston. and come upon the peace of Graham Place, and the little stepped narrow twisting alley called, quaintly, Khyber Pass! Somehow, these managed to exist into the twenty-first century, and they gave a vivid idea of Stromness in its first innocence and charm... '

* * *

But, thank goodness, no such history will ever be written.

Football Matches

25.5.1976

There was a lot of football on TV last week. We watched, enthralled, the European Cup Final at Hampden between Bayern Munich and St Etienne. A wonderful game in every way it was—the French team all verve and ebullience, the Germans applying a cold efficiency to the match, as if it was a chess problem or a bit of mathematics. And which was the better side it was hard to say; it depends what you expect from football. Myself, I like the French style, but the Munich team won 1–0.

Next morning, on the radio, I was astonished to hear the *Glasgow Herald* football journalist, Ian Archer, saying what a dull game it had been. He's one of the best football journalists in the business. Maybe it was one of those games that look better on television than from the grandstand.

* * *

An afternoon or two later, it was the great game of the year, again at Hampden Park—Scotland v England. This has always been a compelling game for me, from the late nineteen-twenties on. We used to listen to it on early loudspeakers—I remember one occasion when the commentator's voice was only a frayed whisper. Yet we endured, ears stuck to the set, as if that whisper was a spell or an incantation.

I was too young for Scotland's greatest triumph, when the 'Wembley Wizards' won 5–1. The very next year they scraped through at

Hampden 1–0, the ball going in from a corner kick (I think) taken by Cheyne the Aberdeen winger.

Those were the days of the legendary goalkeeper John Thomson of Celtic. His death on the football field was as great a tragedy to our boyish minds as Bonny Prince Charlie and Culloden, or Mary Queen of Scots, or the Wallace...

The game that Saturday afternoon had none of the classic precision of the European Cup Final. It seemed an altogether ragged and haphazard affair, to be decided by chance rather than by mind and skill. You felt that either team could win; but the Scots had that extra bit of dash and tenacity that probably made the result—2–1—a fair reflection.

I wondered how John Thomson, Jimmy McGrory, Alex James, Hughie Gallagher, would have come through on a TV screen. In the great football legend, they are heroes, and the likes of them are not kicking a football today.

A Beautiful Month

3.6.1976

I'm writing this on the last day of May; and it has been a beautiful month in Orkney—not like the 'spoiled spring' in Houseman's poem at all, rain-lashed and storm-fretted, where all the doom-laden rustics could do was to sit in ale-houses and mourn their lot:

'Pass me the can, lad, there's the end of May...'

The month has been a kind of pleasant love affair between mist and sun. A morning might be hung about with a grey cloud; but dove-grey, so that you knew the sun was there, somewhere, hidden.

And then, when you were eating breakfast or writing a letter, the window brightened, there was a splash of sun on the floor; and another fine day was about to break.

The only grumble is, when the sun shines you want to be out and about, sitting at some pier or public bench, chatting to the lieges about this and that. But the work has to be done first. And it's much easier to sit at a table and write when the how of winter is in the lum, and the rain is making its music against the window panes.

Yesterday was one of those days. In mid-morning the sun slowly divested itself of the cloud layers—and I knew, over the bacon and egg, that it was going to be a beautiful day. I hastened to finish my tasks. Outside the sky was a blue bowl with tufts of white clouds tumbling over, driven by a fresh southeast wind.

I don't have a garden myself, so I sat in a friend's garden, protected from the wind by a thick hedge, and took the sun's bounty. How pleasant, to sit surrounded by green things growing, and chat easily about this and that for hours on end!

In mid-afternoon we all took car, and headed northwards. At Skaill Bay we ate ice-cream and sat on the greensward. There were cars and folk there, but no bathers, only a couple of girls taking the sun.

North again. There followed a complicated manoeuvre: two of the passengers were dropped at Marwick Bay, to begin walking to Birsay. At the Palace, two more got out and set off in the opposite direction. Since walking is not one of my hobbies, I read the *Time* magazine, and strolled here and there about the village. With the coming of evening—as has happened so often this month—the wind dropped, and the rough sea-texture was all blue silk between Marwick Head and the Brough.

The four walkers were gathered into the car, and we made for Stromness, and the dinner table, and the passing of a can or two...

At midnight the harbour was full of brimming glooms and gleams.

Sun

10.6.1976

That very fine day last week, Thursday, I took the sun at the Museum wall, from which you can observe the flow of Stromness life. On that afternoon it was a particularly tranquil flow, both because it was early-closing day and because a great number of townsfolk, and all the children, had gone to the school sports at the Market Green and the field on the side of Brinkie's Brae.

However, one or two folk came drifting by, and stopped and chatted for a while. The first was a pleasant lady from Franklin Road who is the keeper of an endless store of episodes about Stromness and its people in the nineteen-twenties—a fascinating time for me, for I was growing up then, and only interested in football, chocolate, and *The Wizard*...

While we were chatting, along came the man who is probably Stromness's best-known citizen, ex-Provost George S. Robertson. He was smoking an enormous cigar. Before we had time to ask him whether he had 'come up in the pools', or otherwise inherited a fortune, he gave us the reason: 'I'm eighty-nine today,' said he. (May all our friends be as active of mind and body when they reach the verge of ninety.)

Mr Robertson has, of course, been postmaster of Stromness; and he was Provost for many years. But for him, the golfers might still be playing golf at Warbeth. Golf has always been his great hobby. He wrote a fascinating small book about the golf courses of Orkney, which delighted the Poet Laureate when he was here a year ago. (He can still play a few holes on an afternoon.) There is also Mr Robertson's *History of Stromness*... I hope he will think some time of giving us an autobiography; he could do it, he tells fragments and episodes of his life so well at the Pier Head of an afternoon.

An hour later a car drew up, and an Englishman got out with a copy of one of my books ('I bought it for my wife's birthday') for me to sign. Which of course I did with alacrity—it means there are a few more pence between me and the poorhouse. We talked for a few minutes; then he asked me the best way to get to the top of the Ward Hill in Orphir. After I had made a few bumbling suggestions, he asked whether I had ever been there; to which I had to give the honest answer, 'No.' ... (If only he knew the thousands of wonderful Orkney places unvisited by these timid feet of mine!)

The sun shone, warmer and brighter as the afternoon wore on. An English lady approached and remarked that she had seen me on TV. She had taken the day-crossing from Scrabster. 'Orkney is very very beautiful,' she said. I always like folk who say things like that. She lingered, then went back to the heart of the quiet town.

Midsummer

24.6.1976

Midsummer today; and in Orkney there is always something special about that. Today—if the sun is shining—we stand in the full dazzle and drench of light; we approach as near as we can to the fountainhead.

It was always, from the beginning, a time of mystery. I am not going to bore readers once more with an account of the Johnsmas fires that were lit on the top of every hill at sunset on Midsummer Eve; and the dancing and the merriment went on till dawn. In these faithless times, there remains only a simple flicker of light from the summit of Hoy's Ward Hill.

I must say, I love this time of year best of all. But, strange to say, there are folk—and I've spoken to them—who find the long light monotonous, or unnatural, or maybe both. For them, the great thing is the cosiness of lighted lamp and blazing fire after tea—the easy-chair with book or newspaper or TV. They are the winter people; and who shall blame them, in a way? For winter has its own magic: mazes of stars, the changing moon, and rare-come Aurora.

* * *

Light or darkness, the solstices are dangerous times to venture out of doors. Many a young man has seen, on a midsummer midnight, the dance of the fairies, and then has seen no more, for he was gathered into silence and invisibility.

Or you might, in former days, have seen the clumsier dance of the stones at Brodgar; but woe to you if you were seen by some sentry stone, and seized—you would have been ground into a million grains!

A slower more melancholy end happened at the opposite pole of the year, to the man who chanced to see the Watch Stone uproot itself, and trundle down to the loch's edge for a Hogmanay drink. He wasn't struck dead, that intruder, he withered and dwined through the brightening months, and when the shadows began to gather about Orkney again, a last shadow fell on him, and he died.

Nothing exciting happens now, of course. The printed book drove a lot of the magic out of life; newspapers spread a greyness; and the wireless set, when it came, had an overplus of factual information; and the TV, most deadly and powerful of all, bade the communal imagination—what was left of it—begone, and for ever.

Summer Holidays

1.7.1976

Now, when I come downstairs in the morning and draw the curtain, the first thing I see is a sign on the opposite wall—TOILETS 50M. The sign went up last week, and is one of the most prominent things in town. Because, you see, at last the South End has its toilets: and visitors and those in dire necessity no longer have to toil to the Library or the Pier Head.

Some day soon I must go and have a look, and perhaps (to show there is no ill-feeling) patronise the place. This new building is halfway between Mayburn and Faravel, set doucely into the wall; and should prove very handy for those coming home at 10.20 from the Braes, on a cold night.

* * *

School holidays today, as I write. It's more than a quarter of a century since I left school, but the word 'holidays' still rouses a tremor of joy. Seven weeks of summer, to a boy, is an eternity of happiness. How is it, looking back, that all these summer holidays seem steeped in sunshine? It must be a trick of the memory, that selects happy things and rejects whatever is dull or unpleasant. These summer days were spent in rowing boats in the harbour; or fishing sillocks from a pier; or bathing at the West Shore. And this delicious monotony seemed to have no ending.

I remember one golden afternoon in—it must have been—the early thirties. That July day, at 1pm, we had been given our summer freedom. I went away up a lonely by-way, to relish it alone and selfishly; as if the presence of another boy might somehow have sullied it... But, apart from that piece of monasticism, the rest of that summer was spent in communal football, bathing, boating, butterfly chasing; and wondering how we could earn a penny or two to buy Highland Cream toffee, or a bar of Cadbury's chocolate. Poverty was a part of every boy's heritage, and it lay lightly on us.

One of the first things we did was to discard shoes and stockings and take barefoot to the piers and beaches.

Into the midst of this elysium—all sunlight and buttercups and birdsong—returning from Warbeth beach, a boy said suddenly on the dusty road, 'Three weeks, and the school goes back!' I have never heard such bleak words—the intrusion of time into timelessness.

Heatwaves

8.7.1976

More than myself will be thinking, with deepest sympathy, of the south English frying in temperatures of 95°. And to go on, like that, day after day! The nerves of millions of people are shredded thin; stations and supermarkets are thick with snarls, sweat, shouting. Even at night there is no respite. At 80° it is difficult to sleep with comfort.

All the elements are misbehaving. The sun-struck people are desperately short of water. If one of them drops a lighted cigarette, a whole woodland is liable to blaze up. A terrible state of affairs altogether—and even the most avid Scottish Nationalist must wish a little sweetness of rain, and pleasant breezes from the sea, upon the suffering English.

I am remembering England on the grill with sympathy, because last August we had a mini-heatwave in Orkney. Day after day of unclouded sun. I expect it was pleasant for children and those going among holiday rockpools with nothing to do—but, after the first two days, I got to dislike that heatwave intensely. To sit inside, and try to work, became very difficult, knowing that that unclouded flame was in the sky. The truth is, I suppose, that we cold northerners cannot take too much sun. It upsets us, mind and body. Last August, at any rate, I found myself longing for a grey cloud, a cluster of raindrops, a little salt-laden breeze from mid-Atlantic.

On one of the hottest August days of 1975, I came on an American friend at the Pier Head reading his newspaper headline, and loud with merriment—'Orkney swelters in 75° heat wave'. In his part of America, he explained, 75° is just an ordinary summer day, rather cool on the whole. And there were we 'cold northerners' with our shirts sticking to our backs!

These August days last year—we looked forward so eagerly to the coolness of evening. And what did the evening bring, day after day, but millions of midges. (They say the people in Rackwick, Hoy, had to make their cottages fortresses against those minute torturing enemy hosts.) The midges (Orkney, 'mudjecks') are, according to this morning's wireless, out early this year. If this good weather holds, it looks like being a spectacular year on the midge front.

To Rackwick

15.7.1976

The morning did not look promising at all. When I got up at 7.30am the sky was grey, and wind moved and moaned about the corners of the houses.

I have never done a more hurried packing in my life. Fortunately, in February when I was preparing to go to Perthshire and Edinburgh, I had made a list of essentials—the clothes, the paper and pens, the medicaments, the toilet things, the refreshments—so that morning, with that chart before me, I could lay my hands swiftly on what was required; and pack them into two old carrier bags. Instructions also to switch off the electricity at the meter and pen a note for the milkman NO MILK (but I forgot that, so I expect three half-bottles of crowdie cheese on the doorstep on Monday).

A quick breakfast of fried fish, toast, and tea; and all four of us (one small child, very excited) were approximately ready. We bundled into the loaded car. The day was greyer than ever. 'It looks,' said somebody at the Pier Head, 'like a change in the weather.' … The spirits plummeted a bit further.

In the *Scapa Ranger* I conversed all the way across Hoy Sound with the genial Hoy minister. When we rounded the block-ship in Burra Sound, there were the Hoy hills licked with first sunshine. Looking behind, Graemsay and Stromness lay in a cold shroud.

Sunlight, in ever more generous splashes, as the red van took the Rackwick road. The Dwarfie Stone, the Hammars, the peat-cuttings, first glimpse of the high green west face of the valley, the little bridge, the fork on the road. When the van stopped at the hostel that was once the school, Rackwick was brimming over with light and warmth. We deposited on the green sward the vast impedimenta of food and refreshments that were to see us through the weekend. Other valley inhabitants gathered round for greetings and talk. (Still other valley inhabitants—the clegs—began their first tentative attacks.)

We munched huge sandwiches of cheese and tomato and lettuce beside the open door of North House. A wind began to stir in sudden rallies, that died away again. Later, there were many winds, blowing warm and boisterous from a variety of airts; they scattered the clegs.

There was a huge dinner of sausages, eggs, tomatoes—Rackwick whets the appetite like no other place. Later, there was a happy and convivial visitation of friends from a house at the shore.

On the night it must have rained. The grass next morning was a treasury, a jewelled hoard.

Two Buckets of Water

22.7.1976

There were quite a few folk living in cottages in the valley. Every day last weekend brought a new throng of tourists. They appeared at the throat of the valley, and were quickly gathered into silence and vastness. Miles over the crest of Moorfea, the Old Man beckoned them. Under the huge red eastward cliff, the crescent of saffron sand lured them. But this year, for some reason, the crescent has shrunk very thin; the sand is waiting, out in the bay, for winter gales to hurl it shorewards again.

What a common thing water is, even to dwellers in Kirkwall and Stromness—how tasteless and boring! First thing every morning, after I had put my bedwarm feet on a cold flagstone and dragged on some clothes, I took a bucket in either hand—one enamel, one plastic—and walked across two fields to the burn that comes tinkling down from the bracken above. Already the sun was up, and the dew in the grass glittered, and the first clegs were about. Five minutes it takes to fill the buckets from the drought-shrunk burn. Then back across the field with those heavy brimming glittering precious circles. With this water, tea has to be brewed, faces washed, dishes swilled. In Rackwick, water resumes its royal status among the four primal elements.

There was a small boy, two and a half years old. He comes from a city, but he took to Rackwick as if they belonged to each other. There was no need to entertain him: everything was new and precious, the stones, the wild flowers, the sand and breakers on the beach. Sometimes, in an idle hour, I would take him among the out-houses—hard well-built stones, the roofs fallen in.

We knocked on the side of an old corrugated structure. 'Can we come in, Margaret-Anne?' (Margaret-Anne was a fairy. She was not at home that day.) We shouted in at the byre door, 'Are you home yet, old Willie?' (Old Willie goes to the sea and fishes.) But no, old Willie was not yet back from his lines; when he did come in, he would leave a fish on our doorstep.

So, just before this small boy left Rackwick, after six days of sunshine and boundless freedom, he went and said 'Cheerio, Margaret-Anne,' and he called 'Cheerio, old Willie,' in at the byre door.

Song of Iron

29.7.1976

It started two days ago, an iron music like some new symphony by Stockhausen; it was so intense it made all the inhabitants of Mayburn Court reel. Was it some new ultra-modern Shopping Week event, unscheduled in the programme? We looked out—it was two of the burgh painters chipping away the ancient encrusted paint and rust from the handsome Mayburn railings. The whole of the South End was possessed, till knocking-off time, by the din and the clangour. It was like a torture chamber working to capacity—a few screams and moans added, and you could well have imagined yourself in Torquemada's dungeon or a fairly hot circle of the Inferno.

At 9am next morning, when I was turning deliciously over into another swoon, the Iron Symphony began again, in all its power and stridency. The birds of morning fled away, songless. It was like the striking of huge discordant bells.

And yet the cacophony is very necessary. Eight years ago all we Mayburners moved in, on the very day that the last sections of railing were being welded in place. How smart and clean and lacquered they seemed, those railings! I even entertained notions, some Shopping Week, of having poetry readings from the end of that high balcony, in the quiet of evening. It seemed possible, alternatively, that an open-air play, or concert, could have been performed in the courtyard below, with an audience watching from above, leaning on the black-painted balcony.

But of recent years the salt has begun to eat into the paint and the iron, until last week the children were stripping flakes off the railing; it was all patched, peeled, rusted, crumbling. High time for the painters to move in with their scrapers—even if it meant competing with the dulcet sounds of Shopping Week; even if it meant setting the teeth of the entire South End on edge.

We will have our smart railing, almost new again, soon.

Even as I write, the painters have had their lunch, and they are laying into the diseased railing with might and main, and with unbelievable power and complexity of sound.

Tourists

5.8.1976

We are at the very height of the tourist season. Some Stromnessians say, 'There aren't so many tourists as last year!' Others declare, 'Did you ever see so many tourists in your life?' ... Whatever the truth of it, the *Ola* seems to bring hundreds with her every time she crosses from Scrabster.

I rather like to see all those new faces on the street; especially when they are obviously interested in Orkney and the many-faceted life of Orkney. Even if you didn't know, you can tell these 'good tourists' by the way they drift and linger through the street, very much taken with this roof angle and that cracked stone. Whereas the Stromnessians go about their business with a single-minded directness.

There is the other kind of tourist, who after getting off the *Ola*, is appalled that ever he pushed so far north, into barbarism. Where is the betting shop? Where is the amusement arcade? Why is there so much sea and sky? (They don't usually stay beyond a day or two.)

My door-knocker fairly rattles at this time of year! Out of self-preservation a couple of days ago I rigged up a notice and pinned it to the door: 'Be home 2.30pm' (in the mornings I try to earn my bread and butter with the pen).

So, those last few mornings, I have been able to work undisturbed; troubled to be sure by a random thought that perhaps I had shut out somebody delightful or good or beautiful; but then, if people really want to see you, they will come back.

On the very first day that I pinned the notice on the door—and it is equivocal, I admit; you can read it any way you like—I happened to be along the street, doing something or other, till well after 2.30pm. It was nearer 3.30 when finally I returned to Mayburn. I noticed that my sign had been despoiled. An old school friend of mine, on holiday, whom I would have loved to speak with, had scrawled with his pen, 'Boy, are you never at home?' and signed his name and the exact time of his calling. (He had made two or three fruitless attempts already.)

So it goes—you can't always win.

The Salmon

12.8.1976

What a delightful present to get—an 11lb salmon newly out of the Pentland Firth. A Caithness friend who has corresponded with me for over a year now, and who also works at the salmon fishing, arrived unexpectedly last Thursday evening, when I was (of course) out visiting.

It is no easy matter to lug a huge salmon here and there in Stromness, trying to track down somebody who isn't there. Eventually the Braes Hotel was mentioned to her (my salmon fisher correspondent is a woman) and there she tracked me down half an hour before closing time, discussing books and writing with two holidaymakers—a student getting ready to study English at Cambridge, and an Australian school teacher. (The salmon had proved too awkward to trail around; it was lying in a friend's house, in a plastic bag. I fervently hoped that Panther the cat had not yet begun to feast on it.)

We had a drink or two to celebrate the salmon.

* * *

What does a single man, with only a middling appetite, do with an 11 lb salmon? There it lay, the next morning, in Hopedale kitchen, a magnificent dead fish, covered with a beautiful burnished pattern: a knight among fish, honourably slain.

It would have to be shared out—that much was clear. With a sharp knife my Caithness friend sliced off head and tail (Panther would have these, at any rate); and then gutted it, a gory and necessary business. Then she sliced it into four roughly equal sections.

I kept the tail to myself; other segments went to Thistlebank, Hopedale, and a caravan at Ness where a delightful French couple—more old friends—and their baby are staying. At home, a large pot was produced and filled with cold water. The tail section was reverently sunk in it. Vinegar and salt were added, and the heat turned on.

* * *

It turned out to be an afternoon of visitors—the busiest of the summer. While they came and went, the salmon slowly simmered until the firm pink flesh crumbled at the touch of the fork. Then—except that it had to grow cold again in the stock—it was ready.

In the evening an Edinburgh friend arrived unexpectedly by air. We ate the cold salmon with bread and butter, and lager beer (Danish). There was plenty left over for lunch-time next day; but by now we had risen to the luxury of wine, squeezed lemon, and salad. (Let no one say again that tinned salmon is better to eat than fresh salmon!)

The fish seemed inexhaustible. I ate the last of it for breakfast, this morning.

Gerard's Manse

19.8.1976

Most Orcadians are guilty, on fine days of summer freedom, of sticking to the same old well-beaten tracks: Skaill, Waulkmill, Birsay Links, Aikerness, Yesnaby. There are scores of other places, equally beautiful, that remain unvisited.

Last Wednesday, day broke with a fairly dense sea-haar, and the wind south-east. It looked as if it might be one of those cold blind days which is a possibility at least a score of times in an average Orkney summer. But no: as morning wore on, the lead showed scrapings here and there, scraps of brightness. At last, there was the sun, about the size of an old half-crown, gleaming through the high swirls of fog.

Half an hour later the sun had the blue sky to itself.

My French friends arrived with their Renault. I always (of course) make for the left-hand door. I ought to know better by this time... In under an hour we were crossing the Churchill Barriers. South Ronaldsay was the last of the Orkneys that day to shrug the fog off. There was still shreds and coils of it in the hollows. (Our hostess told us, when we arrived, that that morning when she woke up she couldn't see the rose-bush in her garden; so much for our planned picnic on the beach below the house!)

We took the Cara road that strikes through the east of the island. For the second time in a week we had some difficulty in finding the by-road (there are three or four of them) that leads towards the shore. At last there the cottage was, halfway down a wide fertile slope, rich that day with two immense fields of changing barley... For me, it was a totally new part of Orkney. On the shore, a mile to the right, was St Peter's

Church, which a century and a half ago was graced by a remarkable eccentric of a minister, Rev John Gerard.

The cottage is being restored, with taste and austerity. It smelt of new pinewood. It has a beautiful stone floor, and a new stone fireplace. It soon began to smell of delicious ephemeral things—chicken, salad, pâtés, wine, ground coffee. (It was reckoned, after all, to be too far to carry the picnic basket, plus a year-old baby, to the beach.) We ate indoors; and drank coffee afterwards outside, while the sun (a trifle muted still by fog) shone, and a mild south-easterly blew over our dreaming heads.

Afterwards we walked down to one of the most beautiful small beaches in Orkney. It curves, a golden-grey crescent, right below Rev Gerard's Manse. The sea that breaks on it is green and cold and translucent.

(I hasten to emphasise again, it is difficult to find—in case, next time I go there, it should be crammed with picnickers and sun-bathers!)

Sunset, Moonrise

2.9.1976

Sunlight, day after day. It has been a beautiful summer in the islands. These golden days seem all the more precious for the patches of rain and coldness in between. What could be more earthy-blissful than sitting in a garden in the sun, sipping cold ale and talking with friends? That has happened oftener this year than for some summers past: in this Stromness garden and that, in Rackwick, in South Ronaldsay; and there's a month of summer still to go.

* * *

There's a little mushroom village to the south of the town, all caravans and tents. Some of the tents are so low it must be impossible to sit up in them. I try to imagine, and fail, what like existence must be in such frail dwellings when days of wind and rain come. But there they dwell, young people from—it seems—every nation on earth:

happy, suntanned, carefree. They cook their sausages and brew their tea over little gas stoves, in the open air.

In six weeks, or so, that little community will have packed and gone, except for the permanent caravans. Stromness will be an elderly sedate town again.

I didn't know, till I actually sat in one last week, what a marvellous view those Ness caravan-dwellers have. The evening I called on Hervé and Marie-Antoinette was particularly beautiful. The sun had just set in the north-west—the sky over Brinkie's Brae was rich and radiant. Of course, the harbour water takes all that beauty of light to itself. On this late evening the sea was calm, with only a slight swell and motion. It was a luminous bridal of air and water.

It seemed, while it lasted, as close to perfection as transience can get: in half an hour it would be dark. Hill and harbour would be a cluster of shadows. While we spoke over our coffee and liqueur, a point of silver shone suddenly at the top of one of the Orphir hills. It was the tip of the almost full moon. As we watched, it rose silently and quickly, and soon it had the whole eastern horizon to itself. It threw its coins and spangles on the sea from Cairston to Ness. The rich remnants of sunset were still there. That mingling of the two lights was pure enchantment—something to make a catch in the breath.

Even man made a contribution that night. Not everybody likes those sodium street lights of ours but such a perfect stillness of sea as we had that night gave them back to us, out of the mirror, rich wavering nets and labyrinths of light.

Friends of Newbattle

9.9.1976

One of the happiest times I remember—perhaps the happiest—was that spent at Newbattle Abbey College in the early fifties. It was such a change from Orkney, in the first place: an ancient beautiful house hung about with history, a sylvan valley with a river meandering through it, fellow-students from all over the world. Not that Orkney was entirely absent: the kindly dominating presence was Edwin Muir. After almost a half-century out of the island, he had kept his Orkney speech. His words had that quiet and serenity in them that you still get from the mouths of certain Orkney country folk... Few who met her could forget Edwin's wife and literary collaborator Willa—her kindness, her flashes of earthiness and fun, were always there.

Many of the Newbattle students formed close friendships, after (I suppose in most cases, certainly in mine) an initial period of shyness.

We got to know each other in the classes (which were always more an easy weave of amity than strenuous exercises in concentration and note-taking) and at mealtimes (which had the distinction and luxury of a very good hotel), and especially at evening in the huge crypt of the Abbey, gathered round the log fire. Then everything under the sun was discussed with considerable passion—religion, economics, politics. There we read our favourite poems to each other.

It was perhaps in the Justinlees, a fine old pub a mile up the road, that we swore eternal amity, over mugs of beer. We would never lose touch with one another. We would write. We would visit.

It didn't, of course, turn out like that at all. Time weakens everything. Precious things fall away. Over two and a half decades, I now hear, only occasionally, from a very few of my Newbattle contemporaries.

The other day, I was glad to get a letter from an ex-student friend in Edinburgh, who is now a tutor at Newbattle. He wrote to say that a 'Friends of Newbattle Abbey College Association' has been formed—and would I join? The 'Friends' are to publish a news bulletin twice a year, 'with news of the College, former students, etc' ... Annual subscription, £1.

Why did nobody think of that in my time at Newbattle? It would have kept all those good friends in touch with one another. Twice a year we would have been quickened with a breath of youth and springtime. It might not be too late, still.

The Record Player

16.9.1976

It lay in a corner of the living room for two years, gathering dust. 'Really,' I used to say sometimes, when my eye caught it, 'that thing should be put out to the dust-cart!'... For the record player was old, and two years ago it began to function so erratically that I washed my hands of it. It was played out—it was about to die.

So the rented television set had the evenings all to itself. And the record player slowly rotted on the floor, festooned with a superabundance of wires. And they slowly withered on their shelf too—the delightful records of the Corries, Beethoven, Harry Lauder, Dylan Thomas, Sibelius, and a host of others high and low.

Sometimes the vague idea would drift into my mind that I ought to get a stereo system; and then it would drift out again. For where, in the already crowded book-choked room, could one set those two speakers? More wires, more impedimenta, more clutter! No thank you.

The TV set, well-pleased, had the complete monopoly.

Then, a few weeks back, I had a visitor. While I was out of the living-room one day—either in the kitchen or the bathroom—I heard familiar half-forgotten music. It was one of my abandoned records! Sure enough, when I got back to the living-room, there was the old record-player booming melodiously forth, as fresh (almost) as the day it was brought from Aberdeen.

It was like having a visit from an old friend whom one had imagined dead, or lost in fogs of senility or feeblemindedness. The old friend uttered sweetness after sweetness. It seemed not to resent my long neglect of it. (But the TV set, I think, frowned a bit in its corner.)

So now the records get sifted through regularly. Two years' dust gets blown out of the grooves. They are placed, reverently, on the turntable...

In all honesty, I must admit that things are not quite perfect. The two years' neglect has taken its toll of the battered old machine, after all. The arm, pressed into action, does not drop on the whirring rim of the record, but about five-sixths of the way in; so that I have to correct it manually.

It is a small price to pay, for the joy of hearing Lauder 'Roamin' in the Gloamin'', or the organ-voice of Dylan Thomas, or Beethoven ('out of the strong came forth sweetness'...).

Neglected Seafood

23.9.1976

Fishermen have long been famous for their superstitions. Not so long ago, some of them would turn back from launching the boat if they saw certain women in the street. It's well known how they dreaded ferrying ministers from here to there; the great sea principalities and powers, presumably, being jealous of the priests of another religion. Even the language they spoke at sea was studded with 'taboo words' which it was highly dangerous to utter. Substitute words had to be used—some very interesting 'kennings' resulted. Of course, a boatman never turned his boat withershins—it had to veer in a sunward circle.

Goodness knows how far back in time these beliefs are rooted. They must be pre-Christian. Life at sea was so hazardous for early fishermen that the observance of proper rituals gave them at least a feeling of security—'If I do this, and say that, the chances are that I'll get home to fire and board, candle and bed, this night'...

But why, I wonder, do the fishermen of the north have an aversion to mackerel as an item of diet? They use mackerel, of course, for their lines and creels—but that is as far as they'll go.

Our French friends are astonished, whenever they visit Orkney, by the hoarded wealth of shellfish that is all but ignored by Orcadians. They themselves had a rare field day near the Brough of Birsay in late July, among the whelks and mussels and limpets: delicious sea items for them.

But to return to the despised mackerel. I remember tasting the fish only once, a quarter of a century ago. The other day my friend who is helpful to me in many ways arrived with a couple of mackerel he had gutted and filleted himself. By good fortune Roger, on holiday from London, arrived. On went the frying pan, with plenty of cooking oil.

The slices of raw mackerel were set among the sizzlings, and soon the kitchen was full of a unique aroma.

With toast and bread and butter, we had no complaints whatever about our meal. Perhaps mackerel isn't so good as trout, but it is in a higher class altogether than cuithes or sillocks. We finished with coffee, and a little whisky, and sat in chairs beside the fire and spoke about books and people, and were quite contented.

Poetry and Verse

30.9.1976

Sometimes I get tired of reading verse. (I say 'verse' deliberately, rather than poetry.) I seem to have been reading nothing but verse since the summer's beginning. The reason is that I occasionally review books of verse for *The Scotsman*. *The Scotsman* therefore sends me all the review copies that come its way. I have never had so many parcels in my life. It is one of life's great joys to open up a parcel, no matter what's inside.

Poetry is much rarer than verse, and always has been, and always will be. Poetry is the occasional thin vein of ore in the solid rock of verse. One rejoices, of course, when (rarely) one comes across it. It calls for celebration—in my case, a few inadequate complimentary words in a review. I often feel like writing to the poet personally; but presumably he gets a photocopy of the review anyway, somehow.

But you have to smash up a great deal of rock, and sometimes there is no ore there at all: not one little speck or glimmer—nothing but tough backbreaking stone.

Then another parcel of review copies arrives, and as like as not they will be rocks and stones that don't even look as though they carried ore. But you persevere, bringing down the hammer of the mind, in the hope that there may be a sheer elusive glittering vein. Sometimes there is; not often. Then all the labour and the disappointment have been worth while. There is no greater joy than to come suddenly on a new poet with something strange, beautiful, and true to say. Thanks to the man in *The Scotsman* who sends the parcels, I have had hours of rare pleasure in the few months past.

I think the trouble with a great many verse writers is that they don't take enough trouble. Page after page of obscurity and shapelessness is a weariness to the spirit. Just this morning a very young English schoolgirl, who had spent her summer holiday in Holm with her parents, sent me three poems, along with a delightful letter. The poems are like patches of blue in the sky. I reproduce one, without permission.

MORNING

Morning breaking over the horizon,
Grass and leaves shimmering with dew,
Little flowers unfold their petals.
All the world looks new,
Swirling birds greet the opening of the new day.

The name of the poet is Victoria Sowerby. I wish all the verse I read gave me such pleasure.

The To-fro Drift

7.9.1976

There are Orcadians—maybe more than we like to think—who have no great opinion of the islands. Where are the dog-tracks? The casinos? The discotheques? The massed football excitement of a Saturday afternoon? The high-rise flats? The spaghetti junctions?—And a thousand other things that Orkney is too poor and scantily populated to support.

I suppose the famous 'drift from the isles' was, in part, a response to all those allurements. Why should we stay in a quiet backwater, bored most of the time, and miss all the glamour and excitement the twentieth century had to offer? And so in the fifties and sixties, many Orcadians went off to work in car factories, etc.

Now nobody ever speaks about 'the drift from the isles'. The tide has set, with a vengeance, the other way. It is the city dwellers who are coming, in large numbers, to taste our solitude and silence.

Other city dwellers, it is true, are coming for other reasons: for oil, so that the cities do not perish; maybe, in the future, for uranium, when all the oilwells are dry. So far, we have not bothered to tap the immense resources of the sun and the sea. (It was Bernard Shaw, when he visited Orkney in the early 1920s, who declared there was enough power in the Pentland Firth to supply the wants of western Europe. The Firth must have been in rampant form the day he crossed in the little old black *St Ola*.)

* * *

One Sunday afternoon at the end of summer, I was sitting on the green bench at Mayburn Court, feeling quite relaxed and contented in the sun.

Occasionally somebody would pass, going north or south. If I knew them, we would exchange a few drowsy words. If they were strangers, it was always courteous to give them a nod of the head.

While I sat on, sun-tranced, and wondering what the beer was like at Thistlebank, a car drew in to the car park, loaded with a family: father, mother, two small girls, a smaller boy.

Dead silence everywhere except for the lapping of water on the stones and the sleepy cry of gulls. (Dead silence!—I should of course have written 'a living breathing marvellous silence'...)

The following dialogue ensued:

The Tourist: 'Do you live here?'

GMB: 'Yes, I do.'

The Tourist (with heartfelt envy and longing): 'YOU LUCKY MAN!'

The Need to Praise

14.10.1976

Nobody seems thankful for anything, any more.

When England, and half of Europe (and even Orkney, a little) was parched with drought a short while ago, I felt concern, with thousands of others. I couldn't keep the awful idea out of my mind: what if no rain clouds came for a whole year or more—if, as scripture says, 'the bottles of heaven were stayed'?... It's only when we are brought face to face with drought, or famine, or fire, that we see how perilously and finely balanced the elements are; plants and animals and men live in the midst of them, but only from day to day, and with no sure guarantee that the balance will work in our favour for ever.

When the rains came at last, it was wonderful. The drought-stricken people would see, many of them for the first time, the beauty and preciousness of water... But it didn't seem to work that way at all. It was announced that rain had fallen over England in great dollops and torrents, and was continuing to fall; and you might have thought that the announcer's voice would be touched with lyricism! But no. And when the rain continued to fall, and the streets began to be awash, then the 'precious element' was, once more, a nuisance.

This quality of thanklessness seems to pervade our whole modern outlook. It is rather frightening. Turn on the radio at news time, and black gloom and hopelessness gushes out. 'Interest rate'... 'mortgage rate'... 'the sinking pound'... 'inflation'... 'national bankruptcy'.

Sometimes I think it would be best if there were no radios or newspapers at all. Did our great-grandfathers worry about the huge economic depressions and recoveries of Victorian Britain? Not one iota, because they didn't know they were happening. They had enough to do, keeping a few fields fertile and tarring the boat on the noust.

When a great drought came, it was an anxious time. The whole community was caught up in the crisis, about which they could do not a thing. When at last the rain came, as it always did, and a flush of green went over the cultivated land, and they knew that the corn was safe, there was a simple thankfulness, perhaps too deep for utterance.

An industrial society has lost the need to praise.

The Sunday Paper

21.10.1976

Most of our friends from the south are amused when they hear that we poor Orcadians only get our Sunday papers on the Monday. That's what it is to live in one of the backwaters of civilisation. (Actually, this week, the Sunday papers only came on Wednesday.)

Sunday or Wednesday or Monday, it is all the same to me. I have the problem every week of getting through that vast quantity of newsprint. It's hopeless, in the first place, ever to think of reading it entire. The mind has to he trained to select only those 'stories' or articles that it is really interested in; the rest must be ruthlessly jettisoned. Yet the mind has its reservations and its bouts of conscience. It keeps nagging, 'Here's an article of world-shaking importance—you must read it'... 'Everybody says what a brilliant journalist this person is—give him/her another chance'... 'Wouldn't you really like to know what makes football hooligans tick—it concerns you, and everybody—it is a symptom of our times'...

Beware of such gambits—they lead to an endless waste of time: they bruise the eyes. Stick only to what your mind is hungry for... Sometimes, to tell the truth, there isn't that much nourishment.

Sometimes I think I ought to cancel that paper. I think: 'Here I sit, in my rocking chair, with my feet up on a stool, and the Anglepoise lamp at my shoulder, chewing over this woodpulp, when I could be reading a short story by Thomas Mann, or a few poems by Brecht, or a chapter of *Howard's End*; or trying, yet once again, to unravel one of Pound's "Cantos".'

It was that same Ezra Pound who said that literature is news that remains news. That's to say, Homer and Chaucer will still be vivid reading in a hundred years' time: whereas the famous journalist begins to be stale the day after his stuff comes out.

Our friends from the south may be right when they scoff at us for reading the Sunday paper on Monday. I can imagine how they will double up with mirth when they get to know that this week I went through that great white waste of paper on Wednesday!

We poor Orkney folk are so touchingly innocent...

Breakdown

28.10.1976

Under Brinkie's Brae the *Ola* lay at her berth, while the east slowly encrimsoned.

I had woken at about 6am, and heard the wind prowling among the roofs; and had thought, with a qualm, that the Pentland might be a white and grey tempest. I was intending to make a crossing, the first in eight months; and from Scrabster by car to Edinburgh.

But the harbour was calm when we stood on the pier. Once on board I could see that silently opening rose over Orphir, which soon became a point of gold, and then the sun slowly heaved itself clear of the hills. Stromness, smitten with early light, is more beautiful than at any other time of day.

The Pentland crossing was quiet. It passed quickly and pleasantly in conversation with friends.

At Scrabster, we descended into the bowels of the *Ola* and sat in the white car; and presently drove over the ramp on to Scrabster pier.

Firstly, we dropped a friend at the station; he hoped to be in Ayr before midnight. Was it ominous that we had a slight difficulty finding the station? The car was going sweetly and well.

We crossed Caithness on a north-east diagonal, making for Wick airport. There we picked up three passengers who had decided not to hazard themselves on the Pentland Firth.

The sun, so beautiful at dawn, had long since been covered in clouds. It began to rain.

We sped through the Caithness moors going south. The flat moors give place to Berriedale, one of Scotland's beautiful places: the road winds perilously among hills and valleys with dizzying prospects of the North Sea below. The road has been made straighter of recent years, but is still spectacular.

Somewhere among these hills a windscreen wiper dropped off, and the window blurred. That was fixed quickly. The car descended into Sutherland. All around, desolate moor, in a moving smirr of rain.

It was somewhere in this 'blasted heath' that the engine gave a kind of gurgle; there was a stench of scorched rubber. The car stood stricken.

It was stricken more seriously than we thought. That is why I'm writing this in the lounge of a Sutherlandshire hotel, under a starker hill than Brinkie's Brae; just before taking a train to Edinburgh.

Edinburgh Exhibitions

4.11.1976

One of the paradoxical things about a city, where there are so many wheels and such urgency, is that one walks immensely longer stretches than in Orkney. And the endless climbing of stairs—up and around and about! In Orkney, when you have been living there for a year or two, you forget how much more effort and energy city people have to put into simple daily living.

The weather, apart from one day, was not good. Edinburgh—so beautiful at this time a year ago—was wrapped in a dank cloud. The streets were squelchy with damp foliage.

The weather drove us into exhibitions. Near the foot of the Royal Mile is the museum that tells richly, with maps and drawings, models and tableaux, the history of the city. Further up the street, we stumbled on a new thing—the waxworks exhibition. Nearly everyone of note is here, including, of course, the Royal Family. Scotsmen famous and infamous are depicted in lifesize form—Robert Louis Stevenson, Mary Queen of Scots, Burke and Hare (with the beauteous Mary Paterson, one of their victims, lying white and dead in a recess). You are warned not to enter 'the chamber of horrors' section if you have weak nerves. We went in, and emerged with regular pulses.

In Chambers Street we saw an exhibition of the history of medicine in Edinburgh—one of the epic stories of Scottish achievement. And there, among portraits of famous medicos, etc, far back in a glass case, stood, once more, Burke: but in skeletal form only.

Another afternoon—the bleakest dankest one of all—we stumbled, partly for shelter, into a gallery in Charlotte Square where there chanced to be an exhibition of 'naive art'—that is, by painters who had had no training. I couldn't help being impressed by the vigour and directness of these 19th-century paintings about bulls, horses, boxers, rat-catchers—in which the artlessness is part of the strength.

I always blanch slightly at the very idea of vegetarian food. That same evening, cold and miserable on account of the weather, we had a vegetarian meal in a place in Hanover Street. It lingers in the memory as one of the most delicious meals ever. (Steaks and salmon may not be indispensible after all.)

You get used to those huge flights of city tenement stairs after a time. Adapt your heartbeat to them, and after the fifth or sixth time, you arrive at the top quite cheerful.

Train Journey

11.11.1976

I stayed for a long weekend in a beautiful hospitable house on the south shore of Loch Tummel. ('Sure, by Loch Tummel and Loch Rannoch and Lochaber I will go'...) The sun that had been a miser with his largesse in Edinburgh, now poured out treasures in abundance. The rich trees, tall against the skies, dropped their leaves, singly or, when a breath of wind flawed the crystal, in sudden saffron showers. The world was getting ready for winter.

My hosts, Colin and Kulgin, capped their kindness by driving me twelve miles, at 1.30am, to Pitlochry station. I am so stupid about these things that I would probably have been waiting at the wrong side of the track when the train drew in. But they were there to keep me right. The train was rather empty. I got a compartment to myself all the way to Inverness; except when a bleary-eyed young man entered, asked if we had reached Inverness yet or passed it: and disappeared, uncertain, again.

You try to read, but the head nods over the page. In the end it is best to resign yourself to the urgent rhythm of the train.

Inverness station, between 4.45am and 6.15am, is not the most cheerful place in the world. Of course, again, if I had known better, I could have sat in the warm lighted train for most of that time. Instead, I changed it for a cold, dark, forlorn-looking one; having first ascertained that THURSO was pasted on the side of the carriage. (I have got that wise.)

No use to get out and walk about. There's nothing to see. Every place is closed. I managed to get a bar of chocolate from a machine. I looked at my watch a score of times.

At last lights came on, heat began to seep through the train, and with a powerful lunge she was on her way north.

Suddenly everything became beautiful. The sun got up just north of Inverness. It lay radiantly across fields and mountains and firths. There was not a cloud in the sky.

But even such a rare morning couldn't keep the eyes from closing and the head from drooping.

You arrived in Thurso like a cloth wrung dry long since, and gone slightly mildewed in a drawer.

The sight of the *Ola*, from the bus, cheers the heart up somewhat. She was half an hour late in leaving. The Pentland Firth, between Dunnet and Hoy, heaved gently. It is a good way to come home.

Brinkie's Brae and the Black Crag

18.11.1976

I'm ashamed to say, I haven't been to the top of Brinkie's Brae in 1976, and it looks like I won't be going now, at this cold dark time of year. (The other day I spoke to a man on the street who climbs to the top of it nearly every day.) The trouble is, once you get into a rut you never want to go anywhere, even to Brinkie's Brae or the Black Crag. Not even the promise of a beautiful view can lure you from the rocking chair and the TV.

From the summit of Brinkie's you can see, in a wide wheel, 360°, a breathtaking view: Scapa Flow and the islands, the Atlantic beyond

Hoy, the lochs and stones, the wine-dark moor of the West Mainland. with here and there a kestrel.

(I ought, really, before embarking nearly a year ago on this column, to have first visited Brinkie's Brae and obtained its blessing. I will go in 1977.) That other local eminence, the Black Crag, I was rather afraid of. It's pleasant enough to gather mushrooms on the side of it on an autumn evening, or to walk beside a rich Outertown cornfield that surges halfway up. But climb to the crumbling coastguard hut, and qualms begin to take hold. The ground slopes down steeply, and doesn't stop until it reaches the cliff edge. Even to stand there and think about it for a second puts a hollow feeling in the stomach. 'Imagine,' you think, 'if I were to stumble now, and fall, I wouldn't stop rolling till I was in the Atlantic, with seals and lobsters'... Those folk who hazard themselves on the sheer verge—I don't know whether to think of them as idiots or heroes.

When I was a boy there was a saying: 'The Black Crag claims a victim every seven years'... As far as I know, nobody in my lifetime has gone over there. So, we clever moderns are apt to think superiorly: 'So much for those old tags and saws'... I wouldn't dismiss a piece of ancient wisdom so summarily. Fate may blind us, the more spectacularly to strike. No, the Black Crag has claimed no victim for more than half a century; maybe longer. But I can't help imagining, say, a merry picnic party eating their sandwiches and quaffing coffee from flasks, some innocent bright summer day, near where that sombre slope meets the sheer perpendicular. The Black Crag may give a little shrug, or it may decide to pay tribute to the Atlantic with a little swift erosion. Where will the picnickers be then? Where the plastic mugs, the crusts, the orange peel?

Time

25.11.1976

In Orkney in the old days you didn't need a watch or a clock (or a calendar, if it comes to that). The Birsay crofter and the Rackwick fisherman looked up at the sun when they wanted a general idea of how the day was wearing; ten minutes here or there didn't matter.

When they were going to or coming from 'the lasses', the stars guided them, or gave some indication of time's precious passing.

But modern Orcadians are thirled to the tyrannous precisions of time. I have been wearing a watch since I was about nineteen. Not the same watch, of course; a succession of them that one after the other went the way of all metals: through a hole in the pocket, or a clot of dirt in the works put an end to it, or a violent fall on a paving stone.

Of late years I have entrusted myself, as far as time goes, to a firm of cheap, reliable watch manufacturers. You expect their watches to last for three or four years, before they yield themselves to timelessness. (Nobody could ask for more.)

The other day I was working in the kitchen when the watch catapulted from my wrist on to the floor. It had been mortally wounded. Minute hand and hour hand were frozen on the still face. I gave it a shake or two; it spilled out a few seconds, then died again.

Well, it had given good service and I wasn't complaining. But I couldn't envisage life without a watch. So along I went to the jeweller's the next afternoon and bought (from the same reliable firm) a new one; with, if you please, a little square in the face that tells you the day of the month.

I was in business again, as far as time was concerned.

There it lay on the living-room table, the dead watch that had been such a faithful friend for years. Once or twice I gave it a little toss in the air, in the hope that its encounter with the table-top would shock it into life. Not a hope.

There used to be a young Israeli on television who could bend spoons and sort watches by stroking them gently. I may have been remembering Uri Geller unconsciously when, in an idle moment, I picked up the ruined watch once again and stroked its stainless steel back with my forefinger. It began to go, at once. The second hand got into its long circular stride. The little metal heart, inside, pulsed healthfully. And it has gone on, telling the time faithfully, ever since.

Now I have two watches, one on my wrist and one on the mantelpiece. Plus a clock. We have come a long way from the old Rackwick fisherman whose timepiece was the unfailing sun.

A Winter Drive

2.12.1976

There's not much time, on a winter afternoon, to see very much of Orkney. My friend from Northumberland arrived in a hired car at 2pm. Unfortunately the light wasn't good—the sky didn't have that heraldic Wagnerian quality of Thursday: all gold and darkness and smoulders. Instead, it was a queer eerie light—a thin fleece of grey rain-bearing clouds over all the sky, except the north-east. 'Stronsay and Sanday,' I thought, 'will be having a fine afternoon.'

There was not much choice of itinerary especially since my friend had been to Kirkwall and across the Barriers to the Hope in the morning. Northwards the route lay. We stopped and got out at Skaill Bay. My friend was impressed by the iron-grey light on the inshore curving breakers, and further out. Of course he ought to see that western sea on a summer evening, near sunset.

North again past Marwick and Oxtro and Boardhouse Mill and down to 'the P'lace'. For the hundredth time I tell some things about Mary Queen of Scots' half-brother Earl Robert, and his bad Latin that got him hanged.

We turned at the beautifully-sited public convenience at the burn, and drove out to the Brough. No getting across that afternoon; grey-and-white waves were washing the causeway. Besides, the rain was falling spasmodically, a light thin smirr. There was time enough to say something about St Magnus and what happened to him on the last day of his life.

Along the beautiful north coast—Swannay, Costa, Evie—and a brighter sky above. The road was dry under us. Westray rode the Atlantic dim and distant. The Rousay hills looked grand and bleak in this winter light, and the 'roosts' were fairly ramping around Eynhallow. The islands opened like a fan—Egilsay, Wyre (where the two famous poets of Orkney[1] lived above the same foundation), Gairsay (where the ghost in the long yellow dress is said to drift, perhaps one of Sweyn's Irish captives). We saw the ancient and new peat cuttings along the Lyde Road, in the failing light. My friend got

1 Bjarni Kolbeinson and Edwin Muir.

out to perambulate the Brodgar Stones, which in that light look most impressive of all.

We swung round the Loch of Stenness and enjoyed a pot of tea at Tormiston Mill; with the burn tinkling and gurgling underneath. Earlier that day, Mrs Robertson told us, it had been full of trout.

When at last we came out, it was very dark. A thin moon looked spectral through the high cloud-fleece. Stromness, from the Clouster road, was a net of lights.

The Craft of Writing

9.12.1976

I don't know how many times a year people, known and strangers, come up and say, 'What inspires you? What drives you to write?'

It might be a beautiful morning, and I am sitting at Johnnie Flaw's pier watching the sea and the swans. Then, as like as not, I am joined on the seat by somebody; and he/she will say, 'I bet this is inspiring you!'

In fact, it's not inspiring me at all, though I like it. Nothing inspires me. I am driven to write by the necessity to eat, drink, and pay the rent.

Nobody would dream of saying to a joiner, 'What inspired you to make that door?' Or to a baker, 'Do you only bake loaves and cakes and cookies when you feel inspired?'

We are all tradesmen together, and we work because we have to keep body and soul together for as long as we can; and a roof over our heads; and dependents from starvation.

To write, therefore, all you need is a writing pad and fivepenny ballpoint pen. (Of all trades and occupations, the writer has the least expensive tools. Nor does he have to crate his goods, or stow them in boxes, and pay expensive transport costs—an envelope and a sixpence-halfpenny stamp will do the trick.)

When you sit down at the writing table, after breakfast, with the butter and breadcrumbs and honeypot still on it, some mornings you have no idea what to write about. It sometimes requires a little patience—a little blank of silence—before an image presents itself, or it may be a sequence of four or five words. Out of that germ everything comes, or crumbles into failure.

Some mornings, of course, you take up what you had been at the day before, and then everything is straightforward enough. The rhythms and the pattern are there already; you simply work to them.

Nor do you know when you pick up the pen, whether what will come will be a poem, a story, or a bit of dialogue.

The pen goes over the paper for about three hours or so. You know you are reaching the end of your stint because you begin to make mistakes: spell words wrong, lose the sharp edge of language, feel a numbness in wrist and brain.

That's what 'inspiration' is: hard work. And, if it has been passably done, a glow in the mind that might last for half an hour or so.

The Loaded Rowan Tree

16.12.1976

Is it going to be 'a coorse winter'? After three mild winters I think we should prepare ourselves. The rowan trees in Rackwick were loaded with berries this year—the sure sign, they say, of a hard winter to come.

Already, at the beginning of December, we have been sheathed in frost. The afternoon sun made no impression on it. Going up to the Lookout, I had to take care with every footstep. I am fast approaching the time when bones get brittle. Good though its reputation is, I don't want to spend Christmas in our hospital.

Safely on the summit of the Lookout (to which the fisherman used to climb regularly, to see if there were any poaching trawlers on the horizon) the view is beautiful. Impossible to take it all in—it has to be divided into segments: the Atlantic with curtains of falling snow here and there; white capes about the shoulders of Hoy; Flotta with the first of its myriad million-dollar lights beginning to appear; the long fluent sweep of Orphir; and right beneath us, the town and the harbour.

Lovely, but heart-piercingly cold. We went home by another circuitous ice-perilous country road, under purplish high-piled snow clouds, away from the fading primrose of the west.

* * *

Little or no snow fell out of those clouds a fortnight ago.

When I went to bed last night the street was dry and hard as bone. I woke this morning to an unexpected radiance on the ceiling. It could only mean one thing—snow. The stuff—which some consider ethereally light and beautiful, and most (alas) consider a nuisance—must have fallen while Orkney slept.

I haven't been out in the snow yet, but I must go, on certain urgent errands. The street below this house is not inviting—it is all churned-up slush, the very stuff to harbour the germs of influenza and arthritis.

I remember a marvellous snowfall in Orkney five or six winters ago. In the midst of all that blue and silver radiance, alternating with the soft grey cold heart of snow clouds as they drifted across the town, people kept lamenting: 'O what a day! O what dreadful winter weather!' ... It was, in fact, utter pure enchantment.

In half an hour I'll have to be out along that same street. The fact that, this afternoon, I shrink from it, may be a sign that I, in my turn, am getting awkward and perverse and old. 'Where are the snows of yesteryear?'

Yule

23.12.1976

There was magic in the air for weeks beforehand. The stark air of winter held a different kind of enchantment from anything summer could offer: darker, more intense, more thrilling.

The first intimation came, perhaps, in school. We in the 'higher infants' class, with bits of coloured paper and pots of paste, made our own decorations. Finally the day came when the paper chains were hung about the classroom wall. At once it was a place transformed—the austere classroom had become a magic palace!

In the Sunday School, we began to sing 'Once in Royal David's City' and 'Away in a Manger'.

At home, of course, the main things happened. It had started in mid-November with the baking of cakes: one blond, and full of nuts and raisins and cherries, the other a dark rich heavy bun coated with a thick crust.

From some attic or cupboard last year's decorations were dredged. Some had got tangled and torn—out to Rae's shop then to get a few new ones, a penny each! In some kind of random pattern the decorations were pinned to the ceiling. In the centre beam the paper bell was hung. A few pieces of mistletoe were cunningly hidden in the coloured folds.

There were no Christmas trees in the nineteen-twenties that I remember.

An all-important letter had to be written to Santa. No boy or girl seriously questioned the existence of that generous spirit; who was much more than a spirit: he was a real, stout, apple-cheeked, white-bearded, merry-eyed visitor from the North Pole, with a red hood and a red coat. He halted his reindeer on every rooftop where a child lived; he climbed down the chimney with his sack of presents; he filled your stocking in the darkness. (Woe betide any child who deliberately stayed awake to see Santa at work—he might get a stocking filled with cinders...)

There were far fewer Christmas cards a half-century ago; those that did drop through the letterbox seemed (if I remember rightly) to be all celluloid and gilt ornate lettering. A parcel was a rarity.

Halfway through December, ginger wine had been made, and stowed away in bottles. My taste buds still remember that sweetness, nuttiness, spiciness.

The letter was despatched up the lum and sometimes it dropped again, half-scorched and grimy with soot. Never mind—let it burn—Santa had got the message.

The great drama built up to a climax.

The blond cake was marzipaned and iced. The huge naked goose was stuffed with oatmeal, ready to be sent to the baker's in the morning.

Amid shouts and yells, in the darkness of Christmas Eve, the youths and men dragged north or south, as Fate decided, the 'Yule Log'.

There was an occasional mistletoe kiss—great laughter—the promise of a pair of gloves or a pair of socks...

Then it was time for children to be in bed; to sleep; to waken early to the great mystery of giving: made tangible in the stocking by a game of Ludo, perhaps, with orange and apple, bag of sweeties, a threepenny bit, and a full day of wonderment to come.

1976

30.12.1976

1976, like most years, has been 'a mingled yarn'. There was that golden August, with only minor worries about drought (compared, that is, to the scorched south). Through that golden time drifted floods of tourists, most of them young. One 'day tourist' brought me a gift of an 11 lb salmon. In the caravan of two young French tourists, late one night, we watched a peerless sunset, and immediately afterwards a magical moonrise over Orphir. There was no sheen on earth like the harbour that night, in the high tide.

I managed two trips south, almost a record: and each time visited Perthshire and Edinburgh. In one beautiful Perthshire house, before dinner, we tasted malt whisky that had been a full hundred years in the bottle. We visited a churchyard with the oldest yew tree in Europe—3,000 years, a piece of riven darkness. In an Edinburgh hall we heard marvellous Orkney-inspired music... But Edinburgh, in February, was in the grip of flu. Everywhere people were either getting ready to crawl greyly into bed, or were making miserable recoveries, or having relapses. The astonishing thing is that I, who am open to every germ and virus, escaped with a whole skin...

In Rackwick, one lovely week, we drank home-brew and ate sandwiches in the sunshine, in a little patch of green above the sea.

Speaking about home-brew; there was one frantic disappointment. A brew I put on at the end of March—traditionally the best month for brewing—went bad on me. What sorrow, to have to empty the tainted stuff down the sink! It put me off brewing for seven months. You could call it, as far as I'm concerned, a year of books. I was asked to review verse for *The Scotsman*—since when hardly a week passes but a cascade of review copies of new poetry comes through the letterbox. Of course, you just select the books you want to review. But the trouble is that this house is half-buried in books now: most of them never to be read by me again. There must be a way of disposing of them: so that I can move freely without knocking over a column of books, as tall as the Old Man of Hoy.

One afternoon I was sitting in a friend's garden. The sun shone. To while away the idle hour, I sketched out a story about a black kitten called Fankle. In the following days, event after event happened to Fankle and his friend, a girl called Jenny. In no long time the first draft of a book was on the table.

Besides which, just when I thought the muse of poetry had deserted me, I began to write verse—I daren't begin to call it poetry until a year or two has passed—in astonishing profusion. I'll always remember 1976 for that.

Hogmanay

6.1.1977

Tomorrow (as I write this) is Hogmanay: a night to which ageing people—like me—look forward with a mixture of dread and curiosity.

There has always been a mystery about this festival—if you can call it that. Even the name is strange; no one is sure as to the derivation. How did it, then, suddenly appear in the Scottish calendar as a major feast, instead of just the seventh day of the twelve days of Christmas, that ends with Epiphany, the 6th of January?

It seems certain that, in the course of the 17th century and perhaps later, attempts were made to stamp out Christmas altogether, as being an occasion for gluttony and sloth, a lurid papish remnant. This assault on the feast of Christmas was so successful in parts of Scotland that within the past century Christmas Day was just an ordinary day, with shops open and folk going about their business. It looked as if the magic—good or bad—had been well and truly dispersed.

There is a stubbornness in the popular will and imagination, however, that is not to be ruled by decrees, ordinances, or acts of parliament. 'Very well,' said the devious mass-mind, 'if they want to abolish Christmas, let them. Good luck to them. But we, the people, are halfway through a hard winter. The darkness has worked itself into us, flesh and spirit. Dance and drink and sing we will, whatever they say. It is a token of both thankfulness and hope. What about in a week's time?—We dimly remember a pagan feast round about then—it was called Hogmanay, or some Pictish name like that...' So the winter feast took place after all, in the dark vennels and the straths and isles of Scotland. But it lacked all the marvellous ingredients of Christmas—the great story, the treasury of carol and ceremony. Hogmanay was an altogether more primitive communal event shot through with darkness and fate and excess.

Nowadays we have both Christmas and New Year; which, it might be argued, is a double ration—two celebrations for the price of one. But our peasant ancestors, whom we consider so 'ignorant and brutish' compared to our enlightened selves, had a better time of it than we can ever imagine. Christmas was not a single holy-day for them, it was a feast twelve days long, filled with most beautiful ceremony and ritual in their own houses and barns and byres. Those interested in what has been lost should read *Orkney and Shetland Calendar Customs* by Mrs M. Banks (The Folk-Lore Society).

Oranges, Snow, Fire

13.1.1977

One morning, twixt Christmas and Hogmanay, as I lay cosy in bed, I heard a knock at the door. It was too cold to get up. But when I did get up, what was lying on the doorstep but a crate of orange juice! I had not ordered a supply of orange juice, being at that time of year interested in more seasonal liquors. Had the crate perhaps been delivered to the wrong door? From that day to this, I have not heard a thing—where it came from, who the kind donor was... In order not to have the bottles frozen solid, I carried them into the kitchen. Unless someone claims them, I will keep my veins pure with orange juice until the spring comes... (Later: I found a phrase in a letter that clarified the situation.)

* * *

Hogmanay was a good night for traipsing about. In a hospitable house we had in the evening the traditional supper of salt herring and tatties and melted butter. Nothing like that for buttressing you against excess!

And indeed, after a good few drams, I walked home on steady feet; and felt well next morning.

* * *

Will this winter be called the winter of the many snows? There have been three or four blossomings already—a joy to children, a nuisance to cats and taxi-drivers.

The suddenest and most beautiful came on the late afternoon of New Year's Day, in the first fold of darkness. I opened the door to let in first-footers—the street was dry. Ten minutes later a friend came with a summons to dinner; he came in with crumbs of snow clinging to him. After we had toasted each other, we went down to his car in the courtyard, through inches of bright crisp sudden snow. The problem then was to know if the car could tackle the frictionless hill. It managed, just. 'Another ten minutes,' said the driver, 'and we'd have been stuck!'

We rejoiced in a glorious dinner of roast goose.

* * *

Always those festive nights, coming and going on Ness Road, you see an island lighted like a birthday cake. The other islands are meagrely illuminated. It is the rich island of Flotta, in the middle of Scapa Flow, that is so outglorying its neighbours.

Jeremy Rundall

20.1.1977

One of the most passionate Orkneyphiles of recent years was Jeremy Rundall, radio critic and travel correspondent of *The Sunday Times*. His greatest delight was to step off the plane at Grimsetter and take car or bus to Stromness; and, some time later, the ferryboat to Hoy.

Jeremy Rundall had the gift of friendship. Scores of Orcadians quickly got to know him and like him. He had great charm and humour, and he entered into all the island activities with gusto—fishing, walking, or just looking at the changing seas and skies.

Whereas most folk turn their faces to the sun and the south whenever they can, Jeremy was a northern man. Lapland, Sweden, Iceland, the Faroes, Greenland, Orkney and Shetland were his territory: places where the great drama of light and darkness is played out through the year, and where to live at all often calls for courage and endurance. He wrote a book about his northern travels, which I hope will be published some day, there is so much good robust stuff in it.

Like a bird he had the freedom of the far northern skies; which is one way of saying that he was a devoted air traveller. No one ever made more enthusiastic use of BEA and Loganair.

He wrote a good deal of verse which he only showed to friends, but it is also well worth publishing. This is the great age of crossword puzzles in verse, and obscurity masquerading as depth; and complexity, and shapelessness. Jeremy's verse was mostly about people and places; it has the breadth and clarity of northern light, and a true heartbeat pulsing through it.

Recently his health had given grounds for concern. He had had several serious operations to his foot. Even though cripple, he wanted to spend Christmas in Orkney; though travelling north, and getting around in the islands, would have been extraordinarily difficult for him.

He died suddenly in Oxford, one Sunday a few weeks back.

Right up to the end he had written his radio columns in *The Sunday Times*—criticism concise, observant, generous.

His wish was that his ashes be scattered in Orkney. This melancholy duty, when asked, I could not refuse. And so, this afternoon, in a clear wintry light, with the shadows of snow clouds on the immense stillness of Hoy Sound, the dust of Jeremy Rundall was given to the air and earth that he loved so much.

Which Party Would Burns Support?

27.1.1977

How shameful!—the 25th of January (Burns Day) will have come and gone ere this appears. I hope it is not too late to make amends. One always likes to honour that truly great man.

It is intriguing, I thought, reading *The Orcadian* advertisements, to see that Burns Suppers were celebrated by both the Orkney Liberals and the Orkney Tories, as well as by parishes, Kirks, WRIs here and there. I could not discover whether the Scot Nats were honouring the bard too: one might think the 25th January would be a red-letter day with them. And Labour seemed curiously coy; though more than one Labour supporter will assert vehemently that Burns was a socialist (the word 'socialist' had not yet been coined in his day).

Well, then, what party would Burns have supported had he been alive today? No doubt, going by the evidence of his written work, the Nationalists have a very strong case. No one was more eloquently patriotic, although those poems of praise ('O Scotia! my dear, my native soil') rarely reach the level of his greatest verse.

Money, honours, profit had no appeal to him at all. Could you really see him sitting on a right-wing platform? His sympathy was entirely with the poor and the suffering. (And this is not to say he would have attended Labour meetings either, in these days of 'each segment of society for itself'; and to the strongest the most.)

The circle of his sympathy extended beyond humanity, to embrace all created things. People nowadays sometimes cavil at the 'Mouse' and 'Mountain Daisy' poems. Read them again; apart from the triumph of the craftsmanship, the images are superb and exact: the whole flow of the poetic argument inevitable and deeply moving. The communists claim him too. Did he not, at the time of the French Revolution, donate a gun to the Revolutionaries—at great personal risk to his job as a civil servant. Yes, but the same man, when there was a threat of French invasion in the air, wrote stirring verses calling for the repulse of Napoleon's forces. In this he resembled his contemporary, Beethoven, who also rejoiced in the tearing down of a rotten political structure; but who later, when Napoleon declared himself Emperor, tore up the dedication of the Third Symphony.

The wise thing is not to try to fit such men into any political stable: narrow cribs and boxes cannot contain them.

Instancy

3.2.1977

Writing my diary for yesterday, five minutes ago, I noted that I had 'instant tomato soup' as a first course at dinner, and I finished off with 'instant coffee' (very expensive nowadays, too). Afterwards I sat down to do some work, and had a visit from a friend who presented me with an 'instant razor'—i.e., you use it a few times, and throw the whole thing away when it's finished. The instant razor is made by the same firm that manufactures the ballpoint instant pens I write with.

We are living ever more in an age of immediacy. We can't wait, like our forebears, for the slow shapings and consummations of time. On the screen, instant sensation—the mandatory bedroom scenes with no attempt to show how love strikes, roots, develops, flowers. (There just isn't time, it seems.) Jane Austen would have been shocked, not so much at the crudity of the actions depicted as at the ineptitude of the art.

It all started a long time ago, this appetite for rootless immediacy, with newspapers. Here were the superficial actions of men and peoples—read them, wonder for a moment, throw the sheet away when it's finished. Ezra Pound once said that literature is news that remains news always... But to make any work of art that has perennial value, there must be a craftsman with skill, patience, understanding, imagination.

These craftsmen are getting rarer and rarer in this world of instant objects. Things are made to wear out fast.

When my cheap watch falters, I don't send it to the watchmaker; I throw it away and buy a new one that will go for three or four years; the watchmaker's repair might be more expensive.

Whether we deplore it or not, we are all caught up in this shallowness. The past—whenever we Orcadians think about it—is Vikings with winged helmets and glorious boasts. (They were probably far less interesting as a people than the subtle ingenious race that built Maeshowe.)

And when we visit any place nowadays, it is hardly ever to attempt to understand the place or the people. Not a summer passes but some American or German 'does' Orkney in a couple of days, and moves on fleetingly to some other fleeting place.

Having a slight cold in the head this morning, I have used, and thrown into the bucket, a snowstorm of instant handkerchiefs.

Three Sunsets in One Day

17.2.1977

Three days now the east wind has gone racketing round the house; draughts come, little grey daggers, through every crack and seam. There is a kind of melancholy contentment, watching the scrolled grey and silver harbour water, and the savage circles of white-maas. February is February, and we must expect saga-like weather.

There have been one or two days like golden lyrics in the midst of all this stern stuff.

It isn't often that I make the West Mainland itinerary so early in the year: Yesnaby, Skaill, Birsay, Gorseness, Lyde, Stoneyhill, Stenness, and home again. Never fear: I have no intention of inflicting one more account of that journey, although it was made on a beautiful day and in pleasant company. Sufficient to say that we took one appalled look into that fearful sea chasm at Longaglebe, Birsay; and enjoyed Guinness and cheese sandwiches in the Standing Stones hotel.

The fact is, my friends were looking for possible locations for a story to be televised[1]. Sometimes it only occurs to one, after the journey is over, that such-and-such a place would be perfect for a particular scene. That's what happened over the Guinness and cheese sandwiches.

In mid-afternoon, that same sun-tranced day, we had a look at the marvellous cluster of old houses at Kirbister, Birsay; and afterwards at the gracious profile of Smoogro, Orphir.

The sun had just set over Hoy as we emerged from Houton: there were springs and fountains of intense light from the underside of the hill. Then, as the car sped on to Stromness, the sun appeared in the cleavage between hill and hill, attended by rich heraldries of cloud. It was so beautiful we stopped the car and looked until the Coolags took the sun into its keeping. The car started up; we made for Stromness again. Incredibly, somewhere along the Ireland road, the sun appeared again. It hung just over the sea horizon, a perfect golden sphere, quite naked of the clouds that so often cover its going; and dropped slowly, splendidly, silently into the ocean.

I think last Tuesday—the day of the uranium march—was the first time I had ever seen three sunsets in the space of fifteen minutes. I hope it is a good portent.

Fankle the Black Cat

24.2.1977

Like human beings, some animals are smitten with the wanderlust, and others are 'sweet stay-at-homes'... There was a litter of kittens born in a farm at the back of Stromness one day at the beginning of winter. They were all black, like their mother, except that each one had a little patch of white somewhere about him or her.

Eventually the kittens were weaned and adopted by this household and that. The black tom kitten with a white spot on his chest went

1 *Miss Barraclough*, shown on BBC television, June 1977.

to a house at the South End. You would have thought that such a tiny creature would be only too glad, on cold winter nights, to sit blinking, and purring and washing himself in front of the fire.

The spirit of Ulysses must have entered into that kitten.

We were all celebrating New Year in another hospitable house behind the town, when first-footers arrived, one of them carrying a black kitten. He had found it in Graham Place, drifting around and wishing all Stromness 'A Happy New Year'. Graham Place is a considerable distance from Ness Road, and the kitten was very tiny.

A few nights later he vanished again, and wasn't seen for days. All hope was given up for him (though a forlorn advertisement was put in this newspaper). A caravan-dweller turned up at the door, carrying a little black purring bundle.

Surely it had had its fill of adventure! Some animals, and folk, pack all the excitement of their days into a first few hectic months; then retire prematurely into serene complacent respectability.

Nothing like that for Fankle (that is the kitten's name). A week or so later he was discovered in Stromness Academy, sitting on the deputy rector's desk and going studiously over his papers...

It's never the lowly unimportant places he seeks out. Just the other day he deigned to call at the Town House, no doubt to see for himself how the affairs of the municipality were going. A phone call, a car-ride, and the adventurer was home again.

To see him sitting licking his paws in front of the fire, you'd swear you never saw anything so sweet and domestic. Until suddenly a black gale goes through him and he throws himself at your hand, all teeth and claws!

This Fankle has a sister called Gipsy. Now Gipsy, you'd think—with a name like that—would be another wanderer. But no, Gipsy loves to sit and sleep in the rocking chair. She takes an occasional sedate walk, blinking with wonderment at singing birds and tall grasses.

Old Famous Houses

3.3.1977

I was walking homeward along the street one day, with a bag of messages and a heavy cold on me, when I happened to meet the doctor right in the door of the chemist shop. What could have been more providential? I got my prescription on the spot for the yellow tablets that, like shafts and pools of sunlight, quickly disperse those dark damps and vapours that invade the bronchial tubes twice or thrice a year.

And then the doctor invited me to come in his car to Orphir, where he had one or two calls to make.

That beautiful afternoon, we went along three or four side-roads where I'd never set foot (so unadventurous some of us are, sticking firmly to the highway). We miss a lot, that way. Rendall, for example, from that long straight road, looks a dull flat parish. Take the narrower sea roads of Rendall, and there is beauty and interest everywhere.

The Hall of Clestrain—I see it every day from Stromness, a finely-proportioned building across the Bay of Clestrain. Fascinating history attaches to it—it was there that Gow the pirate and his scoundrels arrived unexpectedly one day in the winter of 1725, and proceeded to sack the house; going about their business ruthlessly, and caring nothing about the laird's wife Mrs Honeyman and her terrified servants. They found nothing of value. Mrs Honeyman had spied them coming in their small boat, rowing, and, prudent woman, she had hidden the valuable silver plate and quaichs and all the sovereigns and crown pieces under a huge heap of feathers in the attic, which the pirates passed without a second look. They weren't interested in stuffing for pillows and cushions...

And in the same house was born Dr John Rae the explorer, who (with his Orkneymen) gleaned from an Eskimo the story of the last days of the Franklin expedition that was to seek out and navigate the north-west passage 130 years ago; but their two ships, that had last made landfall in Stromness, were crushed in the huge mills of ice.

Surely, we thought, such a famous house—and so gracious too, even in decay—ought to be preserved as a keystone in our heritage. And another building sprang to mind, Breckness, where Bishop George Graham had his house in the early 17th century.

The truth is, I'm sure, that both Clestrain and Breckness are too far gone to do anything with, more's the pity.

Inflation

10.3.1977

From time to time you hear people in authority saying that inflation is slowing down at last; soon it will be quite manageable.

From the worm's eye point of view (which is our line of vision) that is all nonsense. It seems to be getting worse, if anything. I got my electricity bill the other day—and it was like getting a blow between the eyes. Surely you remember the '40s and '50s when the Hydro bill might come to £2 odds a quarter in summer; never much more than £3 in winter (at least, that's how it seemed to work out in our house). But I wasn't the only one by any means to get an 'electric shock' this week.

I went to pay the weekly rent on Monday—being very punctual—and was handed a billet-doux in the Town House stating that the rent of this house is going up from £4.50 to £5.25 in April. I'm not complaining. But when I moved in here first, in 1968, the rent was 18/6 a week.

You must remember when you could buy a large jar of coffee for about ten shillings (50p for the benefit of children under twelve). It has climbed lately to four times that price. And tea, coffee's sister, is drifting along in the same direction... Soon you will have to relish every drop of coffee you roll around your tongue; like every luxury.

And to buy a plane ticket to Aberdeen or Edinburgh: perhaps in the old days it did make you think twice, but the benefits and advantages outweighed cost. No longer—there's little chance of a poor man, unsubsidised by state or corporation, taking to the air.

Home brewers used to rejoice in the cheapness of malt (to say nothing of its other advantages over canned beer). Is memory really playing tricks, or did I use to buy a 2½lb tin of malt for 4/6 (22½p)? Last time I bought one, it was £1.30. I admit, the finished product was good.

There used to be a fairy tale when I was a boy. Workers in Germany in the nineteen-twenties wheeled their wages home in wheelbarrows. Those of us who collected stamps were inundated with mint German stamps, value 1,000,000 marks. On some, the '1 million' would be overprinted with '3 million'; the dreadful fairy tale was true, after all, for some people.

I dread the day, some time about 1984, when I go into a shop for a box of matches and pay for it with a £1,000 note (no change).

Great Days

17.3.1977

1935 was Silver Jubilee Year (that is, of King George V). 1937 was Coronation Year. The events came so close that they run together in my mind: the fine distinctions are blurred. There were mugs, possibly on both occasions. Lemonade was poured into them—into hundreds of mugs—in the playground of Stromness Academy, as the pupils walked past the mug-laden table in single file. Also a thick chocolate biscuit was put in your free hand.

I have a photograph to prove it, but whether of 1935 or 1937 I could not be sure.

Where, oh where, are all those hundreds of mugs now? I haven't seen one in a Stromness house for twenty years. It was certainly the Silver Jubilee that drew us to St Peter's Church (now the Community Centre) to hear over the radio a commentary about what was happening in London, along the route from Buckingham Palace to Westminster Abbey.

Nowadays no schoolboy would waste a free morning on such a broadcast, full of cracklings and sound-surgings like the sea. But there we sat most of the morning in our Sunday suits, straining our ears. In 1935 the wireless was still a magic box. Not every family owned a set; hence the need for a communal 'listen in'. (I think it was 1936 that the first wireless came to our house.)

Was there a bonfire on Brinkie's Brae in 1935? I really can't remember. There was certainly a bonfire in 1937—and a grand sports day at the Market Green—and a fancy dress parade through the street that left behind it a wide wake of laughter and awe and delight.

I do not know if there were mugs in 1937 or not—I rather think there were—but there was certainly 'the portrait of the King in bronze'. That fine phrase was uttered by Provost J. G. Marwick to the assembled schoolchildren, standing in that fine early summer day in the stony playground. Provost Marwick announced that, in addition to the other gifts bestowed on us, he was going to present each and every one with a portrait of the King in bronze. It sounded so marvellous; I suppose other pupils than myself imagined something like a sizeable bronze plate. It turned out to be a mint penny, with the new King's head on it, circumscribed about the rim with his titles in Latin... D:G:BR:OMN:REX F:D:IND:IMP.

It turned out—May 12, 1937—to be a day of boundless freedom and light and joy. We were not to know that, two and a half years later, we would be at war, and liable for the call-up. Through that delicate summer web poked the skeleton finger.

Fires

24.3.1977

For one who sits most nights in front of an electric fire, there is no greater pleasure than visiting a house where they burn coal. How the eye revels in the red and yellow dance of the flames, and in the mystery of wreathing smoke. Even if there was no heat, the mere look of it puts a glow about the heart.

That electric fire of mine—what a cold clinical hostile heat it gives off! It makes a Sahara of the bronchial tubes and the lungs. After a few hours of it, you long for a breath of cold outside air on the face.

There is no reason why I shouldn't have a coal fire. There the grate was when I moved into this new house eight and a half years ago.

And, true enough, I burned some of the remnant of the Well Park coal in it, and was quite satisfied.

But then, people like me are out quite a lot. How easy and quick the electric fire is to switch off and on! In the morning the wave of heat strikes your knees at once. Whereas, with a coal fire, you have to crumple up paper, and chop sticks, and make a cunning top stratum of coal lumps; and even then, in the old days, the fire sometimes died on me... Then there is the business of raking out ashes and dust, with blue hands on a cold winter morning. The coal fire is a cheery soul when all is going well, but it has its awkward unpleasant times. A gust of wind blows down the lum—your newly spring-cleaned house can hardly be seen through the fug!

The electric fire appeals to the lazy man in all of us. 'Come, you'll have no trouble with me. I'm always at your service, a silent obedient heat-giver...' But (as I said) it's cold and clinical and joyless, like some efficient character out of the twenty-fourth century.

Often folk urge me to return to the lively blessings of coal. And often enough I'm tempted. But the lazy man inside always wins: 'It's too much trouble. Who'd be there to poke the fire and keep it going, the many times you're out? Besides, your chimney would have to be thoroughly swept: don't you hear the birds singing in their nest a third of the way up? Coal, indeed! You might as well go really primitive, and dig red peat from the flank of Brinkie's Brae. Then, half-broken with toil and weather, you'd see what a good friend the electric fire is!'

The First Orcadians

31.3.1977

Life, said one seventeenth-century pessimist, is brief, brutish and nasty... It never struck me that way until I saw the recent archaeological programme, *Underground Orkney* with Dr Anna Ritchie and Professor Colin Renfrew in fascinating form about our remote ancestors.

It was astonishing to learn that the folk of those primitive tribes rarely lived beyond the age of thirty. Twenty was probably the average lifespan. For some of those brief years, if you had been an Orkneyman of 4,000 years ago, you would have been plagued with arthritis, among other things. No doubt often they went hungry and cold. No doubt their days were haunted by fears and dreads that we have outgrown (or have pushed deep down into the cellar of the unconscious, whence they emerge from time to time in dreams) 'Brief, brutish and nasty', life indeed must have been for them, we conclude. Since life was so short and uncertain, death was the solid stable reality. Death they saw at work all round them. Infants died, old thirty-year men and women died, the young hunter fell under the wild boar on the hill. The birds and the fish were killed, but this kind of death had a strange paradox in it; it kept the flame of life going for the people. Death must have seemed no negation of life, but a necessary part of it, beautiful perhaps, and to be welcomed. The bone and the breath intermeshed.

So it seems they lavished far more care on their 'houses of the dead' than on the huts and hovels they passed their days in. The dead had gone, not into nothingness, but 'into another intensity' (as T. S. Eliot put it).

There, perhaps, the meaning of their miserable few years on earth was made plain to them. There, perhaps, they existed in a timeless beauty, nobility, heroism.

Maeshowe remains, when most of the dwellings of contemporary Orcadians have vanished. Is it pressing the point too far to see it as womb-shaped, and as a huge green circle like spring sun? Enough has been written about the fleeting splash of the setting sun on one Maeshowe wall at the time of the winter solstice: a seed of renewal.

Brief, certainly, their lives were: but it seems they had vision and they had hope. Where those positive attitudes flourish, there is so much the less brutishness and nastiness. Soon we might be living to a hundred and over in a clinical world without any life-giving imagination at all.

A Rose by Any Other Name...

7.4.1977

Today is April the first (as I write). So far, nobody has said to me, 'You have a black smudge on your face,' or 'Look at that flying saucer—no, not there, over there!—In the sky'... And then, when I jerk puppet-wise in response, they cry 'Hint a gock!' And then they laugh to see you so taken in and crestfallen...

It hasn't happened yet, for the simple reason that I haven't seen a living soul since I got up this morning. Since breakfast I've been sitting at the kitchen table answering a pile of letters. There's hardly a clear space, for masses of paper, envelopes, stamps, pencils, paper clips, rubber bands.

I've just changed the calendar on the kitchen wall from March to April. A lady from England sent me a beautiful calendar at Christmas, published by RSPB (the Royal Society for the Protection of Birds). It is a long slim calendar, with days and figures down one margin and plenty of blank space in the middle for writing notes, comments, or haikus (mini-poems). Each month has a beautiful painting of a bird by Robert Gilmor. I have just changed the goldcrest of March for the dabchick of April.

April—I think it is one of the loveliest words in the language. The sound it makes is exquisite—a little song. It is a poem of clean springing images: daffodil, lamb, garden, eggs, warm glowing showers. The poets have always seen April as a girl, eager and laughing, but quickly moved to tears. Perhaps they have been a bit sentimental about the month (which is why, no doubt, the young iconoclast T. S. Eliot began his most famous poem with 'April is the cruellest month...').

But I still like everything about April: the sense of sap and surge everywhere, the swift-encroaching light, men in shirt sleeves planting tatties, women beating the living daylights out of mattresses.

Perhaps April is a beautiful word only by association. When you think about it, May, June and July are also little miniatures of poetry (not quite so perfect, perhaps, as spring's first-comer).

Here is a mystery of art, which it would take a big thick volume to thrash out fully: if April fell in some dark period of winter, and not when she does, would we shudder at the sound of the name?

This Is the Way the World Ends

21.4.1977

I suppose the first thing most of us do, when we wake up in the morning, is switch on the transistor beside the bed. In the morning, first thing, you look for a cheerful voice like the sun to break through the mists of sleep. Once or twice, lately, wonderful communications have come on the early morning radio waves.

Only this morning it was a thing about dogs. I have never liked or trusted them at the best of times (except for an individual dog here and there). The voice on the wireless said that dogs carry some germ or worm or micro-organism inside them that can make children blind, or mentally retarded... A good happy thought to start the day with: especially when you remember how dogs make the public street their lavatory.

A few mornings back an expert was saying how, billions of years ago, the earth was bombarded with heavenly bodies, which caused great circular craters on the surface; points of weakness. This is why South America, for example, broke away from Africa; they fit into each other neatly across the South Atlantic, like pieces of a jigsaw. The west coast of Norway exhibits the same clean break, also Australia.

Everybody wonders, sometimes, how the world began, and how (if at all) it is to end. The Bible speaks of the moon turning to blood, and the stars falling down; but of course we all pooh-pooh such non-scientific fantasy nowadays.

But, nags the mind, if it happened once before, when there was probably no life on earth at all—or only life so simple-celled as to be hardly worth the name—why can't it happen again? We live in a universe of the purest chance. If the earth reeled under an assault and swarm of heavenly bodies long long ago, why is it impossible for another such blind swarm to blunder into us some time in the future?

It could happen, and there is nothing we could do about it. Since there is nothing we can do, we're not likely to lose any sleep worrying. Space is so vast, and even the greatest stars such dust specks with a near infinity of space to themselves, that nothing of that apocalyptic kind is likely to happen in our time...

If it did happen, we wouldn't need to worry about next quarter's electricity bill; or the fact that the brewers want to put another 2p on the price of the malted water they call beer.

Saga Translations

28.4.1977

Some wise man once said that every house in England should have copies of Shakespeare and the Bible. In the same way, I suppose most Orkney homes would like to be graced with a copy of the *Orkneyinga Saga*.

The first translation was made just over a century ago, by Hjaltalin and Goudie. It was at a time when interest in the past of the islands was stirring in every intelligent Orkney man and woman. I remember John Mooney the historian telling me how eagerly he devoured the saga, lying one summer day somewhere on the Scapa coast. The translation he read was probably the Hjaltalin & Goudie one; but it could have been the Dasent translation of 1894. Whichever it was, there in front of his eyes was the backcloth against which those larger-than-life Orcadians enacted their roles. John Mooney must have felt very much like Keats opening Chapman's translation of Homer for the first time: 'Then felt I like some watcher of the skies...'

Earlier Orcadians knew vaguely that the islands had once been part of a Norse medieval empire. The ministers who, ardently or dully, compiled the statistical accounts of 1795 and 1840, speak of 'Danish lords', etc who once lorded it over the Orkneys; but their information was dim and scant.

No doubt the generous amount of space given to the Dasent translation in *The Orkney Book* of 1909 gave many a young Orcadian his first taste of the great story, and whetted his appetite for more. But Orkney had to wait till 1938 for the next translation—a very scholarly work by A.B.Taylor, in which the apparatus of introduction and notes outbulks the text. Dr Taylor's was a worthy translation, much more supple and colloquial than earlier ones, which had a kind of Victorian ornateness and weightiness about them. Sadly, Dr Taylor was working on a new edition when his death intervened.

I am happy to say that later this summer there will be published a completely new translation, by Hermann Pálsson and Paul Edwards, both of Edinburgh University. A proof copy was sent to me the other day, and I have dipped into it here and there. It will be a handsome volume, and the prose will fall true and sweet on twentieth-century ears which, nowadays, might be put off by Victorian 'thees' and 'thous' and 'wouldsts' and 'dursts'.

Hamnavoe Names

5.5.1977

The names bestowed on local places are endlessly fascinating. Some are pedestrian enough: calling one section of our street after Queen Victoria, and another after one of her sons (Alfred, Duke of Edinburgh) who happened to set foot in Stromness. Some (Dundas Street) smell of sycophancy a little. And will nobody ever enlighten us as to the John of John Street? (I remember wondering about this before.)

Some names are half-forgotten, like Plainstones, that section of the street just below the Church of Scotland. Plainstones is now incorporated in Victoria Street; but it never should have been, it is such a beautiful and fitting name. Was it called that because it was the first part of our street to be paved with flagstones?

It was a fine inspiration to call the central square in Stromness after our hero, Alexander Graham. His house forms the east side of the square. Poor Graham, who died in poverty—we were late in making reparations to him, small as they are.

You would think that tortuous by-road between the main street and the Back Road should be called Rae Road, rather than Franklin Road; because Dr John Rae is the real hero of that tragic episode in the Arctic ice. As for Franklin, he only called at Stromness to get water from Login's Well for his ships. (I must admit, Rae Road is not so euphonious as the other.)

I don't suppose John Gow the pirate will ever get a close named after him.

We come into fascinating territory with forgotten names that still linger on in the town's memory. Who was the Speeding of that tall building at the North End? Who was the Downie of that road that meanders up the side of Brinkie's Brae? Who, if it comes to that, was Brinkie, who gave his name to the hill? (I think there was no man called Brinkie: possibly it means 'the hill of burning'.)

Cooper's Slap: I remember that name from childhood. The old men used to say that Cooper's Slap in Cairston marked the town's northern boundary. I think it may be a mistake to try to fix names of closes, like 'Leslie's' and 'Christie's', for close names and pier names tend to change generation by generation. Khyber Pass—our most notorious local place name—was once Garrioch's close. What we used to call 'Copland's Pier' was formerly 'Ronaldson's Pier'—I wonder what the young folk call it nowadays?

Poetry at Skara Brae

12.5.1977

I rarely read verse aloud, even to myself. I wouldn't go on a platform and read verse to an audience for a fortune.

Sometimes, to earn some money, I read it into a microphone for a BBC recording. But that is different: there's nobody there but the producer, and beyond a thick glass panel, technicians etc.

Once, nearly five years ago, I made a recording for an Irish Record company, in a high room at Stromness Hotel. Again, there was only Paddy Maloney (of Chieftains fame) present. Every time a car revved up at the Pier Head fountain, we had to stop and start again. We managed to do twenty or more poems, and a story, with the help of a sup or two of whisky. (That record has just been published, and is so good technically that there's not a car engine to be heard, not the least breath of Highland Park.)

Along comes the Norwegian TV producer Erik Bye, the other day, and asks could I read some poems at Skara Brae, in front of his cameras?

Well, as I said it isn't a thing I relish doing, but one will go to some lengths to oblige our friends and cousins from across the North Sea.

Across a green field the Norwegian minibus lurched and bumped, towards a little village of huge TV trucks. Into one of them I was invited. (I do not understand mechanical or electrical marvels at all; but I gathered that this was some special 'video' form of filming.) Anyway, there, on several screens inside this mobile studio, was Skara Brae and those concerned with this part of the programme; gesturing, expounding, pointing out this stone bed and that stone sideboard— in, of course, Norwegian.

Outside, it was one of the coldest days of this spring of 1977. A bitter east wind, the magnificent waters of Skaill Bay a dull pewter, grey clouds hugging the hill tops.

Soon it was my turn. Normally, walking on to that green hillock at the centre of Skara Brae watched by TV cameras, I would have felt like a man going out to his execution. I suppose it was the cold that made me indifferent; it may have been a sip or two of Highland Park that cheered me up; but I think mostly it was the kindness of my Norwegian hosts. Anyway, I read the three poems—one of them rather long—with serenity and with only one minor mistake.

Immediately afterwards, inside the warm mobile studio, I watched my performance—it proved to be both a disconcerting and a reassuring experience. I think of all events it must have been the first poetry recital in Skara Brae for 4,000 years.

Radio Orkney

19.5.1977

Welcome and congratulations to Radio Orkney.

It is pleasant to wake up in the morning, switch on the radio, and hear all about the previous night's football results, the beef prices, whether the *Ola* is to leave or not (a boor, that must be, to intending travellers in Deerness or Evie), what the weather's likely to be: together with pleasant voices singing new Orkney songs, and the no less fluent controlling voices of Howie Firth and Liz Davies.

Of course Radio Orkney is only experimenting yet, and new and even more pleasant things will evolve in the future. But after only three days, it can be called a success.

I am wondering if some of the comical characters of Orkney fiction, namely the inhabitants of Stenwick (Chon Clouston, Godfrey Ritch, etc) could not be given a new life in Radio Orkney. These stories, when they appeared weekly in *The Orkney Herald*, were enormously popular in Orkney and far beyond. The trouble is that Orkney Radio's programme time is limited, and it would take Godfrey Ritch, that immortal veteran, a good ten minutes to work up his home-brew thirst. (It is just a suggestion.)

There must be a large archive of past Orkney radio programmes, many of them of outstanding interest. I think, for example, of the late Tommy Wishart, Double Houses, Stromness, describing the wreck of the *Shakespeare* at Breckness so long ago: how a tattoo of horses' hooves on the south end cobbles brought the first news to Stromness (was the horseman the farmer of Breckness?)...

That, and scores of other items, were heard once and once only. I know that hundreds of Orcadians would welcome the opportunity to hear them again.

I go to bed thinking how nice that new awakening is. (What by the way, is Radio Orkney's signature music?) This morning—Thursday May 12—I woke at 7.15, and turned over to sleep again. How disgusted I was to wake up, look at my watch, and discover that it was 8.50am! Nothing on the wireless but boring parliamentary debates! I had missed the morning treat. Nothing for it but to turn over and have another snooze.

Towards Changing a Name

26.5.1977

I have received a delightful letter from a lady in Kirkwall that is well worth reproducing. Being shy, she has put a pen name at the end of it. She writes vividly and well.

'Dear GMB—For many years I have read and enjoyed your "Pier Head" and "Under Brinkie's" columns. As bairns, our father, once or twice each year, took the family to Stromness to visit his mother who lived in an old house up one of the closes She gave us pennies to buy "claggam" in a shop across the street and our father always took us a scramble to the top of Brinkie's Brae which, in those far gone years, swarmed with blue butterflies. He always hired a "brake" and an old nag from P.F.Thompson in Kirkwall and left the outfit at Park's Blacksmith's premises. I can easily recall the Stromness Hotel being built. But this is NOT the reason why I am writing to you.

'It is about the event that will be upon us before long—Shopping Week—I believe the title is odious and offensive to many people, as if profit and the making of money was the chief and only concern. I have never heard your opinion—one way or the other. Couldn't we find another and more suitable and pleasant title for Stromness's Gala event? Many young people feel embarrassed at the present title in front of tourists, holidaymakers, "hippy" people and the townsfolk themselves... Could not the students in the Academy vie with each other and attempt to contrive a more desirable name for Shopping Week? Hamnavoe Festival, Hamnavoe Gala Week ... or just leaving in the Stromness and forgetting the "Shopping". Of course the decision would be up to the Town Councillors in the end. Many thanks for enjoyable reading throughout the years. Yours, "LIZA O'BAREBRECKS".'

I have never been comfortable with the name Shopping Week for the same basic reason as 'Liza o'Barebrecks'; though perhaps I wouldn't put it quite so strongly as she does. One or two suggestions have been sown, but have borne no fruit so far. I remember especially Professor Ronald Miller opening the Week six or seven years back and suggesting that 'St Olaf Week' might be a good title. It is the Chamber of Commerce, not the District Council, that has the say in these matters.

It may be, however, that the name, after nearly 30 years, is now so ingrained that 'Shopping Week' it will be to the end, whether we like it or not.

The Death of a Small Queen

2.6.1977

Erik Bye, the Norwegian TV producer, is such a modest man, that when he was in Orkney three weeks ago, he didn't tell me he was a songwriter. By a curious coincidence, the Norwegian TV team had hardly left the mists and rains of Orkney for home, when a parcel came to me from a friend in Kristiansand, Norway, Liv Schei[1].

The parcel contained a gramophone record of Erik Bye's songs, *Veg Vet en Vind*. One of the most beautiful in the collection is called 'Margareta's Vise'. The Margareta of the song is the daughter of King Alexander III of Scotland, who crossed the North Sea to marry Erik, the boy-king of Norway (she herself was at the time a mature young woman).

My Norwegian friend writes: 'The story of Margareta is dramatic and moving. Her marriage contract must surely be one of the strangest of its kind. It states flatly that if the marriage is not consummated when Erik reaches manhood, it will have the following consequences: (1) If the fault is Margareta's, Norway will get Man and the Hebrides back (ceded to Scotland in 1266), (2) If Erik is to be blamed, Norway must cede Orkney to Scotland ... I refused to believe it when first I heard of it, but this marriage contract is one of the documents to be found in *Diplomatarium Norvegicum* ... Neither of these alternatives had to be further considered, as a child was born of the union when Erik was fifteen years old. Margareta died in childbirth. Their daughter Margaret became Queen of Scotland at the age of three, when her grandfather Alexander III died. Sent to Scotland when she was seven, she either died on the voyage or on arrival in Orkney. I believe she is known in Scotland as the Maid of Norway ... King Erik later married Isabella Bruce, the sister of Robert Bruce ...'

That little web of innocence, statecraft, and death is indeed one of the saddest stories in history. Even today the heart stills with sorrow for that little queen lying dead in the cabin of her ship that was anchored off St Margaret's Hope, 700 years ago.

---

1 Liv Schei's translation of *Greenvoe* was published in Norway, autumn 1979.

Erik Bye says on the sleeve of the beautifully-produced record... 'I am enchanted by Margareta. She was a small touch of light in our history, and brought beauty and spirituality and rich impulses to a hard country and a stubborn people... '

The song, based on an original Gregorian wedding hymn, begins:

> King Erik, the young man, rides to Hakon's Hall
> Margareta, lovely maiden, you who were Scotland's pride
> Margareta, lovely maiden, you are our Norway's joy.

Faintly, in the background, is to be heard the sound of bagpipes.

On the Holms

9.6.1977

I suppose there may be some Kirkwall folk who have never been inside St Magnus Cathedral. It used to be said that in the old days some Newhaven fisherfolk had never taken the short walk up to Princes Street and Edinburgh Castle. Can it be that some Stromnessians, though they see the two familiar green islets every day, have never set foot on the Holms?

It's nine years, come Dounby Show Day, since I was there; and that was to a splendid supper, with plenty of young folk at a long table... But in my childhood when the house on the Inner Holm was a ruin and nobody cared, we must have visited the Holms a dozen times each summer, to bathe and run around. Even then, how beautiful I thought Stromness looked from the far shore!

My friend Roger from London, who has been to Orkney so often that we think of him as a naturalised Orkneyman at least, is staying at the Holms at present. The last good day (it has been dull and foggy ever since) Roger rowed across the harbour in the little boat *Jimmy* and beached her at the Mayburn noust while he did his shopping. What he wanted to know was, would I like a row in the harbour?

By the time my morning's work was done (an essay on Kirkwall, of all presumptuous things) another friend, Stan from Wideford Hill, had dropped by. It was 'three men in a boat' who made the brief crossing, rendered exciting only when we bobbed about in the bow wave of a fishing boat.

At the Holms, and *Jimmy* tied up, we wandered in the huge ebb across to the Outer Holm, where I hadn't set foot for forty years or so. It was a beautiful end-of-May afternoon. Terns circled, scolding us. We sat for a while beside the well. Clumps of marigolds blazed richly in the sun. A single ewe with her lamb avoided our company. Near the end of the island is a blank flagstone upright in the earth like a tombstone, with a kerb around. Who, if anyone, is buried there? And why, since there is a kirkyard across the bay?[1]

As we sat outside the front door drinking Coca-Cola, little shreds of fog began to spill over Brinkie's Brae. They thickened into hanks and fleeces, and in no time blotted out Hoy Sound. We did not want our kind host to be lost, coming back from setting us ashore at Flaws' Pier. So Stan and I decided to go home via Garson shore.

How we made that passage I dare not say: we have our dignity to consider.

It had been a marvellous and memorable afternoon.

Jubilee

16.6.1977

Growing old and awkward, I didn't look forward to the Silver Jubilee with much enthusiasm. A bunfight for Londoners and children it would be for sure, I thought. As things turned out, it was all cheerfulness and gaiety (except for the shadow of General Amin). What a relief it was to switch on the wireless, or the TV, and not hear anything of the mournful endless litany of strikes, inflation, the spiralling price of coffee and tea, pundits prophesying doom and disaster, etc.

It seems there's a spring of cheerfulness in the nation yet, when most of us had thought it choked with dust and stones. Now that the spring has come up once fresh and glinting in the sun, let's give it a chance to increase and mount a bit higher. I'm sure that journalists and 'newscasters' could

---

1 I was told later, this is the grave of a dog.

find much for our cheer and comfort. Alas, it is the bad things that happen, to people and nations, that make the good news stories.

The Jubilee season drew some good old films to our TV screens. After dinner last Monday evening I sat through *Scott of the Antarctic*, which I'd seen before in the Town Hall a long time ago. But it was worth seeing again. I was just wondering whether I had the stamina to sit through *Henry V*, which I'd seen two or three times and hadn't tired of by any means, when I got a summons to watch the Jubilee bonfires... Where better to see them than from the wide eastward facing window of the Braes Hotel? The first fire to stir into life was Orphir: but the flame must have been on the far side of the ridge—all one could see, in the late summer evening sky, was a plume of dark smoke... Then Hoy's Ward Hill was tipped with flame. Columns of smoke climbed from invisible fires to the north: Stenness probably, and Sandwick. Then the green island, Graemsay, which hardly rises 100 feet from the sea, blossomed with its little flame-flower. Out of Flotta, bursting rockets made hieroglyphics of dropping light over Scapa Flow; that drifted and died.

What of our own fire? We viewed it after closing time from both sides of Brinkie's Brae, and it was a creditable blaze, with flames that crackled and smoke that stung; a huge red writhing muscle. People drifted athwart it like shadows.

Think: a century ago all of Orkney would have been a network of such fires at midsummer, except that in those backward ignorant times they encouraged the flames with fiddles, dancing, and ale. On and on went the feast until dawn broke.

Perhaps it would do us all a world of good if there was a nationwide Jubilee every year.

'Old Orkney' Whisky

23.6.1977

I have not yet been to this summer's Museum Exhibition (Lifeboats)—I'm saving that enjoyable experience until I can share it with friends.

But in one of the Museum's windows there is a mini-exhibition on 'Old Orkney' Whisky.

It must be one of the saddest losses Stromness ever experienced when our local distillery stopped operating, some time after the First World War. I remember, when we were boys, how melancholy that particular section of the street was; deserted, padlocked and decaying. Two immense lead 'worms', like fantastic modern sculptures, adorned one gable end. It was an area of ghosts: the only living person who moved about in it was the caretaker.

And in the field behind, where Faravel is now, the huge warehouses lay and rotted; and right at the top of the Mayburn was a little square reservoir that had supplied the distillery with sweet Stromness water.

I don't suppose I will ever have a chance to taste either 'Old Orkney' or 'Old Man of Hoy'. It's said there are a few bottles in existence still, but to those who possess them they must be precious antiques indeed, not to be broached until the day that Stromness is proclaimed a Royal Burgh. (There used to be a single bottle of it above the gantry of the St Ola bar in Kirkwall.)

But, this last little while, the old fragrant ghosts have been having their own tableau in the Museum window: here are bottles of 'Old Orkney' and 'Old Man of Hoy'. Even in those days, the distillery issued gifts to their patrons: ashtrays, decanters etc. Even in those days, they set out to allure with beautiful idyllic advertisements—a young stylish pair in a boat in the harbour, languorous, lips locked, the love light in their eyes; another rich sophisticated couple in a winter drawing room, fire lit—one can almost hear an Edwardian ballad being played on some mute piano. The lady has flaming piled pre-Raphaelite hair.

That museum window is steeped in a marvellous period flavour.

In time, of course, something was done to that blank piece of Stromness, the distillery. It was pulled down ten years ago, and in its place rose Mayburn Court and Faravel. I write this, maybe where the barley was turned on the malting floor, or perhaps where the exciseman had his little office.

A Summer Idyll

30.6.1977

It was a dull Sunday morning: one of those grey-cowled mornings that look as if they will be melancholy all day, and perhaps turn wet and awkward in the end.

We were due to go to Rackwick in midmorning. As we all boarded the *Jessie Ellen*—that broad commodious new inhabitant of Stromness harbour—the day indeed turned nasty. Rain lashed the boat's windows and pitted the harbour water. All but the young and hardy sought sanctuary inside.

In Hoy, at Moness pier, it was raining harder than ever. (In Hoy, whatever the reason, it either shines or rains with more intensity than in other Orkney places.) Hair and coats already streaming. we piled into a fleet of waiting vehicles—and off with us into the dark valley of the Dwarfie Stone. The rain lashed down; we were as cheerful as we could manage.

And then Rackwick, that enchanted place, performed one of those little miracles that make the valley especially dear to its devotees. As the minibus swung round past the peat-cuttings, there came into the sky between the two huge dark cliffs a little pallor, as if the day might after all decide to cheer up. The pewter sky became silver, with shifting gleams. When we got out of the minibus the rain had stopped: only the ghost of it was left, a little gentle drifting haar that made everything mysterious and evanescent.

The rest of the day was very happy. The company split up into parties that set out here and there. It is easy to lose people in the green vastness of the valley; and yet, in terms of size, it is only a little bowl, sea-tilted by the powerful scarred hills.

We wandered for an hour and more along the fertile western slope: to the old crofts beautiful even in their ruins—Scar, Quernstones, Crowsnest. (Our only discomfort was that the early rain had soaked the fields, and our feet quickly got wet—but that was a minor inconvenience.) We came on a young sheep helplessly tangled in a piece of netting; but Jack Rendall, told about it, quickly set the terrified creature free...

Meantime, while the majority of us were drifting about like butterflies, some of the party had been very busy. Outside Mucklehouse, above the shore, a barbecue corner has recently been built; and there, over the grill, the two expert chefs were producing seemingly endless sausages, steaks, chicken portions to feed the returning wayfarers. A noble meal it was in the open air, washed down with home-brew or wine (or both). Soon enough we entered a sweet timeless Nirvana.

When we got back to grey Stromness, we discovered that there it had rained pell-mell all afternoon.

The Transistor

7.7.1977

Now I am without a wireless, and can't hear Radio Orkney, 'The World at One', Alastair Cooke, or 'Pick of the Week'—a sad business altogether.

I must say, my transistor has been ailing for quite a long time. First, about three years ago, the long slender pull-out aerial got rheumatics in the joints or some kindred complaint; it lost its resilience and elasticity; it only creaked up to half its maximum length.

Then, more recently, the little VHF button turned temperamental. The voices and the music in the green box would become, all of a sudden, low and remote. It was simply a matter of twiddling the button until the volume came on again rich and full.

Such complaints we could live with.

It had a strange personality of its own, that transistor. To plug a new battery into it was like giving it a huge meal to eat. It was full of joy and well-being; too full, for sometimes it had devoured the battery in a few weeks, and after that only groans and raspings issued. Sometimes, with other batteries, it behaved doucely and rationally, spreading its power over several months. You could never tell.

I think that transistor must now be about seven years old—maybe the allocated span for such things.

When I tried to switch it off a few mornings ago, it refused to shut up (and it had just been given a new battery a day or so before). The switch had gone. Perhaps there is something to be done with broken switches; certainly not by me.

The question is—what kind of transistor will I get now? Advice pours in from all directions. Some say I should get one that plays tapes, and records special radio programmes. Buy a Japanese model (they insist), or a German model, or a Norwegian; or be patriotic and keep some British worker occupied for a day or so... Open a newspaper: all kinds of contradictory slogans, from this manufacturer and that, are hurled at one.

One thing remains sure—I can't remain long in this state of utter newslessness. My little house is drained dry of music and information. A voice whispers in the ear, 'Be honest, you don't miss them all that much!...' To tell the truth, I don't—and if it wasn't for Radio Orkney I might have owned my last transistor.

Tatties

14.7.1977

At the end of May they have thick coats and long bluish curling shoots, and are soft and plushy to the touch. In June some time, a new generation of them arrives, from Cyprus or Egypt or the Canary Islands: like all things exotic, they are very expensive. Still, one takes them into the cupboard, a few at a time, to get a first taste of summer (along with far-travelled tomatoes and peaches). They are good enough on the palate, if rather thin and flavourless, as if they had been bred in shallow sun-drenched earth.

I am speaking, of course, about new tatties.

Yesterday I was going home with my few expensive messages in a plastic bag when a kind friend asked if I would like a boiling of new tatties? I stood in that sun-smitten garden, watching the fork dredge up a vivid green shaw. There, scattered on the mould, were ten or a dozen pale globes of various sizes—the first Orkney tatties of 1977.

I ate them, along with an Arbroath smokie, that evening. I let a little gold nugget of Claymore butter melt among them. That was as good a meal as I've eaten for many a day.

All praise to the Orkney tattie. You can taste the dark earth-strength in it; the sun; the sweetness of rain. (That can't really be said for their cousins from Cyprus or Egypt.)

It's hard to think of a time when the tattie was not a staple item in the Orkney diet. You hear more than one say he hasn't had a right dinner unless there are tatties, and plenty of them, on the plate. Yet, I suppose, two hundred and fifty years ago tatties were just beginning to be planted in Orkney soil—no doubt with much stubborn resentfulness, to begin with, from the crofters. (The earth worker is always the most conservative of men.) After that initial resistance, how marvellous the new American vegetable must have tasted, with boiled cuithes or roasted bacon! How the home-brew greeted it, and saluted it, and made it overnight as much a thing of Orkney as peats from the hill or dulse from the shore...

Another exotic import that took to Orkney at once was the tomato. (Many thanks to the Cherokees and Iroquois for both these gifts.) That is another moment of summer to look forward to, when the first Birsay tomato crumbles delectably between the teeth.

Milk Carts

21.7.1977

What a strange thing: our milk supplier for all Stromness has dwindled to one; and that source is away in the east, in St Ola parish!

In my childhood Stromness rattled and clip-clopped with horse-drawn milk carts, twice a day: there was a whole cavalry of them. Castle, Dale, Croval, The Mill, Quholmsley, Westhill, Redland, Burnside, Brownstown—the housewives adhered to one or other of those dairies. Besides which, there was a little milk shop in Alfred Street, that opened of evenings.

Sometimes I stood in as milk delivery boy for Tommy Firth of Castle Farm. I would wander up Hellihole Road about 8am. Presently, coming along the Oglaby Road (what we boys called Oglabrae, a fine place for sledging in winter), I would hear the smart clop-clop of Tommy's horse and cart. They would draw up, generally near the gate of the Old Kirk Manse (now St Peter's House), and I would mount and sit on a tiny wooden seat at the edge of the cart. Tommy never sat. He stood on the cart, delicately holding the reins, and occasionally uttering little sounds of encouragement or rebuke to the mare. There was a huge metal urn of milk secured by ropes in one corner of the cart, with a tap on it. When Tommy turned on the tap, out came the sweet new frothy milk into the pint measure. From there it was decanted into tin cans of pint or quart size. And the day's business began.

The Back Road first; then the long stone surge of the street, where the cans made a brave morning music. Generally the housewives had put a bowl on the doorstep, covered by a plate with twopence on it; into that bowl you decanted, carefully, the milk. But sometimes the milk boy had to come unbidden into the kitchen, where the family were sitting round hot plates of porridge waiting for you. And, 'Here's the milk-boy at last!' the lady of the house would cry resoundingly. The cat would give out wails of utmost desolation and yearning.

Down piers, up closes, all the way from the North End to the South End we stopped and started, till the milk in the great urn had ebbed almost dry. Then, when the last housewife and cat were served, I was free to go to school: a sad boring business after the morning's ringing transactions.

Once something frightened the horse on the street, and she bolted, eyes staring, hooves thundering on the cobbles, the cans making an urgent harsh music never known before. Finally Tommy got her under control, shivering and sweating, the poor beast. That was the greatest thrill of my life, up to then.

Ernest Marwick

28.7.1977

This is being written towards the end of Shopping Week—and, for weather, what a dull cold week it's been coming to full grey-bleak flower this morning with rain! I hope, for the sake chiefly of the thousands of tourists in Orkney—the bed-and-breakfasters and the tent-dwellers especially—that the sun shines splendidly tomorrow (Saturday).

There is a blank in Stromness this July. Stromness's friend, Ernest Marwick, always took his holiday in Shopping Week, and stayed in the Oakleigh Hotel with his wife Janette.

I have many happy memories of Ernest and Janette during Shopping Week. Never an afternoon passed but they were at the North Pier to see the *Ola* coming in, in sun and rain... Ernest got to know—I suppose—most Stromnessians over the years, and he relished the particular kind of character that flourishes here best, and the things we enjoy and laugh at. So, he always had his tape recorder there, in case a really good fragment of reminiscence or lore came up...

I remembered how Ernest entered into the spirit of the week; which at the time I thought rather strange, he being a shy man who loved quietness and retired places. But he obviously enjoyed himself, even under the loudspeakers braying out pop music. I met him, one Saturday evening when the Fancy Dress Parade was unaccountably late, sitting patiently (with scores of others) outside the Bank of Scotland. Was it the same Saturday, near midnight, that Janette and he and I watched from the Oakleigh pier the fireworks writing their Chinese ideograms across the night?

He was very proud at being asked, a few years ago, to open Shopping Week. Of course he did so with a brilliant speech—possibly the best opening oration of any.

There was one evening, soon after he had got his car and passed his driving test, that Ernest (after we had enjoyed one of those delectable Oakleigh high teas) invited me for a run. Four of us in all, including of course Janette, drove to 'Happy Valley' in Stenness—I think that was the first time I had ever been there. But that might have been in the lull following Shopping Week; for Ernest always stayed, if I remember well, for another week after the festivities—the pop groups and barbecues and fireworks—were a memory.

Lawrence Millman

I have always found books about Ireland intriguing: *Twenty Years A-Growing*, *Juno and the Paycock*, the poetry of Yeats, *The Well of the Saints*, *Ulysses*, *The Deserted Village*—and hundreds more. The Irish, it seems, have added more to literature in the past century than England, Scotland and Wales put together.

Three weeks ago, through the post from America, came a new book about Ireland called *Our Like Will Not Be There Again*, by Lawrence Millman. I read it through, quite enthralled. It is about the vanishing storytellers of the west of Ireland, whose Gaelic oral art is on the way out—killed by newspapers, books, TV, radio.

The American author visited that dying breed, and was quickly accepted by them. He got on especially friendly terms with the tinkers of Sligo and district; he describes their talk and customs with great vividness. Their earthy joy communicates itself in the writing. (Most of those storytellers of the old high tradition, going back as far as Homer the Greek, are quite illiterate. You really don't need education to understand art.)

I had hardly finished reading this entrancing book when there came a knock at the door one afternoon. 'Another visitor!' I sighed, and went to open the door... 'Good afternoon,' said a young bearded man in a pleasant American accent. 'My name is Lawrence Millman. I wonder, did my publishers send you a book of mine recently, called "Our Like Will Not Be There Again"?'

So that was the start of four days in the delightful company of a man who is almost certain to be a famous writer. (This present book is his first.)

Scotland enthrals him almost as much as Ireland. He had been, before he came to Orkney, to several Hebridean islands, in search of stories and real-life characters. Before he goes home to teach in the University of Minnesota, he intends to visit the writers in Scotland he likes best, and also the tobacconist in Perth who blends his favourite pipe tobacco.

He spent two wet days in Rackwick, and tramped fifteen miles all over North Hoy, with bread and Orkney cheese for sustenance. He loved every moment of it. When I said goodbye to him, he was intending to spend four days in North Ronaldsay.

If, out of his Scottish wanderings, there comes a book half as good as *Our Like Will Not Be There Again*, we have something to look forward to, I assure you.

The Old Man of Hoy

11.8.1977

I had a visitor a few Mondays ago—a seventeen-year-old whom I had met in Orkney two years ago; but who had grown so rapidly and favourably that it took me a good ten seconds to recognise him. The news he was bursting to tell me was that he and his pals had just, after five days' work, climbed the Old Man of Hoy, assisted by three other teenagers who had not planned to reach the summit. Chris[1] (my young friend) was a bit awed and delighted with this achievement. He was quite honest too: he told me how scared he had been more than once during the ascent. Now, starved of sleep and substantial food, they were all five staying at the Hostel before catching Tuesday's *Ola*.

It seems not long ago since BBC television screened one of its major spectaculars—the three-day epic climb of the Old Man of Hoy by such renowned mountaineers as Bonnington, Haston, etc. Was that in 1967? It seems that once something seemingly unattainable is achieved, the bell is rung again and again and again.

I remember, a long time ago, writing an article in *The Orkney Herald* about possible fantastic headlines in *Heralds* to come. One of the headlines was OLD MAN OF HOY COLLAPSES INTO SEA... For some reason, a few readers took this bold headline for stark fact; and anxious 'ex-islanders' in the south phoned and wrote, enquiring just exactly when and how the catastrophe had taken place.

Of course, in the next issue the matter was firmly cleared up.

---

1 Christopher Murray from Ayrshire. His father, Brian Murray, originally suggested the publication of *Letters from Hamnavoe*.

But it seems that, in fact, the imaginary headline may not be so utterly fantastic, after all. During Shopping Week some of us spent an agreeable hour or two listening to Professor R. Miller's talk (with slides) on 'The Natural Environment of Orkney'. One of the slides was of the Daniell print (1814) of the Old Man of Hoy standing on two legs. When one of the legs collapsed has never, to my knowledge, been recorded; but some time in the mid 19th century, with an almighty thunder and ruin of falling stone, the cataclysm took place.

Did anyone—a passing fisherman or seaman—happen to be looking when the Old Man lost one leg? It seems not. But Hoy must have been an awed island next morning... When, some day, the whole stack slithers under the waves, the whole world will be shaken—such is the fame that that column has achieved in the last ten years.

Adam the Shetlander

18.8.1977

I heard a very touching and strange true story the other evening from the lips of a consultant psychiatrist who, happening to be on holiday in Orkney, got in touch with me.

It concerns a Shetlander who, at the age of thirty (round about the turn of the century) suffered a severe mental breakdown. He was taken as a patient to the mental hospital in Montrose, to which all Shetland patients went in those days. He remained there for fifty years, and died aged eighty, in 1950.

He had been a farm worker, and had (like so many Shetlanders) musical gifts. He had also literary gifts—his letters to the Shetland newspapers are well and clearly written. He objected, for example, to the Boer War—a remarkable attitude to take in view of the prevailing jingoism of the time.

In hospital in Montrose, after quite a long time, he began to make things: straw eggcups, kaleidoscopes, a fiddle. Then, quite suddenly, in his mid-fifties, he began to carve in wood and stone, using such crude tools as a nail or a piece of broken glass. On the panel of a tea chest (plywood) he carved 'the battle of Clontarf', which Dr Keddie assured me is a striking piece of work.

But his main energies went into stone carving. He was very prolific, and gave away for nothing the finished works of art to anyone who wanted them. The staff of the hospital used them to decorate their gardens. (Unfortunately, many of them were broken up and used to make a new car park at the hospital. But quite a few survive.)

As works of art, those stone heads are vivid and powerful in the way that untutored art springing from deep urgent roots often is. One head is, it seems, a self-portrait, and at the base he had carved 'Jubal', who, it seems, was one of the first musicians mentioned in scripture. So, he proclaims himself to be an artist; and pays tribute to the first flowering of his art in music.

Now the works of this gifted and tragic Shetlander are being shown in exhibitions. No doubt there will be a quickening of interest in him. Much has been lost and forgotten, but enough of Adam the Shetlander's work remains for us to wonder at.

It is a very moving story. Some day we may be able to know more.

Insects

25.8.1977

Where have all the clegs gone? And the spiders? And the earwigs? And the midgies? There aren't nearly so many flies about as when I was young—then every ceiling in Stromness was hung with fly-papers, and hundreds of coagulated flies on each had come to, literally, a sticky end.

Nor is the song of the bluebottle heard as often in the window.

Perhaps we have upset the balance of nature, with our DDT and our spray guns; and creatures infinitely more sinister are biding their time before issuing forth to make our summers a stew of misery.

1947 was the great year of the earwig or forky-tail. They were everywhere. Every night before you went to bed you had to shake the pillows and examine the sheets. Ten to one a few of them were lurking in the folds. People went to bed with cotton wool in their ears; for there is an old wives' tale that earwigs will crawl in and chew an eardrum to shreds. (Indeed, a neighbour of mine actually woke up with one inside his ear; he still has his hearing, though he had a terrible job getting the insect out.) That year, they even crawled into the hollow barrels of razors. They were in your hair and shoes and eggcups... What caused such an invasion of earwigs is, I suppose, a mystery. Since 1947 they have only appeared harmlessly, in ones and twos.

August is midgie month; but I haven't been bitten once, so far. Tales have been brought to me from Rackwick, however, that there they are out, on a still evening, in hosts innumerable. In that most beautiful valley the midgies are said to have teeth like sharks. Nowhere in the world breeds them so savage.

To be out of doors for ten minutes, at midgie-hour in Rackwick, is like having a blowlamp played over the face and hands. The creatures burrow down to the roots of your hair. They are said to live for only a day—but oh, boy, what a time they have of it!

I have only seen one spider in the bath this summer. When finally it disappeared, after several porcelain days, I was not heartbroken.

Our other friends, the clegs, have not been active either. The cleg is one of the most furtive and sinister of creatures. At least bees, and other stinging things, give fair warning of an impending attack... Not the cleg: like a footpad he steals up behind you, silent and deadly, with a knife; and before you know it the poison is in you.

Cold bleak summer of 1977, at least you have kept such creatures away.

A House in Birsay

1.9.1977

Strange, to visit a house that you haven't seen for thirty-four summers, a place where you were happy for a long month, and which is now empty and delapidated.

In August 1943, being rather unwell, I was invited to stay in a hospitable house at the North Side of Birsay. Mrs Johnston, who lived alone there, could not have been kinder.

Perhaps memory deceives me—it sometimes does—but it seems to me that those summer weeks were steeped in sunshine. It was the middle of the war, but apart from an air-force man coming and going (the RAF had a camp nearby) nothing could have been more peaceful.

The north coast of Birsay is indented at two places by immense frightening geos. The first time I looked into them—I have never had a head for heights—earth and sky seemed to dissolve about me. And that first night I had nightmares of falling, falling endlessly. Yet I forced myself to walk to Longaglebe and Kerraglebe every day at least once; but never to within a man's length of the fearsome brinks. In little clumps, that August, mushrooms grew in profusion; each morning there seemed to be a new crop of them. There were far too many for Mrs Johnston and me to eat; I would take what was left over in a basket down to the Palace, to the Miss Coopers' (those kind and gentle ladies immortalised in the poetry of Robert Rendall).

For the rest of the golden time, it was all reading books at the end of the house, or visiting the farm houses round about. (Where is there to be found, anywhere, such courtesy and kindness as in a Birsay farm?)... And each evening, before I went to bed, my hostess heated a bowl of ale for me, which led to quick felicitous dreamless sleep... Not in any bar on earth is it possible to buy ale of such quality.

Two afternoons ago we were showing two German girls round Orkney (I have mentioned the old usual itinerary before, which I go through twenty times a summer). This time I said, 'What about going to a beautiful frightening place?' So we drove down the road to the North Side and stopped beside Longaglebe. They were suitably impressed by the narrow chasm, sheer precipitous walls, the floor of moving azure, though we found none of the mushrooms I had half-promised.

It was the last beautiful afternoon before this present hideous spell of rain and cold north wind set in. We walked through long grass lush with wild flowers, to the cottage where I had been so happy thirty-four summers ago. The once well-kept garden was a tumult of nettles and weeds. Inside, rusted, was the stove on which my 'night cap' had been warmed in a pot. There was the pleasant little north-facing room I had slept in; to wake each morning to the blue Atlantic glitter through the window. The roof here and there had begun to sag dangerously. But still there lingered everywhere the old kind wholesome atmosphere.

Lammastide Rain

8.9.1977

Lammas is the time for thunderheads, cloudbursts, sudden 'demptions' of rain.

Last Monday I was along the street getting 'my few errands' (as the old wives used to say) in a kind of mild drizzle. So I had put on a plastic mac and I was of course wearing my summertime 'Hush Puppies'. I had just got my stamps from the Post Office and was walking home when the rain came crashing down, without warning. I took shelter in the doorway of the fish-and-chip shop. Just then a little car stopped and an English lady got out and asked me to sign a copy of my *Selected Poems*. I always do that with alacrity; it means, with the profit, I can buy a pint in the Braes, the Royal, or the Stromness... Pen in hand, poised to write, the rain steadily increased in volume and power—it sheeted down, crashed down, came in long diagonal ropes. It almost washed pen and book out of my hand. I only hope the signature on the title page is not one blue blot!

Fortunately, the lady was going my way. She kindly drove me south in her car and dropped me at Mayburn Court. Even so, I had to change trousers and shoes at once. As for that plastic raincoat, in such Lammastide weather it might as well have been sewn together out of Kleenex tissues...

Now we are into September, and the saturating weather goes on. Last night, driving out of the beclouded East Mainland, we saw ahead blue splendours of light in the west. Hoy loomed so close and brilliant it seemed we could see every heather-bloom on the Ward Hill... But couched all along the horizon, like a beast waiting to spring, lay a huge blue-black cloud. It contained three or four hellyifers.

* * *

Next Tuesday, if there had been no World War Two, would have been Stromness Lammas Market Day. It used to be one of those times, like Christmas and Hallowe'en and the first day of the summer holidays, to make the heart of a child dance with delight... You sallied out to the Fair at the Pier Head like a young Onassis with four or five shillings in your pocket, fruit of long diligent saving, augmented by the 'fairings' of neighbours and friends... Till the naphtha flares were lit along the enchanted piers at sunset, it was all one gaudy whirligig of joy—the swingboats, the roll-the-penny stalls, the coconut shies, the rifle-shooting booths, the cheap-jack, the Indian sellers of silk, the Wall of Death, the apples and chips and ice cream, Charlie Riccolo, Guilio Fuggacia...

An Operation

15.9.1977

For weeks I had had a swelling, like a pimple or a small boil, inside the left eyelid. It wasn't really sore, but sometimes momentarily it blurred the vision (not that the sight of that eye is anything to shout about, at the best of times).

In due course I got notice to attend at the Balfour Hospital, at noon yesterday (Wednesday). I made my mind a blank; it's best not to think about such things.

As I was walking along the street, between heavy black showers, to catch the 11am bus, Dr Mary More stopped her car to chat; and so I got driven to Kirkwall in style, under a marvellous heraldic skyscape of surging blue and silver and grey... It was too early to go to the hospital, of course; I wandered around inside the Cathedral for half an hour, reading the old tombstones and the memorials of the Victorian great. (Thank goodness, in the late 20th century we seem to be a bit more modest, or less pompous.)

I started out vaguely in the direction of the Balfour, going by the Watergate, and soon found myself in a warren of housing schemes, with Wideford Hill showing between the gaps from time to time. After drifting along in this aimless fashion for twenty minutes or so

I realised that the appointment time was only ten minutes away, and still no sign of the hospital; the Kirkwall housing schemes had got me into the heart of them; I was lost in a labyrinth.

Finally two kind ladies directed me down Pipersquoy Road: at the end of which was, of course, the Balfour. I hurried in through the main gate; but this was a mistake too: the department I should have been in was a distance away, along a complex of corridors. At last I arrived at the desk and handed in my appointment card. A male nurse said (perhaps jokingly) 'You're late—a black mark!'... But in actual fact I had made it with one minute to spare.

As for the minor operation itself, it was carried out with much kindness and unerring skill by a lady doctor, assisted by a male nurse. In a few minutes the cysts—there were two of them, one big and the other small—were removed, with a minimum of discomfort. I felt it was an accomplished piece of work.

I emerged with a white cotton-wool patch strapped to my eye. I hesitated to sit in a bus and walk through Stromness wearing such piratical costumery, for fear of possible stares, questions, remarks, jokes.

In the end I got myself driven home in a taxi, and a few hours later I was able to dispense with the eye-patch.

Surnames

22.9.1977

I was doing a bit of work yesterday afternoon when a knock came to the door. The visitor was a pleasant middle-aged man with a Canadian accent. He gave his name—Corston. 'Well,' I said, 'that's a good Orkney name, right enough.'

Mr Corston from Nova Scotia told me that his grandfather had emigrated from the parish of Firth well over a century ago. What he really wanted to see me about was this—in a story of mine called 'The Ballad Singer' the name of the poet who recites the 'Lady Odivere' ballad in the Palace of Birsay before Earl Robert and his ladies is given as 'Corston'...

Now, asked Mr Corston, is that situation based on fact—was there a real poet called Corston in the late 16th century?

Of course I had to disappoint him. The story of the ballad-singer is a piece of fiction; the name Corston was arbitrarily chosen. In fact, no one knows who composed that magnificent ballad. Like all the great ballads, it is anonymous...

Mr Corston from Nova Scotia turned out to be a pleasant person. He couldn't stay for long; his wife was waiting for him in the Library. But we spoke about the surname Corston, and how it had completely died out in Orkney. He himself had two children, but they were daughters. However, he did tell me of a cluster of other Corstons in (I think) Ontario...

It is very interesting that a name so common once in Orkney should have vanished completely from the islands. (Corston is, of course, like the majority of Orkney surnames, derived from a district or parish: Linklater, Isbister, Rendall, Costie, Halcro, Firth, Twatt, Heddle, etc.)

I thought, over breakfast, of other names that had died out: Bimbister, Knarston, Hemmigar, Richan... There must be several others. (Strangely enough, three of these names, including Corston, are originally districts in the parish of Harray).

Other thoughts occurred. Why was nobody given the name of Evie, or Birsay, or St Ola, or Stromness, or Hoy? There is a mystery here that some of our local philologists must tackle.

It seems that at some definite time in history, surnames, either by decree of custom or law, became fixed. The simplest way was to call yourself by the place you lived in; and this, it seems, happened in most instances. But for some reason it was not universal.

The Happiest Day

29.9.1977

The Autumn equinox is here—light and darkness hang, evenly balanced. We are poised for the take-off into winter. It all sounds cold and cheerless, especially since the summer just past has been nothing to write home about: long bleak periods interspersed with a golden day here and there. We had been spoiled by three warm sunny summers in a row. The summer of 1977 was quite like old times, a bit of a skinflint with the sun. In spite of its miserliness the tourists came in their thousands: bird watchers, amateur students of archaeology, people with postcards, guidebooks, binoculars and cameras. There was a couple of very pleasant American ladies, sisters, who came because they loved islands; the last lot they had been to were the Canary Islands... There are still a few hundred tourists around—most of them students who have spent the high summer working at this job or that, and have taken to wandering in September before university classes resume.

If I was asked to pick out the happiest day of the summer, I think it would have to be that marvellous day, towards the end of June, when a boatload of us went to Rackwick. Peter Maxwell Davies, at the end of the St Magnus Festival—the first of many, to be sure—threw a party for performers, critics, helpers, friends, at his cottage Bunertoon, poised high on the cliffs above the Atlantic.

The sun shone from morning to night, at that time of year, when summer decides to be generous, the world is drenched in light. The *Jessie Ellen* went cleaving through acres of blue silk.

When, from various little private expeditions and meanders, the company assembled at Bunertoon, the delicious food and wine were consumed outside, sitting on benches, stones, and in the little fenced vegetable garden (now blossoming again after half a century's neglect). The talk flowed as sweetly as the excellent wine. It was one of those idyllic days that happen only six or seven times in your life.

We recrossed Hoy sound in the late afternoon, blessed with the sun of Orkney and with sun-blessed vintages of Italy and France, treasures of vanished summers.

* * *

But winter has its compensations: friends and talk and books in the firelight—sudden immaculate blossomings of snow in the heart of darkness—over-mastering storms—tea behind warm drawn curtains— hot toddies before bed when the night has a snap and crackle in it.

Betty Corrigall Poems

6.10.1977

I think I have never heard the full story of the Hoy girl, Betty Corrigall, whose body, in a state of pristine preservation, was discovered under the peat moss during the last war.

To have been buried so, between the two parishes of Walls and Hoy, indicates that the girl took her own life. We shall never know the pain, anguish, despair that drove her to such an extreme. We can only surmise. The old classic situation of course springs to mind—a pregnant unmarried girl deserted by her lover, in a climate of intolerance.

In the early part of this summer, I had the pleasure, briefly, of meeting a London man, Nat Gould, and his wife. They had spent days cycling round Orkney, which, if you are hardy enough, is (next to walking) the ideal way to get to know a strange place.

Mr Gould mentioned the grave of Betty Corrigall in Hoy, and how much his imagination had been touched by her bitter death and lonely interment. We had been introduced to each other as poets. Mr Gould promised to send me anything that he managed to write about Betty Corrigall.

In due course, I received a typescript of a group of poems called *Hoy Song: The Poems of Betty Corrigall*. I was moved by the beauty of much of it, and impressed too by the way Mr Gould, after only the briefest acquaintance with Hoy, had succeeded in capturing the atmosphere.

Betty's Headstone

So sweet
So small
Here lies
Betty Corrigall....

Outwith the bounds of kin
They buried her,
And not within.

The burn beside
The brae above
Keep her with more
Abundant love.

In our small space, the above is only a taste of Mr Gould's poem. If poor Betty suffered any uncharity in her last days from her fellow-mortals, here, at least and at last, in *Hoy Song*, are a few words of compassion and sympathy uttered over that lonely grave in the moors—music to soothe her ghost.

A New Headmaster

13.10.1977

When you think about it, there have not been many headmasters in Stromness in a century of compulsory education.

When I and my contemporaries, including Ian MacInnes, crept unwillingly to school in 1926, the headmaster was called Mr MacAulay. He did not stay for very long. (The only thing that binds me to Mr MacAulay was that, in utter innocence, aged five, I used a 'bad word' in his presence—he was so nonplussed that I got off scot-free...) Mr MacAulay was succeeded by Mr J.R.Learmonth, the science master at the Secondary School (as it was then called). His successors were, first Mr William Groundwater, who had been an ex-pupil, and who is still, happily, with us, and second, Mr John S. MacLean, whose sudden death in July so shocked everyone.

Now we salute Mr MacInnes, who, between 1926 and 1939, sat in the same classroom with me. In those days he was a wizard with the pencil, and could with a few strokes draw vivid profiles of anyone within range. Indeed when he was still a boy, he drew weekly for *The Orkney Herald* a series of brilliant caricatures of local characters; the series was called 'Personalities You Might Have Met'. I am the proud possessor of an almost complete set of the originals. Stromnessians of all ages never tire of looking at them, though nearly all of them 'are out of the story' now.

Besides his artistic gift, Ian MacInnes was from his earliest days a fearless spokesman for what he believed. Any hint of injustice or misuse of authority touched him to the quick, and whenever he could he went straight to the source of the trouble. He still has these fine qualities in abundance. No pupil at Stromness Academy will ever lack for a fair and generous deal.

I could say a great deal more in praise of the new rector, which would, I know, embarrass him. For the moment, 'heartiest congratulations' will have to do.

* * *

Before Mr MacAulay was Mr Hepburn, who ruled before my time; he had the reputation of being a good teacher and a strict disciplinarian... In my youth, the old men in Peter Esson's tailor shop would speak sometimes, in awed trembling voices, about the first headmaster of all, a Mr Reith.

The Hermit of Brinkie Isle

20.10.1977

It is delightful always to explore some aspect of Orkney's past: the slow agricultural revolution, the Stuart earls and their beautiful palaces, Summerdale, Norsemen and Picts and the dwellers in Skara Brae.

It may be intriguing, from time to time, to project the imagination into the future. The future of Orkney is an uncharted sea, the mind has perfect freedom to go where it wants. Of course, the ingredients of the future are all here with us today, but only a mind of superhuman wisdom could forecast how things will actually turn out.

Meantime, it is good fun to have a try; secure in the knowledge that what follows will certainly never come to pass.

THE HERMIT OF BRINKIE ISLE

Progress went ahead so urgently and triumphantly in the late twentieth century that suddenly the icecaps began to melt.

The people of Stromness went out to work one morning and found themselves splashing along the street up to their knees in new sea. 'It's only an extra-high tide,' they called to each other with that brightness which water puts on the human voice...

Never a bit of it; the waters still rose. A month later Stromness had to be evacuated; a fleet of little boats took the Stromnessians and as much belongings as they could carry out to a large ship, that presently sailed away west; where, no one knows.

The Holms were no more. Only the spire of the Academy Hall, piercing the hungry sea, marked where Stromness had been. The waters rose and rose. Soon all that was left of the parish was a little island called Brinkie and another called Miffia. They looked north to the deserted islets of Kring afiold and Meeranbloo. There was a cluster of long dark islands to the south called Hoy. There were the three islands of Orphir; Wideford island crammed with rusty masts and pylons; Keelylang isle with its single forlorn monument to Progress.

Presently an old man rowed from the south and built a small rough granite hut on Brinkie island. He did a bit of fishing and fowling; he dug the obdurate earth and next summer had a little rosebush and a row of potatoes. But mostly this old man sat in the door of his hut and meditated long on the vanity of human strivings and aspirations. Often he smiled.

Sometimes, on a still summer evening, the hermit thought he could hear music rising from the sunken town of Stromness; but no—it was only the harp of the sea itself.

In spring, this old man would row over to an islet in the Hoy group, called Kame, to get wild birds' eggs.

A Morning in Deerness

27.10.1977

Here I am, on an early afternoon of 'peedie summer' 1977, stuck in a small yellow Citroën car, outside a farm in Deerness.

My two friends have gone about photographic business to the cliffs below. A tall stone finger reaches into the sky: the Covenanters' Memorial.

An hour ago land and sea and sky were washed with a grey haze (that same haze has wrought havoc with planes and mail and newspapers over the past few days). But suddenly the sun broke from its last scarf of cloud, and now all is golden, except for the indistinct horizon. The old Chinese painters must have revelled in days like this, all mutings and mystery.

The field to the left is littered with grazing cows, black and white. Five minutes ago, a line of white ducks came waddling up a tractor rut, and where one rut had caught the rain in a muddy pool, two ducks had a rare splash!

With the sun the wind has come, ruffling the tall sere grasses, racketing round the little yellow car.

Somewhere behind, a bird sings thinly. From time to time a dog barks in the adjacent farm. The poet Keats, as well as the Chinese painter, would have loved today—'season of mists and mellow fruitfulness...' But we are in the twentieth century. There is the sound of an invisible engine; tractor, or motorbike. Half an hour ago a plane flew over slowly, like a soft moth in the haze, drifting towards Grimsetter.

I shall not enumerate the reasons why I have not gone with the camera to the Covenanters' Memorial, even though I have not been there before, and I was assured that the cliff-line is unique and well worth seeing... I am incapable of sitting and doing nothing, even in a warm car on a rare day of Indian summer. Before my friends walked off, I begged the loan of writing materials, and got a blank envelope and pen with a thick nylon tip. And with these I have passed quite a pleasant half-hour, writing this little essay.

But how much more delightful to be a Chinese artist of five hundred years ago, with a square of silk and quiverful of little brushes and crucibles of coloured inks! There he sits in the door of his pavilion, smiling, while the mists—impossibly delicate garments—drape themselves around distant heights... In the end, he writes at the bottom right-hand corner an exquisite lyric—a far more satisfying conclusion than a signature, with all its overtones of western aggressive self.

Postcards of War

Currently in Stromness Museum is a remarkable exhibition consisting of postcards of World War One (mainly from the collection of the late G.C.Mackay, Oakdene).

There is the confident jingoistic opening. 'Rule Britannia,' shouts out of the cards, as if the end of the conflict (and that a speedy one) was beyond the smallest possibility of doubt. The poet Kipling at his brassiest is quoted.

The scenes on the postcards shift to the trenches and shellholes of France. (It seemed, by that time, that victory mightn't happen by Christmas 1914 after all.)

The conflict got grimmer and grimmer. Barbed wire, rats, poison gas, duckboards across the bloodied swamps of Ypres—no soldiers in history have been asked to go through such hideous and prolonged horror. The postcards reflect this, but in a curious way: the hideousness is covered up in mush upon mush of sentimentality. 'Where has my daddy gone to?'... 'Let me die with my face to the foe.' Then as morning after morning the nation read in its newspapers the endless columns of dead, young men in their full vigour and beauty, the postcards depict scenes of death on the battlefield. 'Abide with me.' The religious note is struck again and again.

Year followed bloodstained year—Mons, the Somme, Jutland, Ypres, the last desperate German onslaught in March 1918. The Germans of course are depicted as the blackest of monsters, or else as fat comical sausages. The Kaiser, even though he was first cousin to our own King George V, comes in for some rough handling. 'Hang the Kaiser!' the news-sheets shouted, but the villain at last went into sedate retirement in Holland. It had been indeed a 'Pyrrhic victory'.

There is a section of Orkney's own soldiers (photographs), that will stir many memories; though not many of them can still be alive.

In a curious way this postcard exhibition parallels the poetry that was written between 1914 and 1918. The glorious beginning—'Now God be praised who has matched us with this hour', through the doubts and questionings—to the ultimate cries of protest against the insensate hellish carnage, from serving poets like Siegfried Sassoon and Wilfred Owen.

So much rich blood had been poured out—enough 'women's tears to water a little field'—that the despoiling of the earth hoarded in bank vaults might lie inviolate, whatever dynasties fell.

The Sun and the Pen

10.11.1977

November has come in with three peerless days in succession. Hallowe'en seemed to pass quietly. I heard one shatter of glass about 7 o'clock in the evening—next day I was told that the telephone box below my window had a broken pane. That poor old telephone box has taken some punishment in its time; and yet I was assured the other day that it's one of the cleanest pleasantest booths in the county. So we shouldn't complain overmuch.

One of the handicaps of my trade is that the sun makes it difficult. In summer, paradoxically, I am thankful for the morning, at any rate, to be dull, so that I can get my daily quota of work done. In November one expects the conditions for writing to be nearly as perfect as can be.

Not November 1977. Yesterday I sat at my table with a scatter of manuscripts and virgin sheets of paper, and tried, heroically and vainly, to resume where I'd left off the day before. The sun poured its pale honey all over my writing hand. Three hours of hard work, and all for nothing. I was more than disappointed—I was angry.

This morning the sun was more serene than ever, I didn't even try to write. After the breakfast pot of tea, egg and toast, I wandered coatless into Stromness.

I sat at a pier in mid-town for two hours and more. The sea was all tremulous blue silk. Occasionally a boat came and went; then, to show how heavy the blue silk was, the stones shook and sounded to the bow-wash. From a score of chimneys smoke went straight up, frail grey plumes. A black cat and a white cat sat sleeping in patches of sun... On the southern horizon, all the same, brooded the storm that has been forecast for two days past; and Hoy was all tangled in purple-grey hanks of cloud.

In Stromness the afternoon ran out, imperceptibly, in gold grainings...

* * *

Whether a man called Guy Fawkes ever sat among barrels of gunpowder under the House of Lords is, it seems now, open to question. But a few weeks ago I remembered his day, 5 November, and I began to save every copper that came my way. In two days' time the children will be coming round with carved turnip-heads. Whether the sun shines that day or not, I won't get much writing done for the continuous crash and rattle of the knocker... I don't mind—I amassed much treasure on account of that same Guy Fawkes in years gone by—I seem to be giving only a small fragment of it back.

The First Travel Book

17.11.1977

There was once a man who came to Orkney and saw it with new eyes. 'Jo Ben' is the man's name as it has come down to us; probably a contraction for John Bellenden, or some similar name. He may have been a wandering friar; there is slight evidence of an ecclesiastical background...

We are so used to visitors saying nice things about the islands that we would have resented this Jo Ben very much. He looked, in the early 16th century, through his new eyes, and what he saw was the monstrous and the surrealistic. Some islands and parishes he had undoubtedly been to; others he was only told of.

He wrote down his impressions in a little notebook, or scroll. And there the manuscript lies, to this day, in the Advocates' Library in Edinburgh.

In Sanday, tired with walking, 'I rested myself at a church called the Holy Cross, and in the churchyard saw innumerable skulls of men, about a thousand ... larger than three heads of those now living, and I extracted teeth from the gums of the size of a hazel nut'...

That's only the beginning. In Stronsay lived the great monster Troicis... 'He was covered with seaweed all over his whole body, and resembled a dark horse with wrinkled skin'...

North Fara he had a better opinion of. 'Cows ... graze on bushes with great satisfaction, and the boys sing to the dull beasts'... (This is an unusual touch of lyricism in Jo Ben's sombre goggle-eyed recital.)

In Eday 'The men sometimes fight with great monsters, which they cut up in dregs ... then they boil and cook into oil...' (Can we discern, through that mist, a whale-hunt?)

Jo Ben didn't think much of the ladies of St Ola: ...'given to excess in luxuries and pleasures; this is supposed to be caused by the abundance of fish. Here is a very high mountain named Whisford.'...

The Loch of Stenness is 'a large lake, 24 miles in circuit. On a little hill near the lake in a tomb was found the bones of a man in length 14 feet'... The little hill was Maeshowe, no doubt.

Jo Ben doesn't have much to say about Stromness: ...'Here is a very dangerous bridge for travellers, called the Bridge of Vaith, where many travellers perish...' Indeed, before the present bridge was thrown across, the passage twixt loch and sea must have been difficult often.

'All the men [of Pomona],' concludes Jo Ben, with a frown, 'are very drunken and wanton, and fight among themselves... If one neighbour invites another and if the invited before his departure has not vomited, he assails his host and there is much strife.'

So ends the first travel hook we have of Orkney, four and a half centuries ago. Later visitors have cast a kindlier eye on us; at least we were human, and did not live on a lurid borderland with monsters and savages, where all the perspectives are awry.

Sheltered Houses

24.11.1977

A few weeks ago bulldozers moved into a hidden garden between the Whitehouse and Alfred Street and began to level and prepare the ground for building. The section of wall next to the street was removed; for the first time the eyes of the townsfolk were able to see that particular slope.

It is to be, soon, the site of a 'sheltered housing' scheme. I assume that elderly people, and people able to look after themselves to some extent, will be the tenants. So, they will have their independence; but there will be a warden to keep a vigilant eye on them.

I'm sure most Stromnessians will be pleased to see well-designed houses on that vacant lot. The street below has preserved one of the ugliest of our wartime scars. Where that concrete scab is, stood prior to 1940 a block of houses. It made of that part of Alfred Street a narrow dangerous ravine; northwards it curved, an abrupt blind corner into Alfred Square.

To obviate that danger (I suspect) as well as to ease the passage for the great lorries blundering through our wartime street, that block of houses was demolished. (I have a feeling that Major Eric Linklater, RE, had his HQ there earlier.)

The concrete scab was thrown upon the wound and it has been there ever since; it is a part of the street that, left to itself, could never sweeten and grow mellow.

Let us hope that the sheltered houses, when eventually they are built, will add beauty and interest to Alfred Street.

My grandparents lived up the close adjacent, in a house that has long been levelled. They were dead before I was born; all I know about my grandfather is that he was a shoemaker or cobbler. I had an aunt who still lived in that house when I was a small boy. All I remember from a few visits there is that there was an enormous white cat, and a black horsehair sofa...

It was called 'Brown's Close', I think. Now the few houses that still stand there are vacant. But the lowest house, next to the street, will (I understand) eventually be occupied by the warden of the adjacent 'sheltered houses'.

Early Snow

1.12.1977

Nobody could have foreseen it. Saturday evening was black with rain showers. The TV weather forecast (as far as I remember) said nothing.

It came in the night, secretly, chastely. The bedroom ceiling when I opened my eyes was a white gleam. Through the mirror the roof opposite thrust up, an immaculate wedge. It was the first snow of 1977, and it had come unusually early.

A light delicate fall, as if some exquisite tracery had been thrown over the world. (All except the street under the window—the cars had churned the snow into a filthy porridge.)

Time, in mid-afternoon, before the sun went down, to dig out of the cupboard under the stair cobwebby rubber boots; and set out to see what the snow had done beyond my narrow confines.

It had finished its work on the hills and fields, houses and gardens, they were all new and pristine from the fingers of winter; and the sea had its own snow-blue; quite different from the summer blue or the harvest blue. The sky was the most marvellous of all; it was scrolled all over with magnificent heraldry. Snow clouds like fabulous beasts moved in from the north. The sky over Stromness was clear, but Orphir was dark, and a piece of the Atlantic was blotted out; and Hoy, with the setting sun muffled now and then in immensities of blackness, looked like the backcloth for some Wagnerian music... Soon over Brinkie's Brae, a snow cloud thrust up, the wind blew sharper, and it was obvious that Stromnessians were to have some more of this snow bounty. It was time to be seeking the shelter of the town. Even so, before we got there, a thousand or so grey pellets had chilled hands and faces, whirling in on the north wind.

In a house in the middle of the town, beside a peat fire, we thawed out with mugs of home-brew. The sea window brightened, and darkened, and slowly brightened again.

How long would the snow last? So beautiful in its beginning, the end of a snowfall can often be a filthy business, with thaw soaking into mind and spirit as well as flesh.

But this first snow of 1977 went away as lightly and exquisitely as it had come, a white dream that 'left no wrack behind...'

On Monday morning, the bedroom ceiling was, again, dull grey plaster. The street was a dark mirror with rain. Yesterday's garden, that had been an enchanted square, was a dead-season sereneness.

What Boys Used to Read

8.12.1977

Yesterday afternoon, among a pile of unwontedly cheerful letters, came one from a schoolmate in England whom I had only seen once, fleetingly, since our schooldays. What I remember mostly about him is that we exchanged boys' magazines for a time. I forgot what I gave him when I'd finished reading it; what he gave me was a delightful weekly called *Film Fun*, full of strip cartoons of Laurel and Hardy, Harold Lloyd, and other screen stars of the nineteen-thirties.

A great deal of our time, as boys, must have been consumed with those magazines (there was a varied collection of them, twopence each). On the whole our elders—parents and teachers—tended to frown on them, as not being conducive to good taste in literature. But 'good taste' means nothing to boys. What they are after, perennially, is immediacy, vividness, characters larger than life, a swift clean exciting storyline.

The firm D.C. Thomson of Dundee published a clutch of these weeklies. On Monday *The Adventure* came out—I never greatly cared for it, a junior version of *The World Wide Mag*. Tuesday was a day to wait for: *The Wizard* enchanted us. You stood with your two pennies outside Rae's shop after the *Ola* came in, waiting for the spell to be cast... Wednesday, for some reason, was a blank day. Thursday brought *The Rover*. Friday was the greatest day of all—for us it was *Hotspur*-day. *The Hotspur* contained only school stories, and for some reason which I cannot even now explain, I loved school stories best of all. How shall I ever forget the boys of Red Circle School, for example and Mr Smugg, the dreadful master?... On Saturday *The Skipper* came out; but I was tepid about that too.

In addition to the D.C.Thomson publications, from other presses came such joys as *The Gem* and *The Magnet*, one of which featured Billy Bunter—like Falstaff and Sancho Panza one of the fat immortals... For boys preparing (all unconsciously) to tackle Hemingway and the tough school of writers, there was *The Champion* and others. Boys obsessed with sport went for *The Topical Times*.

Of course in those austere 1930s we were lucky if we could buy only one weekly. The rest were devoured, or skimmed, by means of exchange—a quite complicated barter system... So, we lived for much of our time in another world of marvels, heroes, villains.

Thanks to Jackie Chalmers' letter, that particular era of reading has all come back vividly to me.

Maeshowe at Midwinter

22.12.1977

If you can possibly manage it, turn your face today in the direction of Stenness parish.

Why Stenness? Because the most exciting thing in Orkney, perhaps in Scotland, is going to happen in Stenness, this afternoon at sunset. You come to a wide plain between the hills and the two lochs. In few other places even in Orkney can you see the wide hemisphere of sky in all its plenitude.

Stop at the Tormiston Mill, with its rushing burn and joyous ducks. Across a green field is another hemisphere, but small, solid, earth-fast.

The winter sun hangs just over the ridge of the Coolags. Its setting will seal the shortest day of the year, the winter solstice. At this season the sun is a pale wick between two gulfs of darkness.

Surely there could be no darker place in the bewintered world than the interior of Maeshowe. It holds, like a black honeycomb, the cells of the dead.

Stoop through the long narrow corridor towards the chamber of darkness, winter, death. Now the hills of Hoy—strangely similar in shape to Maeshowe—are about to take the dying sun and huddle it away. The sun sends out a few last weak beams.

One of the light rays is caught in this stone web of death. Through the long corridor it has found its way; it splashes the far wall of the chamber. (In five or six thousand years there has been, one assumes, a slight wobble in the earth's axis; originally, on that first solstice, the last of the sun would have struck directly on the tomb where possibly the king-priest was lying with all his grave-goods around him...)

The illumination lasts for a few minutes, then is quenched. It is a brief fleeting thing; yet it is a seal on the dying year, a pledge of renewal, a cry of resurrection. The sun will not renege on its ancient treaty with men and the earth and all the creatures.

Winter after winter, I never cease to wonder at the way primitive man arranged, in hewn stone, such powerful symbolism.

Hogmanay

29.12.1977

Bedtime, on normal nights, was eight o'clock. But on the last night of the year boys were allowed to stay up beyond midnight.

On the dresser in Melvin Place the paraffin lamp burned—a softer, gentler light than gas or Tilley or electricity. There were a few cards along the mantelpiece, all gilt and celluloid. Across the ceiling beams stretched a star of coloured decorations, cunningly stuck here and there with sprigs of mistletoe. You had to be careful not to be taken and kissed under the mistletoe. If you were a man you had to give the lady who kissed you a pair of gloves. The lady thus saluted had to present a pair of socks to the man who had honoured her. (I dare say many a one deliberately took up a stance under the golden branch with the pale berry. I remember, aged eight, kissing a spinster lady in the ritual way; and I'm sure I got a fine pair of stockings for my venturesomeness...) That sweet old custom seems to be quite dead now.

Somewhere in the house—in the cupboard, I expect—was a bottle of whisky. I was supremely indifferent to it. What did the older folk find so fascinating in that burning liquor? My mother made for Christmas and New Year 'Crestona Ginger Wine', bottle after bottle of delectable stuff, pure magic. It blended beautifully with a slice of rich, heavy, dark, sappy Scotch Bun. The interior of the house was quiet with expectancy all that evening. At ten to twelve it was time to be wrapped in a muffler and overcoat. Then, with scores of other darkling figures, we went (under the gas lamps) towards the Pier Head. The Pier Head, as the seconds ticked away towards midnight, was almost as crowded as the second Tuesday in September (Lammas Market); but now the crowd was, in comparison, silent and motionless. From North End, South End, Cairston, Innertoon, the Loons, more figures moved in to join the whispering throng.

Suddenly, earth and sea erupted! The Pole Star began the feast with a swift succession of rockets that burst over Stromness and dimmed the stars and made enchanted reflections in the water... Every boat at the piers turned on its siren full blast. The people round the Fountain fell upon each other with cries of 'Happy New Year'. The men would offer each other those squat evil shapes with the 'fire water' in them. Some faces were red as apples, some as grey as ghosts under the lamps.

This was only the beginning. After the communal celebration at the Pier Head, the first-footing went on till the sun got up—a strange bizarre rather frightening ritual to an eight-year-old.

We young ones shouted to each other 'A Happy New Year, a bottle of beer, and a box on the ear!'...

The Christmas Card Tree

5.1.1978

Over Christmas, the shops were shut for three days. On the Saturday, Christmas Eve, shopping bags were heavy along the street. Every household had to be certain that there was a sufficiency of the basic things—bread, meat, bacon, eggs, milk, whisky, cheese, butter—to tide them over the lean days following Christmas... As things turned out, the cupboard did not get bare...

Three Yules ago, I bought a Christmas card 'tree'. I was so tired of cards fluttering down like white birds every time somebody opened the outer door. And then, it was impossible to find things—pipe, pens, comb—behind those massed cards on the mantelpiece (and on bookcases, TV set, table, pictures). The card-tree is gold-coloured and has a hundred slots in it. The Christmas cards, as they arrive, are stuck in the slots—slowly climbing the cardboard tree from bottom to top. And that first Christmas, the tree overflowed.

Something must have happened—a rise in the price of stamps, or a number of my old half-remembered friends had decided to blot me forever from their memory, or mere chance—but last Christmas the upper reaches of the card-tree were bare. And I half-resigned myself to a neglected and neglectful old age.

But no, this Yuletide again the cards have come homing in from all quarters of the globe. The 'tree' is overburdened. This afternoon, three days after Christmas, a small flock of more cards has come. Those latecomers will have to stand, till Twelfth Night, on the table; there's simply no room for them on the tree.

There's a fine splurge on television about this time of year. When I said, earlier, that everything had been laid in for the festive season, there was one serious omission: the *Radio Times*, the double issue covering Christmas and New Year. The paper shop had been cleaned out of the *Radio Times*. There was a bleak prospect of groping blindly about in a fog of programmes for a fortnight. Fortunately, a friend managed to buy one for me—one of the very last copies in a Kirkwall paper shop.

On Christmas Eve, there was a superbly produced Christmas Carol (*Scrooge*) and for two afternoons a huge Russian version of *War and Peace*. Unfortunately, I only managed to see fragments of that...

* * *

I hope I won't be blamed for having all this Christmas stuff inflicted on you in the opening year. Dear readers, it is still Christmas until the Twelfth Night (5 January). Our ancestors knew it full well. So did the singers and dancers who performed the old carol 'The Twelve Days of Christmas', celebrated on our postage stamps this year.

Honey Ale

12.1.1978

I had fallen clean out of the habit of brewing—through laziness partly, and partly because of one unsuccessful brew twenty months ago. The rising price of beer—a staple in north European diet for two thousand years, probably much longer—forced me into action in the first darkness of winter.

Out came the blue plastic bin from the cupboard under the stair, and the bucket. The tins of malt extract were cut open. The two kilograms of sugar stood on the kitchen table. Everything went according to plan—the dissolving, the topping up, the gauging of the true temperature, the scattering on of the yeast granules...

At the last moment I discovered a pot of Brazilian honey in the cupboard. Since I am not as partial to honey as to marmalade in the morning, the honey too was added.

The yeast, and that intense sweetness, acted on one another for a full ten days—seething, sighing, whispering, building up vast grey-yellow ravines like some Himalayan mountainscape viewed from a great height. Slowly the mountains eroded, subsided, melted back into the tawny water from which they had emerged. There were a few last whispers; then it was time to bottle the brew.

The time drew on towards Yule. The ale matured, unbroached in fifty bottles. Then one evening—there being nothing good on TV—I was sitting idly in the rocking chair when it occurred to me to taste the brew.

There it lay in the mug with a noble crown of froth on it. A first few sips confirmed that it was a successful ale, and would grow better as the days passed.

Strange things happen—you might imagine I would be contented, so late at night, to drink down that jugful of Lethe and go to bed. It was the spring of Parnassus I was sipping at. The jar was less than half down when my fingers got an urge to hold a ballpoint pen and make marks on a piece of white paper. I obeyed the impulse—imagination took over, with its own sweet laws and urgings—little poems came, one after another, on the page; all clustered like stars about the central theme of Christmas.

I thought, 'This is bound to be nonsense when I look at it with a cold eye in the morning!' But next day, and the day after, the little galaxy of words still sang out of the page[1].

If it was the honey that was the music-maker, I won't be ignoring honey in future brews.

'Burns Lives'...

19.1.1978

Years and years ago, I've heard, some Orkney countrymen in a certain parish were sitting together one evening with their pipes and yarns—perhaps in a smithy or a farm kitchen. It was a winter evening and by and by they got on to talking about Robbie Burns—quoting his verse, telling stories (whether authentic or apocryphal) about the man himself.

Suddenly one of the group said, 'Is he still alive, Robbie Burns?'...

After an astonished silence, the company dissolved in loud merriment. And perhaps—for all I know—the man who had put his foot in it with a vengeance slunk home, red-faced, under the stars.

* * *

But perhaps the man wasn't so far wrong, after all. When you think about it, 'Robert Burns Lives...' has been true ever since he followed the plough and rode about the countryside on excise duties and sat in his garret with pen and paper, 'rhyming for fun'... He caught the imagination of his countrymen as no other poet has ever done.

What Englishmen, when they sit of an evening over tankards of beer, ever speak about Shakespeare? (If one made the attempt, he would he regarded as more than a little 'round the twist'.) Italians with Dante, Germans with Goethe, Russians with Pushkin, Americans with Whitman—it's all the same: poets are excluded from the ordinary give-and-take of conversation.

1 The poem is called 'A Christmas Patchwork'.

Let them be confined to their proper places—the book, the classroom, the university lecture hall.

* * *

It isn't that Scotsmen are more literary-minded than other nations. Mention Henryson, Galt, MacDiarmid to 'the common Scot' and see what a blank look you will get...

Edwin Muir has offered the best explanation so far for the mystery. It is that every Scotsman sees himself somehow mirrored in Burns: the sentimentalist, the religious man, the lover, the heroic drinker, the father and husband, the 'lad o' pairts' dogged with ill-luck, the good companion, the common man who could keep his head and hold his own in the highest urban society, the stout upholder of the rights of man.

The man who, ignorantly, caused such hilarity in that Orkney smithy thirty or forty years ago was right after all. Burns is still alive; and while he lives there is hope for humanity.

Car Rides in Snow

26.1.1978

It's a cold winter night in the second half of January. The wind is soughing in the chimney and occasionally there are blatters of sleet against the window.

Not weather for anyone who can help it to be out. I have a stuffed nose, and a harsh throat, and the weather has made my left ear as dull as a centenarian's.

Yet we seem to be having better weather than in Scotland and England. The TV news, a few hours since, showed storms and snowed-in traffic—the very wildest ragings of winter. It kept today's mail from reaching Orkney—a thing I have mixed feelings about. (Every letter demands an answer, and this week's list is already formidable enough.)

I confess to a growing aversion, as I get older, to going out on winter nights—even on fine winter nights.

Round about the festive time, there was a cluster of invitations, all in the space of a few nights. Going by car to Kirkwall, in answer to one invitation, I observed with apprehension a large silver moth (a snowflake, to you unacquainted with our Norse habit of kennings), fluttering on to the car window and dying a watery death there. And I thought, supposing it is only the first of a billion silver moths, and we end up at two or three in the morning in some vast snowdrift near Maeshowe!

There was no need to worry. Such was the generosity of our Kirkwall hostess, we went home a merry carful; and the night was sweet and dark.

A few nights later, things looked more serious. A black half-gale, filled with sleet, was blowing athwart our road. We sat at another kind board, but outside the storm was getting wilder and wilder.

In other circumstances, I might have asked for a bed for the night; but with a Barleycorn glow inside one, one is ready to face anything... It was, I assure you, quite a thrilling drive home. From time to time the car was wrapped in a dense throbbing blizzard; that thinned out, and lightened; and showed the landscape under a new coating of snow. And there on the horizon another ink-black cloud swelled to engulf us. It was very exhilarating. (On an ordinary night I would have been a bit frightened!) I welcomed the little labyrinth of lights under Brinkie's Brae...

Please, don't expect me to shift far from Stromness of an evening until February is out, at least.

Blizzard

2.2.1978

The great January seize-up began on Saturday morning. I had got up, after repeated knockings, to open the door to a friend from Kirkwall[1]; who stood there, spectral with snow. We managed to have two cups of coffee apiece when the ceiling light gave a blink and flicker, and

---

1 Nan Butcher, who types for me with great speed and efficiency.

another longer wink, and at last died. Outside, you couldn't see the Holms for the grey smoor of snow from the north-east.

Much more serious than the death of the light was that my living room was drained of all warmth. My chimney has been long choked with birds' nests: I have relied for ten years on an electric fire. Now I was paying the penalty.

My friend, having left behind the typescript of some children's stories, departed to catch the 2pm bus back to Kirkwall. I managed to shave, and eat, shivering, a thick cheese sandwich. Then, rubber-booted and wrapped in the old black duffle, I set off townwards in search of warmth. I dropped in past the licensed grocer to buy warmth of one kind.

It was one of the nastiest blizzards I remember. (A blizzard can be a thing of beauty, all driven crystal and swans' down.) This blizzard was wet and grey and altogether foul.

It was pleasant to be sitting, in a short while, in a wide room with a generous fragrant red-chasmed peat fire.

Once, in the course of the late afternoon, the lights blazed upon our twilight and we thought, well, it wasn't too long or too bad...

Then like a black scythe the darkness descended again, but friendly and starred with candle flames.

The children were delighted with this piece of unexpected midwinter drama. It was almost like Christmas all over again, with mystery and excitement moving in the shadows. A paraffin lamp was discovered, and lit on top of the piano; a pure soft radiance. Hungry mouths soon reduced a toppling plateful of sandwiches to crumbs... We expected, always, the great star of Hydro light to explode soundlessly and permanently about us; but twenty-four hours were to pass before that happened.

In a very short time we had reverted to the winter conditions of our great-great-grandparents. We even enjoyed word-play—the game 'The Ministers' Cat' went from mouth to mouth and was hugely enjoyed by the children.

Meantime the great blizzard darkened and hushed over cold benighted Orkney. We thought how lucky we were; we thought of the hundreds of people without light or fire, far from friends.

Next day, Orkney Radio came into its own—and showed (if we didn't know it before) what a very valuable service it can be in times of chaos and crisis.

Things Fall Apart

9.2.1978

What it must have been like, to be isolated in the country last week without power or water, I can't imagine.

It was bad enough in Stromness, for thirty-six hours (and we were never without water, except the farms and cottages on that broad ridge that sweeps out to the Black Crag).

When I finally got home to Mayburn Court on Monday afternoon, it was like the interior of an iceberg. Merrily the fan heater in the kitchen purred and sang, full blast; and waves of warmth moved everywhere. I had a visitor who had just disembarked from the *Ola*, having bravely made that fearsome train journey from Cumbria through the white wilderness of northern Scotland[1].

Over a pot of tea, we discussed the blizzard and what it had done to the sophistications of civilisation that we take for granted—light, power, water. If our materialistic acquisitive culture ever breaks down, some time in the future, will it happen something like last weekend?—we wondered. But in a much more drastic fashion, of course, because the blizzard and its aftermath were only, after all, a slight temporary inconvenience.

But people, when our 'decline and fall' takes place, will know that their lights are out for ever; nor will their fridges, irons, TV sets, cookers, kettles, washers, blankets, fan heaters, toothbrushes, clocks, doorbells ever operate again... We can't conceive of the hopelessness of such a situation. (May it not happen for many generations. May it not happen at all...)

1 Jeremy Godwin, well-known Orkneyphile.

Meantime, with that fan heater purring sweetly in the corner, I foolishly assumed that the TV would be ready to oblige too. Nothing doing. When I switched it on, bands of luminosity was the only response, though I twiddled the knobs for a good half-hour.

In the next few evenings I did more reading than for a long time, and enjoyed the change.

How pleasant, though, to get a black-and-white image on Friday evening early! Because that is the night that *The Mayor of Casterbridge* comes on, and episode one had been marvellously good. I watched part two in beautiful colour, sitting in a friend's house.

The great blizzard had its heroes. In the midst of our discomfort we never ceased wondering at the resource and endurance and dedication and skill of the Hydro-Electric workers.

It can have been anything but pleasant, working against time in the white wastes of western Orkney, last weekend and after.

England Unvisited

16.2.1978

Some of them laugh. Some gape in amazement. Some look with lofty disdain. I have been explaining, for about the hundredth time, that I have never been to England—'that other Eden, demi-Paradise'...

I hasten to say, then, that I have indeed been out of Scotland. In 1968—a full decade ago—I was given a 'travel award'. The stipulation was that I visit a foreign country. A decade ago, if I remember rightly, you could only take £50 out of Britain. I had always been fascinated by Ireland, that land of poets and scholars. (It was the year before the present 'troubles' started in the north.) So my friend Patrick Hughes and I drove to Stranraer, crossed over to Larne, and in early evening light traversed the beautiful Antrim hills to Portrush. It rained in Donegal, and was utterly enchanting. We stayed a few days in Galway, where there are memories of Spain in the stones. In a pub on the outskirts men and boys were speaking Gaelic; while a new TV in the corner blared out the inanest of English.

In the wilds of Connemara—the landscape has a remote visionary beauty—the car broke down; it was the first of our troubles with it. We decided, after a temporary patch-up, not to trust that car overmuch. Instead of driving along all the Irish coastline—and how I was longing to see Kerry and the Blasket Islands—we drove through the flat centre of Ireland to Dublin. We stayed there ten days in the annexe of a hotel where the service was excellent. The car was fixed for £5. We looked in vain for James Joyce's Martello tower.

The night before we left Ireland we had a marvellous evening with a group of Irish poets and singers in Belfast. (And, as I said, the very next summer the bad things started happening in Belfast, Derry and Larne.)

* * *

So far, and no further, the wanderlust has taken me. There have been invitations to the south of France, Wales, England; and just the other day, in a letter, a sweet lady wrote that if ever I was in British Columbia, I was to be sure and call on her!

I fear that I have told a lie right at the start of this article. Once, eight or nine years ago, I was in a car with Hazel and Allison and Pamela. We drove through another enchanted landscape, the Borders. We found ourselves a few miles from Berwick-on-Tweed. Towards Berwick we headed.

Now a Scottish Nationalist would say that, geographically speaking, Berwick is part of Scotland. But to make quite sure I had set foot on English soil we drove over the Tweed and got out on the south bank.

Prince George and the Lifeboat

23.2.1978

Fifty years ago was the year 1928—and I'm sure it was in 1928 that Stromness began to seethe with excitement. None get infected with excitement so easily as children. We knew that some great event was about to take place.

Stromness School was crammed that day with pupils carrying flags of all shapes and sizes. You might have thought we were massing for the Children's Crusade. I remember that my own peedie flag had a red lion rampant on a yellow ground—the arms of Scotland.

Somehow or other those teeming hundreds were marshalled and marched down to the street, and there we formed two immensely long lines, facing inwards, flags fluttering, all the way from the South Pier to the Lifeboat slip.

It seemed we had a long time to wait. We brandished our flags. We chattered like birds. (And of course—I ought to have mentioned this earlier—there were arches of flags all along the street, from chimney to chimney. Our grey town was enchanted for one day.)

When would the prince come?

At last there was a hush along the street. I was standing with my small fellow-pupils almost opposite the Lifeboat shed, at the door of Mrs Birch's house (but then it belonged to a man called Adam Mackay).

Was this the prince at last?

I remember feeling a vivid pang of disappointment. I must have been expecting a storybook prince, a Grimms' fairy-tale prince, on a prancing horse perhaps, with a golden circlet about his brows.

What appeared on the crest of Hutchison's Brae, moving towards the Lifeboat slip, was a group of men, very important-looking certainly, but sombrely clad. And which of them was the prince? We had no means of telling. We recognised, certainly, Provost Corrigall; because we saw him every day of our lives. There was a young man in naval uniform walking along beside Provost Corrigall. Was he the prince?

We waved our flags and shouted.

Presently the group of important men turned and descended the steps towards the Lifeboat shed.

That was the day, some time in 1928—half a century ago—that Prince George (later the Duke of Kent) came to launch the Stromness Lifeboat *JJKSW*... Somewhere in my drawer of photographs I have postcards to prove that it was no dream.

Fuel, and Fires

2.3.1978

Finally, a few days before Christmas, the kitchen fan heater gave out. The kitchen is where I eat and write (passing half the day), so it was a serious business.

The fans whirred on and on, but out of the heater came only intense coldness. Had I caught flu? Had a ghost entered the premises? No—the element had gone dead.

Fortunately, a friend lent me hers, and so there was nothing extreme in the situation. I took the sick heater to the electrician, and waited for a new element to be sent from the south.

We are more dependent than we like to think on those modern contraptions. And yet, at our doorsteps, there's enough fuel to keep every fire in Orkney merry for a century or more. (I am not speaking about oil.) Maybe, if some awful catastrophe overtakes civilisation, we will be only too glad to go out and dig peats once more—inferior though they may be—from the Loons and environs.

* * *

In my childhood, the first step towards sophistication, and away from the natural wealth lying everywhere about us (which is therefore apt to be despised) had been taken. In every Stromness house coal-fed stoves heated kitchen and living room; except in the posher houses, where they had grates.

To show what a precarious step it had been, in 1926 occurred the General Strike—which was 'general' only for a short time—but the miners held out for longer; and so there was a dearth of coal. One of my earliest memories is of our lamplit kitchen in Victoria Street in 1926; there was no coal, but my father had got 'pitch' from somewhere, and I remember the strange smell and the dripping frightening yellow soft cold flames. It was an altogether alien fire; I was very glad when the coal boats started coming again, and the bell-man went about the street calling, 'A cargo of best English coal has arrived... '

In a farm kitchen, from time to time, our nostrils got the smell of burning peats, one of life's most enchanting fragrances.

In 1947, I bought a one-bar electric fire for my room. What could be said in its favour?—only that it was supremely useful. Character or charm it had none.

That fan heater did have a kind of character—purring away in a corner of the kitchen like a contented cat.

Now it is back again, completely recovered (for the time being). The peats in the Loons lie waiting for Stromnessians of the doomed 21st or 22nd centuries.

Decimals

9.3.1978

Decimals everywhere. Soon it will be no good wandering into a shop and asking for a pound of tea, or an ounce of tobacco. You will quaff your beer by the litre. If, some summer soon, a stranger asks, 'How far away is Kirkwall?' and you reply, 'Fifteen miles,' the stranger will gape at you as if you were some kind of dinosaur who had somehow or other escaped the Ice Age.

It has become fashionable too, when writing the figure 'seven', to put a horizontal stroke through the diagonal, after the continental fashion. This I refuse resolutely to do. (I suppose the idea of transfixing the '7' in that disgraceful way is to distinguish it from the figure '1', which in France and Germany has a little curl or forelock descending from the top.) But when I went to school in the primary department of Stromness Academy, there were no such flourishes. 'One' was a simple vertical stroke, 'Seven' was the diagonal with the peak: there was no possibility of them being confused. And so I will go on making these figures in the traditional way, Common Market or no.

It is interesting that they have never tried to decimalise time. There is no reason, on the surface, why the day should not be divided into a hundred hours. It would cause some initial confusion; but we learned to forget £sd soon enough.

But here, in the austere mysterious realm of time, we come slap-bang against cosmic measurements, which are different from ours, and can never be tampered with. It would gladden the hearts of bureaucrats the world over if the earth took exactly one hundred days to revolve round the sun. But to the everlasting joy of trees, waters, children, animals and artists, the number of days in a year is 365¼. And that can never be tampered with. Also the moon performs her marvellous ballet in 28 days.

But I wouldn't put it past them to make, some time soon, a ten-month year. What could be more disordered than the present calendar with its twelve months of varying length? The revolutionaries of France two hundred years ago imagined beautiful new names for the months. I don't think we would get 'Fructidor' or 'Humidor' nowadays—it would be 'Month One', 'Month Two', 'Month Three', etc. So drained of poetry is the age we live in.

Bombs in Springtime

16.3.1978

Be sure, if you prod the memory, a swarm of images come buzzing around.

Three weeks ago I tried to remember the visit of Prince George fifty years ago to launch the Stromness lifeboat *JJKSW*.

The lengthening days remind me of a more recent highly dramatic totally unexpected event—the bombs at Brig o' Waithe.

It was a Saturday evening in March. I was alone in the house with my father. My mother was in the town shopping. (The shops stayed open longer in those days.)

What could be more quiet than the weekend in Stromness? There weren't even pubs in March 1940. You sat at home, reading or listening to the battery wireless.

Suddenly, in the twilight, earth and sky erupted! The houses shook and trembled. (I suppose there must have been an air-raid warning previously.) We were not supposed to, but we went to the back door that looked out over Scapa Flow. There was now a continuous uproar of anti-aircraft guns, and against the dark hills around Scapa Flow scarlet and orange stabs of fire. And in the brief pauses, a very sinister noise—the faint wavering drone of German bombers. The sky was full of little puffs of anti-aircraft smoke.

This, I think, was the first large-scale air raid over Scapa Flow; at least it is the one I remember most clearly.

The council house dwellers stood at their back doors, faces tilted up at the menacing sky, and that Wagnerian uproar going on and on. We were more thrilled and excited than frightened. (Were we ordered inside, sternly, by the air-raid wardens? On other occasions, certainly, we were. I was vividly aware of being a spectator at the clash of nations.)

As the spring evening darkened, the anti-aircraft flame from the hill stabbed more starkly—the earth and the sky melled with each other more fiercely—the drone of the high bombers swelled and thinned...

Suddenly—I seem to remember—it was all over. A great peace descended with the oncoming of night. We drew down our blackout blinds and lit the gas lamp. My mother came home at last with her bag of rations.

* * *

It was only next day we heard that a man had been killed, and other folk injured, in the hamlet of Brig o' Waithe.

A troop of us boys walked there that afternoon, a bright tranquil Sunday. Here and there in the grass were the fins of the incendiary bombs that the German pilot had scattered, probably at random, in order to be off and away as unencumbered as possible.

Next evening, Lord Haw-Haw announced on the German propaganda radio that a military airfield had been destroyed at Howe on the Stromness side of the Brig.

A Bowl of Daffodils

23.3.1978

I suppose many folk, like myself, have a special affection for the daffodil, of all flowers. It is one of the first comers (after snowdrop and crocus). It seems to trumpet, soundlessly, a fanfare for spring and summer. It is a small yellow sun, and yet it has this chasteness, as if it carried memories of snow.

On the afternoon of my birthday, away back in autumn, a small girl arrived with a heavy parcel for me. Unwrapped, the gift was a beautiful blue china bowl crammed with earth and bulbs. Judy instructed me what to do—the bowl must be left to winter in a dark place under the stairs, and only brought out in the lengthening days.

There, almost forgotten, the bowl slumbered through the bonfires of November, and the bells and carols of Christmas, and the bottles of Hogmanay, and the great grey blizzard of January's end.

The snow lingered, and melted at last, and the light grew in ever widening circles.

It was time to bring out the blue bowl and set it on the table. 'Water it frugally, only once a week or so,' had been another instruction.

Swiftly the green stalks grew. The tight saffron buds showed themselves, the leaves grew and grew and began to sprawl over the edge of the bowl on to the book-strewn table. Perilously the buds hovered in the air—then they too made slow descending arcs.

It was high time to do something to keep the joyous company together. There wasn't a stick in the house, but I found a tall thin candle from four or five Christmases back, and that I stuck in the middle of the bowl. I gathered buds and leaves up from their sprawl and bound them with a length of wool. And I gave them a drink of celebratory water.

One morning when I came downstairs two of the golden trumpets had opened and were making unheard vernal music to the books and pictures and chairs...

Now four of them are brightening the living room, and tomorrow there will be a fifth; and still there are many buds to open.

The poets have praised those lyrical graceful flowers, and mourned to see them 'flee away so fast'. But no sooner have the house daffodils packed and gone than the roadsides of Orkney will begin to spill over with golden drifts; that is a new feature of Orkney in springtime, and a very delightful one.

An Easter Bug

30.3.1978

Strange that one should get through all that wild winter without a tickle in the throat or a sniff, and now, when the blue and green wave of spring is breaking over the islands, I get the worst cold for a long time. It is the kind of ailment that spreads a grey film over everything. To do the simplest thing you have to summon up a lot of willpower. All the senses have lost their relish for life.

Colds used to have certain compensations—for example, a hot toddy before bed. But this particular March cold has spread tentacles down to the stomach, so that eating and drinking are no pleasure. And other tentacles up to the brain—my head seems a block of pulsing wood. (It seems that nothing sweet and delightful will ever, ever happen again.)

And sleep—sure solace of those in distress—even that has lost its comfortings. For two nights I have lain tossing and turning; sometimes tangled in a confused drowse with unpleasant dreams; sometimes lying sweating, and longing for daybreak.

And tomorrow I am expecting friends from the south to stay for a few days. It will be a grey spectre, not a rubicund 'mine-host', that will meet those pleasant people in the door. (Still, I will do my best.)

And on some days next week, I am to be concerned in a certain piece of filming; and that, at the moment, seems an utterly impossible thing to participate in...

Cheerfulness keeps breaking in, when we least expect it. The doctor has given me a supply of those magic yellow tablets that put every cold to flight in a very short time. Every four hours I pop one in my mouth and wait for the breakthrough.

I'm very sorry to depress readers at this most cheerful time of year, when the roots are throbbing with new life and the whole golden summer is lying in front of us. But there it is; there is in life no unalloyed delight, just as in the darkest times a bead of light abides unquenchable.

In three days time, I hope I might fancy a fragment of Easter Egg.

A Film Interview

6.4.1978

If they ever take a film of the inside of your house, be sure it is no simple matter of setting up a camera and letting it whirr.

By no means. There is a complex system of lighting to be set up in the first place—lamps set strategically here and there, that shed a near intolerable brightness and a heat that brings out beads of sweat on forehead and upper lip. Anyone passing in the street on two days last week must have been surprised—to say the least—at the midday brilliance from my windows—as if some kind of high revelry was going on. (I hate to think of the hectic hurtling revolutions on that electric meter.)

Then the sound has to be taken care of. A kind of noose is hung round your neck, with a tiny microphone hidden under the jersey.

Soon after that it is time to begin.

Few things in life are as disconcerting as an interview with the cold eye of a camera on you and that microphone round your neck, listening. Some people love it—just watch them on television, how they revel in the exposure and the publicity like trout in a cold rapid burn... To a recluse like me, it is sheer agony

(Why do it, then? To oblige people you like—not to let them down—to attempt once more, in spite of instinctive revulsion, to co-operate with twentieth-century technology; for after all, we are a part of it, whether we like it or not. I would be a hypocrite if I said I was indifferent to my favourite TV programmes.)

And so the interview, in these disconcerting circumstances, began. To make things easier for me, the producers had brought up from Glasgow a young woman poet for whose work I felt a deep instinctive rapport[1]. She it was who did the interviewing; but, as it turned out, fortunately, it was more a pleasant conversation that meandered on and on for an hour or so. Fortunately for me, only tiny snippets of the film will eventually be used.

At last Liz Lochhead and I had nothing more to say, with regard to some of the things I have written in the past.

1 Liz Lochhead

The brilliant lights were switched off. A grey grateful gloom flooded in. Some of the taped conversation was played back—I winced, as always, at the alien sound of my voice.

When and where the film will be shown, eventually, I do not know.

But that evening, I expect, I will watch it in a state of intense quivering privacy.

A Week in April

13.4.1978

SUNDAY: A cold bleak day. Spring is reluctant to come, this year. Have lunch in a kind house on top of one of the little hills between the town and the Black Crag: delicious smoked sausage and cauliflower in a mellow sauce, helped down by a bottle of claret... We look at a sequence of coloured slides of Orkney, as best we can against the window light—many taken from the air, with bold beautiful patterns.

MONDAY: A town holiday. Speaking selfishly, I dislike those monthly town holidays. The whole town lies as dead as Skara Brae for a day. (But if I worked in a shop or an office, I'm sure I'd feel a lot different about it.) The April holiday is traditionally the time to dig the garden: and one day this week there was a group of horticulturists working; away in the garden beyond the kitchen window.

TUESDAY: I have been reading the typescript of an old friend who died untimely the winter before last[1]. This inveterate traveller loved, of all places on earth, the northern latitudes best of all. He wrote down his impressions of Scandinavia, Finland, Iceland, Orkney and Shetland: hoping to have them published in a book some day. The chapter on Shetland has been sent to me—it is altogether delightful and fresh, as if the man was sitting at a table next to me, talking about the shepherds and fishermen of Sumburgh.

If the book is published, it will be a fine addition to our island literature.

1 Jeremy Rundall

WEDNESDAY: Dropped into the Reading Room of the Library to discover that 'all losses are restored'—the papers and magazines that were subtracted, for national economic reasons a year and a half ago, are back on the racks: *Times*, *Daily Telegraph*, *Glasgow Herald*, *Daily Express*, *New Statesman*, *Illustrated London News*, etc...

The first wave of tourists has come and has almost gone. I had a visit this evening from two American young women and an Indian. They wanted books signed. They gave me, in exchange, an apple and a piece of Orkney fudge. A very pleasant conversation altogether.

THURSDAY: One of those rare golden and blue spring days. At an Orphir house, beautifully situated. Looking across to Hoy and Stromness, workmen were busy making extensions. I sipped white wine while my friends ate sandwiches... In Kirkwall, later, spent a soothing hour in Tankerness House Museum. There was a small exquisite exhibition of photographs. We lingered for a while in the lovely garden behind. (Where are the public seats in Kirkwall and Stromness?—I longed to sit down.)... Surely, the tide of spring is rising. We saw, earlier, first lambs in the fields of Clestrain. Going home in the bus late afternoon, there at Tormiston Mill the daffodils, folded still, were waiting to announce from a thousand yellow throats the entry of spring and summer.

Getting to Know Your Toaster

20.4.1978

I used to make the breakfast toast under the grill, which I was assured was a very expensive way of doing it.

So the other day I bought a toaster, a very neat smart-looking piece of hardware that would sit easily on the kitchen shelf.

I looked forward to next morning's toast—but when I brought the toaster out of its box there was no plug at the end of it. The old grill had to be pressed into service again.

In the late afternoon good fortune brought Keith Hobbs (from Evie) to the door, and we drank tea and chatted together. Just as he was about to leave, I remembered how he had fixed something electrical for me in the winter. In no time at all Keith obliged with a plug from an old lamp. 'I'll have two pieces of crisp toast with my chops and onions, for dinner,' I said to myself, smugly. But when I inserted the bread and switched on, nothing happened. Coldness and darkness rose up from the twin mouths of the toaster.

It occurred to me that perhaps the fuse was burned out. It was, indeed. I fixed in a new fuse—so far my knowledge of electricity extends—and enjoyed most delicious toast with my dinner.

Next morning I began experimenting with intensities of heat; there's a little dial on the toaster ranging from 1 to 6. I considered something between 3 and 4 would be fine—I like toast to be well done. Up popped the two pieces of bread with only the faintest burnish on them. That would never do. I pushed them back for a second toasting, and this time, with a fanfare of black smoke, they surfaced on the rather too-well-done side—I had to slice cinders from the extremities.

It takes a long while, getting to know the various 'Daleks' in your house—TV, record-player, cooker, toaster, washer, etc.

'I will make no mistake this morning,' I said to myself an hour ago, and turned the dial up to 5½. Presently, while I filled the teapot, the kitchen was possessed by a dense yeasty floury blue-black reek, and up came two squares of burning carbon. I had to throw the window open wide. My second attempt was more satisfactory. Tomorrow, I hope, I will have arrived at some kind of understanding with my toaster.

Sometimes I think, wistfully, of the coal-burning ranges of the 1930s, and of how we held out bread, on the prongs of a fork, to the glowing ribs.

The Battle of Clontarf

27.4.1978

Out of Scapa they sailed, and down the broken western coast of Scotland. Here and there, in this voe or vik, where they paused to take on water and provisions, a few young men joined the ships.

'There's no doubt about our victory,' said Earl Sigurd to the volunteers. 'My mother has sewn the raven-banner. Once it flutters above the host, there is no question of defeat. Only, the man who carries the banner must die.'

The young men from Orkney, Caithness, Iceland, Shetland, the Faroes, looked with eager eyes at the southern horizon. When would they see the coast of Ireland?

Off Galloway, the rotund thickset Earl, said, 'If only my son Hund were here with us!' But Hund had died in Norway when he was still a boy, a hostage. The small ghost of Hund drifted through the royal palace of Bergen.

When the coast of Antrim broke through the fog one morning, soldiers and sailors cheered.

It was April in Ireland. Birds were building their nests in the woodland. Ploughmen had combed the hillsides to dark furrows. From the ditches spilled daffodils and lilies and new grass.

But among the hills of Ireland were secret movements of men and horses. From the villages and halls and little farms men came together, and mingled, and marched by night towards the town of Dublin.

It was late in the season of Lent. The little bells rang now and then from the monastery towers.

Earl Sigurd and his host landed, with uproar and songs and boastings, on the shore of Dublin. And there one of the many small kings of Ireland called Sigtrygg, whose beard seemed made of spun sunlight, greeted him...

The battle outside the city wall was fought on Good Friday. King Brian, High King of Ireland, was hewn down where he sat in his chair (for he would not bear arms on such a day).

From hand to hand went the raven-banner of the Orkneymen. Whichever hand held it aloft was soon white and cold in death. At last the earl himself wrapped the magical thing about him, and rushed into the red maelstrom: and was never seen alive again.

The scales of battle tilted in favour of the Norse-Irish, and the dead Christian King. The invaders fled in disorder.

One young Icelander paused in the headlong retreat. He bent down and tied the thong of his sandal. The victors, swords reeking, stopped. They asked him, why was he not fleeing with his comrades to the ships? 'I live in Iceland,' said Thorstein, 'and that's a long way off, and I don't think I'll get home tonight.'

It was such a sweet speech, uttered there on the edge of darkness, that his captors spared him.

The Last Day of April

4.5.1978

Sunday afternoon, and the last day of April. It has been one of the coldest Aprils we remember. One day last week I saw a swirl of snowflakes dancing past the window; to melt at once, of course, in the daffodil trumpets and the black new-delved tattie patches.

This morning, coming back from Kirkwall in the car, the sun had the sky to itself, except for (it seemed) one little white tuft-cloud. Scapa Flow had a small flotilla of naval vessels at anchor. Orphir, with its beautiful hills and valleys, seemed to lie at the door of summer. Lambs everywhere, and the ditches spilling with daffodils. On the Scorriedale road, the first brilliant flickerings of gorse.

But when we walked back in early, afternoon, along the high road from Castle Farm[1] to Oglaby, the easterly wind smote keenly and made the hands and cheeks blue. The solitary lamb-like cloud of morning had become a high scattered flock. Shadows went swiftly across the fields and the sea. The road going down from Quildon to the housing schemes was more sheltered, and a faint warmth kindled the flesh again.

The first dandelions were in the ditches—a scattering of small suns. Soon the makers of dandelion wine will have to be abroad, emptying endless teeming galaxies into their baskets. ('Lion's tooth'—how did the dandelion ever come by that name, those flowers that we used to pluck by hundreds half a century ago, wondering always at the milky

1 Tam and Dunnie Macphail lived there at the time.

146

stems?) The daisies, too, are starring the grass—I noticed the first ones today in a sheltered garden.

Dandelion and whin and daisy—a fair gift for the last day of April to give us: and so we forgive it the cold winds and that solitary snow-whirl.

× * *

From the music of time to time's mathematics.

I wrote a few weeks back about decimalisation, and how at least they would never be able to inflict their arbitrary man-made measurements on such an unstable dimension as Time.

Like an echo came back an answer from Mr A. Wylie, Kirkwall, that dexterous craftsman. He said in his letter that he had in fact made a working decimal clock, and to prove it he enclosed a photograph.

It may be the first decimal clock in the world; if so I hope Mr Wylie will get recognition for it, when the day comes for the day to be universally segmented into ten hours.

Edwin Muir and Time

11.5.1978

It is hard to realise it, but if Edwin Muir had been alive this May he would be ninety-one years old. It is impossible, somehow, to imagine him an old man.

Time and the poet Muir had a strange relationship to each other. It might be said that time is the great theme of all his work: he was endlessly fascinated by the nature of time, its flowerings and fadings, its curious turns and twists and loops and returns.

A poet is, by romantic tradition, young. Keats, Shelley, Byron, Rimbaud—all blazed like comets for a short time only, then burned themselves out.

But Edwin Muir was 35 before he began to write poetry. He went on working at the craft of verse, improving all the time, until his death in 1959. It seems appropriate that he was just beyond the psalmist's perfect age for ripeness and departure—seventy: another piece of felicitous co-operation between Muir and time.

Many poets and philosophers have, in the past two generations, been intrigued, like Muir, by time—Thomas Mann, J. W. Dunne, T. S. Eliot, J. B. Priestley. It has seemed to them that time is not just a sequence of seconds, hours, years, centuries. Something far more mysterious is working on us and through us. An experience of great joy or sorrow has an altogether different 'time quality' from the arid hours we spend in office or factory.

But Edwin Muir was haunted beyond any of those other explorers of the nature of time.

The outwardly placid landscape of his life—and nobody I have known ever seemed to be more possessed with tranquillity—masked a battlefield in which two cultures and two civilisations clashed. His first years were spent in the little pastoral island of Wyre. At the age of fourteen he went with his family to live in Glasgow, in the very heart of industrialism. It was a dramatic and highly dangerous step to take. Within a year or so four of the family died. Innocence and experience, the pastoral and the industrial: few writers have had to endure the savage tension of such opposites. He wrote somewhere that he must be two or three hundred years old: such vast changes had occurred in his life.

The child who was born in Deerness on 15 May, 1887, moved about in a world of timelessness. In spite of poverty and hardship—which were the lot of all Orkney country folk in those days—life for the child was irradiated with wonder and beauty and delight.

Those early memories became the poetry of the mature man, once he had learned (in some fashion, at least) to reconcile the 17th and the 20th centuries.

Football

18.5.1978

When I was a small boy in Stromness nearly half a century ago, I and my contemporaries were all passionately devoted to football. We played it along the roads and on the street with small rubber balls—ever vigilant for the approach of the two policemen, Messrs Mainland and Manson.

We played it more formally in fields here and there, with little heaps of coats for goalposts, and imaginary by-lines. The boundaries were so vague, frequently these impromptu games ended in a squabble or a fight.

Ten or twelve times a year, real battle-lines were drawn and matches were played between the North End and the South End. We generally managed a real leather football (small size) for those encounters, which took place sometimes on a lower slope of Brinkie's Park, where the Grieveship houses now are, and sometimes at Ness (now Guardhouse Park). Of course there was no such thing as strips or colours. A few of the wealthier boys wore proper football boots.

The most exciting time of the week was the evening when Stromness Athletic were playing one or other of the three Kirkwall teams at the Market Green. It so happened that our juvenile football fever coincided with the finest flowering of adult football in the west. Stromness Athletic in those days was a feared and famous team: when we saw them running out of the wood and tin pavilion, in white shirts and black shorts, on to the pitch, our hearts fluttered with excitement! We expected, and often got, immense victories. We trudged home late, sated with drama and joy.

How outraged we were if this star Stromness player or that was left out of the Orkney team to play against Shetland! That match was a time of breathless anticipation. (Not that there was the remotest chance of us getting to Shetland—or even to Kirkwall's Bignold Park, the bus fare being too much for us.) Instead, we lingered in Graham Place, near Provost Marwick's tailor shop window. Presently the Provost would stick a notice written on an old envelope in his window—the half-time score, along with the scorers' names. Then, a breathless hour later, the final score. I remember one result from Lerwick that shattered us: Shetland 6, Orkney 0.

* * *

These memories were prompted by something I saw on TV last night—Liverpool against Bruges in the European Cup Final. It was nowhere nearly as exciting, I solemnly assure you, as Stromness against Kirkwall Hotspur at the Market Green forty-five years ago.

Evie

25.5.1978

The Mayburn bench, painted a fresh glossy green, is in place again—a sign that we are on the verge of summer. The sun last Tuesday morning was doing its best, after indifferent grey days. I sat on the sun-warm Mayburn bench talking mainly about books and poems with a friend from the south of England who comes, alas, only too rarely to the islands[1]... She was late for lunch in Kirkwall; she had to leave quite soon, but before going she invited me to a barn party in early September, next time she comes back: which date I have entered in my calendar.

I had to go, too, with two friends; the first of the year's circuits of the West Mainland by car. I have been peevish about this well-beaten path before; but in fact there are new things to be seen and done every time; and besides, who can ever have enough of Sandwick or Birsay?...

Brightness fell from the air (as the medieval poet said). The golden morning turned gradually grey and chilly. But the larks, nothing daunted, ravelled their threads of song over the hills; and sometimes even my indifferent sight could glimpse the pulsing wavering rapture of them.

Discovering that we had some necessary messages to do, we called (for the first time in years) at one of those Orkney shops that sells almost everything you can think of. Entering this one in Sandwick was like a swift nostalgic return to childhood and magic caves. There is still to be found in country shops a courtesy that has vanished from smarter slicker places of trade.

Dave Brock, who owned and drove the car, sat in a kind of torment as we passed Boardhouse Loch, glimpsed Hundland through a gap of hills, plunged down towards Swannay Loch. 'A perfect afternoon for fishing!' he said; and he should know, being a talented trout fisher. Cloudy, a ruffle of wind, scattered larksong. Sure enough, out on Swannay he counted five or six fishermen... They smote the pewter to tiny silver rings.

Aikerness Bay gives its name to Evie parish: 'efja', bay of tideless water with a strong tide-race outside. We sat over sandwiches and apple juice and books in a modern cottage looking out across that bay

---

1 Elizabeth Gore-Langton, who has since bought a house in Outertoon: Garth.

to the tide-sieged isle of Eynhallow and the brown hills of Rousay. The early Orcadians loved this place; their brochs are more thickly concentrated here than anywhere in the north. There, on its grassy promontory, smoulder the strong stones of Gurness.

The day was ebbing. Throats slightly malted with the ale of country inns, we came down the Clouster road towards the first lights of Stromness.

Torf-Einar, Earl and Poet

1.6.1978

When we saw the peat-cutters on the high desolate hills above Evie the other evening, I thought of Torf-Einar. the earl who (it was said) got that nickname because he first showed his people how to burn peats.

But what did the Orcadians burn on their fires before Earl Einar sailed west from Norway: the only one of three brothers willing to rule in the turbulent Orkneys?

They certainly didn't burn logs: the woodlands had long since sunk into the dark bogs. There wasn't much driftwood in that uncommercial age. The first monk at Newbattle in Lothian hadn't yet kicked the first black stone out of his meditative way; then picked it up, examined it, smelled it, and applied his mind to the mysteries of carbon and combustion. (That was Scotland's first coal.)

The folk of Gurness and Wideford and Skara Brae were burning peats long centuries before Torf-Einar, certainly. Why, then, the distinctive name?

Perhaps, like other 'heroes' of that civilisation, Einar had the habit of thrusting a lighted peat into the thatch of some householder he didn't like. That was the simple solution to problems in that age: reduce your enemy to ash.

Einar was the kind of man that we of the 20th century can hardly begin to understand. He was extraordinarily lucky in all he undertook—every skirmish and battle ended in victory for the Norwegian whose mother had been base-born and a slave.

Not even the King's son could stand against him. Haltdan the Norwegian prince fled from the axes of Einar, after a sea battle. Next morning the sharp eye of Einar saw something rising and falling in the ebb of an island. It turned out to be the exhausted prince. First, Einar hacked his ribs from his backbone; then he drew out the lungs, slimy wings, and spread them out to be a victory offering to Odin the God.

All the time Einar exercised his gift of poetry; the part of the saga that deals with him is patched with poem after poem.

And yet—very unusual in those days—this man of violence died in his bed. This perhaps was his only defeat: a long drawn out senescence, all valour and epic long vanished. He wheezed, hobbled, mumbled his way to the end. He sat long on winter days beside the huge fire of peats in the great Hall. And perhaps the girl who tended the old creature said one day, 'More peats! How cold your blood must be, my lord! There's flame enough in here to roast an ox. More peat? No, if you say "peat" again, I'll give you a new name. I will. I'll call you Peat Einar...'

A TV Play at Yesnaby

8.6.1978

Day after day of unsullied sun—not a single puffball of cloud in the sky—along the horizon a thin haze, sign of continuing good weather.

We Orcadians are always taken by surprise at nature's extravagant bursts of generosity. We are used to patchwork weather, not this unrolling golden web, day after day.

Wednesday, today, and the last day of May. Unflawed sunlight again, the heat of yesterday tempered a little by an easterly breeze.

At 12.30 a car came to take me to Yesnaby, where a piece of film was being shot. On the little green hilly peninsula of Brough-of-Bigging a group of colourful figures was gathered: come out of 800 years ago, and Vikings, by their costume and gestures—except for a young boy and a girl from the same Orkney glebe and steading, both in pastoral clothing.

All around this tableau were gathered cameramen, sound recordists, makeup ladies, keepers of the wardrobe. Dominating the proceedings was the lithe alert figure of the producer, Tom Cotter[1].

The wind was freshening all the time. The long hair of the Vikings streamed out. Yellow scripts fluttered here and there on the grass, like panicky hens.

The same scene, about a minute long, was repeated over and over until at last the producer was satisfied; and the other technicians concurred.

The small farm boy, Igor, is looking for his mother's lost sheep. The Viking skipper and his two sailors are looking for a boy to take with them on the great pilgrimage of Earl Rognvald, now, in 1151, about to sail from Scapa. The searches mesh and mingle, in a few brief words. That was the tiny episode that had taken up such a slice of the afternoon.

(We tend to think, looking at a play on TV, how smoothly it unfolds; as if the filming-time and the action itself were of the same length, roughly. In fact, every movement and word and gesture is intensely scrutinised by the director; and often a little cameo—as today—must be repeated over and over again. In an hour there must have been seven or eight retakes.) It should look beautiful on the screen, with, as background, that misty-blue curve of sky and the Atlantic fingering white lace about the bases of the cliffs at Yesnaby. Finally, about 2pm, the episode was in the can. The little army of actors, technicians, spectators, retired to the concrete-and-brick scabs at the end of the Yesnaby road; and there we ate sandwiches, drank out of cans, and conversed.

For me, it was a brief delicious interlude. The TV team would be busy all day at Brough-of-Bigging, in wind and sun; and there, and elsewhere, is envisaged a week of intense activity, over one small fifteen-minute play.

1 Four TV plays for schools: scripts by GMB: directed by Tom Cotter for the BBC: screened in Autumn 1978.

Ally's Tartan Army

22.6.1978

So there we sat, one Saturday evening in early June, in front of a colour TV, and waited for the magic to begin.

After fifteen minutes came the first touch of tartan magic: a goal that set Cordoba in a roar and let loose a sea of lion-rampants. Scotland, it seemed, were well on the way to the promised land; immortal glory in the history of football!

Is there something strange and perverse in the Scottish character that allows the brimming cup to fall and shatter on a stone? What about those battles in history that we were all set to win, until we were fatally lured from our secure position into the marshes and quicksands of defeat?...

The quick moment of Argentinian magic passed. Thereafter the team that had been sent from Scotland with unprecedented raptures and praises on their heads fell apart, disintegrated, became a collection of toiling impotent individuals. The lightly-regarded Peruvians beat us, in the end, 3–1.

What shock, outrage, disbelief! We had been led to think of the Scottish team as virtually unbeatable (even after that 1–0 defeat by England at Hampden: another occasion when the valour and fire shown by the Scots ended in ashes).

The newspapers, that had been lauding them for months, now led the howls of detraction. If you stumble and fall nowadays, in the civilised 20th century, don't expect to be helped to your feet—look instead for a series of kicks in the teeth.

Then the drugs sensation broke, and the media got wildly excited again; this time with a touch of smugness and self-righteousness.

A day or two later, we began to eat crumbs of comfort. We will beat Iran, of course; and then, getting into the victory stride, steal the march on Holland; and all will be well, perhaps, in spite of everything.

I only saw the last twenty minutes of the Iran match. It was so poor I'm glad I didn't see the rest of it. I will carry for a long time the image of poor Ally MacLeod sitting in the pit with his head in his hands.

There is another strange thing in the national psyche: we seem to revel in defeat more than any other nation. There is an element of dark enjoyment woven into our greatest disasters. Think of it: the tragedies of Flodden and Culloden have produced far more beautiful lyric, legend, ballad than have any of our famous victories.

POSTSCRIPT—Dared we watch on Sunday evening? Could we take more humiliation? We dared—and saw at the very last, a splash of the promised magic! Scotland 3, Holland 2—it was almost incredible, but it was true.

A Day between Weathers

29.6.1978

8.15am—and the *Jessie Ellen* lying blue and handsome and ready at the South Pier. The morning was sun-drenched, except that Hoy had built up over its summits a battlement of grey and white cloud; which might possibly contain rain. Hoy-ward, this Wednesday morning, we were bound.

Musicians without instruments and music-lovers arrived from Kirkwall. The *Jessie Ellen* was crowded as it moved out of the harbour at 8.30am.

The huge cloud over Hoy had toppled sideways across the sun. In that shade the air moved cold. We had a serene passage round the east side of Graemsay. There, at the Moness pier, Jack Rendall and Geoff Clark were waiting with their vehicles. The tide brimmed high and blue over the rocks. Some benign fortune gives us, nearly always, beautiful weather in Hoy. Our car passed the slowly growing tree plantation and the ancient peat-banks; and there at last Rackwick lay like a green sea-tilted bowl, full of light.

There was no need to hurry. We walked, singly or in small groups, across the perilous side of Moorfea to the high hidden cottage of Bunertoon. Gulls flashed past our faces from the chimneypots of North-house.

To those who suffer, like me, from vertigo, there are anxious moments in the slow climb across that curving hill, Moorfea. The sea, blue and dazzling, lies far below. Above, the serene sweep of sky. Between, this crazy green tilt where we trod hesitantly along ancient sheep paths. One thinks, 'If I stumble, there's nothing to keep me from plunging straight into the Atlantic!...'

I trod, nervously, the last sheer curve, and there were the roof and chimneys of Bunertoon, with smoke drifting in the lucent air. There is no cottage in the world more dramatically sited.

* * *

Through the long day, till 4pm, we sat around Bunertoon, sun-drenched, talking and eating and drinking good red wine. Groups drifted away towards the Old Man, and drifted back again: as if it was all happening in a blue-and-green-and-gold idyll.

Motionless, as in a dream, rain clouds hung over Caithness, across the Firth, and trailed their slow grey curtains, day-long.

It was a beautiful epilogue to the St Magnus Festival of midsummer 1978. Our host was the composer Peter Maxwell Davies, whose home Bunertoon is.

The Muses, for the second year running, had decided to grant us a peerless day, between two days that dripped and throbbed with urgencies of rain.

The Sea Poet

6.7.1978

There arrived by post the other day *Selected Poems of John Masefield*. In case you don't know who John Masefield was, call to mind those poems you learned at school—'Cargoes' and 'Sea Fever'. Those were two of the crown jewels of a schoolboy's treasury of verse, together with 'The Burial of Sir John Moore at Corunna', 'Daffodils', 'The Sands o' Dee', 'Sir Patrick Spens', 'The Traveller', 'To a Mouse'.

Masefield's 'Cargoes' has a line: 'Quinquereme of Nineveh from distant Ophir': which last name for a time we schoolboys misinterpreted as

Orphir parish in Orkney; until, at last, even our mistily romantic minds had to accept that the distance between Nineveh and Houton was a bit too much for the navigation of the time... How we thrilled to Masefield's marvellous triptych of ships in the poem—the quinquereme, the Spanish galleon, the dirty British coaster 'with a salt-caked smoke stack'... (T.S.Eliot was not the first poet to gain effect by the juxtaposition of the antique and the modern.)

Stromness in the 1930s was crowded with retired deep-sea sailors. It is small wonder that 'Sea Fever' moved us so much, with all those skippers and engineers walking our streets, come to port at last; but they carried distant horizons in their eyes, and their mouths were full of exotic stories:

> I must go down to the sea again, to the lonely sea and the sky,
> And all I ask is a tall ship and a star to steer her by....

I don't know if Masefield was ever in Orkney. But he did write a beautiful ballad about a girl called Morgause who, wandering the shore one day with otters and seabirds, was abducted by strange seamen; and in the far north, 'King Lot of Orkney took her for his bride'. That happened in the legendary times of King Arthur. Ernest W. Marwick included the poem in his *Anthology of Orkney Verse*.

John Masefield the Poet Laureate wrote a vast quantity of verse, including long narrative poems. He was born just a century ago, and to celebrate it this selection of his work has been published by Heinemann at £5.90, with an introduction by the present Laureate, John Betjeman; who himself needs no introduction to Orcadians.

We must thank the sailors' poet for putting bits of magic into our childhood.

Summer Days

13.7.1978

The summer school holidays. For days the children have been drifting round in anoraks and thick stockings, against the mist and incessant drizzle and a cold wind out of the north.

Surely, by the time they read this, the children's grey summer will have broken into blue and green and gold: as each summer was meant to be, if only for their sakes.

* * *

The summer holidays! Half a century ago it was an endless golden dream. (Seven weeks is a small eternity to a child.)

We seemed to spend most of our time either above or in the sea. From the edge of Gray's Pier a line of boys fished with limpet-baited hooks, for sillocks or cuithes. Some show-off would produce a 'ripper', three hooks stuck in a slug of lead; and with these lethal lines the water was torn apart powerfully, again and again... Sometimes a crab would come up, oscillating slowly at the end of a line, and as soon as it touched the pier begin to scuttle, sideways and comically, towards the element it had been lured out of. I remember a boy jumping close-footed, with tackety boots, on one of those little hard-backed seaclowns. A flagstone of the pier was splashed with a vivid yellow star, and fragments of shell!...

Some days we got hold of a flattie or dinghy, and rowed about in the harbour, idly, all afternoon. We were well warned by our elders not to row beyond 'the black buoy', otherwise the powerful ebb of Hoy Sound would take us out into the open dangerous Atlantic. Always, when we could, we dared the bow-waves of the old black *Ola*.

In that little seven-week eternity there was bathing every day; for every day brimmed over with warmth and light. Sometimes we bathed from the piers, innocent of sewers. It was more of an adventure to walk to the West Shore, and immerse ourselves, with bright shivering cries, in the incoming waters. On special days, there might be a picnic to the Holms, or to Warbeth. Never did grouse or salmon or sturgeon taste like those potted-head sandwiches, dusted over with sand. What finest champagne tasted like Gowans' lemonade, even though a fly or two homed in to have a sip before you did!

There seemed to be never one grey day in the summers of the 1920s... But there must have been. Memory is such a sweet deceiver.

William and Mareon Clark

20.7.1978

One evening, late, two summers ago, my friend Peter and I left the car near the Sawmill and walked along the grassy road of Garson Shore. I hadn't been that way for decades. Yet what a pleasant walk it is, and how specially beautiful the town is viewed from the east, with Brinkie's Brae standing guard over it like its good angel.

Other gentler guardians, the Holms, are tidal extensions of Garson Shore... Those natural stormbreaks made it possible in the first place for Stromness to take root, and grow centuries since.

It is a history-haunted road too. Somewhere along this road a man called William Gow from Caithness established a house and business. When I was young we called the ruined boatyard 'Gow's Garden'; so, if there is any truth in legendary names, the Caithness merchant's house and store might well have been there. The respected William Gow had one son—and we all know what happened to him...

We walked back in the lingering midsummer light. Near where the North End burn spills into the inner harbour, we looked here and there for even more interesting stones—a fragment perhaps of William Clark's inn foundation.

Nothing. There is no trace. It has vanished utterly.

Yet, in this Shopping Week, Stromness ought to be honouring William Clark and his good wife Mareon more than anyone. If they weren't the first Stromnessians, they were the first recorded business people in the parish.

With forethought and some daring, William saw the ships of Europe growing larger with every decade and venturing further north and west, stormbound often between Brinkies and the Holms. William, with the Earl in Birsay's permission, built an inn at the very tip of the harbour.

You may be sure, on a stormy winter night, half the languages of Europe were spoken across William's barrel of ale and Mareon's bannocks and cheese!

Towards Sanday

27.7.1978

It was the first time for many a day I had been up and astir at seven o'clock in the morning. The stomach refuses to accept anything, at such an hour, but a scrap of crisp ryebread and a mug of tea.

What kind of day would this be, in the cold rain-swamped summer of '78? There was one little patch of blue, like a fish, in massed whale-schools of cloud, as we set out for Kirkwall in the car. Presently the little blue fish was swallowed up. In Stenness and Firth, the whales stampeded over us, throbbings and lashings of rain.

The *Orcadia* left Kirkwall pier at 8.30am. There were between a dozen and a score of passengers, mostly tourists. I spoke awhile with Tom Towers the engineer and Mr Bain the purser. It was very cold; but the sea was flat calm, a dark brimming mirror.

A smell of frying bacon from the galley roused the morning hunger in me. I had an excellent breakfast of corn flakes, fried egg and two thick rashers of bacon, toast and rolls and a pot of tea; all for £1, which is not bad nowadays. The service was as good as the food.

By the time breakfast was over, the *Orcadia* was nearing Eday. A few passengers got off. A group of young evangelists were seeing some of their friends off, with boisterous good humour. As the boat left the pier, it was wafted away with evangelical choruses.

Having just read the new edition of Defoe's *The Pirate Gow*[1], I was hoping that the boat would pass between Eday and the Calf, where disaster struck the pirate like a thunderbolt from Olympus. But instead, the *Orcadia* struck directly across the Wide Firth towards Sanday.

Slowly the massed clouds thinned out. The huge sky over Sanday showed larger patches of blue, and cold sunlight splashed on land and sea.

At Kettletoft it was high tide. We came down a steep gangway on to the pier. A kind friend was waiting for me[2]. We did a little shopping:

1 Gordon Wright Publishing, Edinburgh: 1978
2 Carlene Mair, wife of Dr James Mair, of Glasgow.

rolls from a delicious-smelling bake-shop some stationery from another shop. In the brimming water seals bobbed their dark streaming heads. Presently our car arrived in the village, and we drove towards the doctor's house at the centre of the island—it is situated near the church, whose spire (so flat is Sanday) is a landmark to the whole island.

The Claws of the Lobster

3.8.1978

What can be seen, or understood, about Sanday, or any other place under the sun, in 24 hours?

All that you can take away are a few hasty impressions.

Approaching the island from the boat, there is the low horizon rim. The farmhouses stand stark and heraldic against the sky, motionless arks above the brimming flood tide.

Weather-wise it turned out to be an indifferent day, for high summer. The sky was a dome of pewter: scraped, polished, blackened pewter: a great pewter scrollwork, announcing rain.

A sea-coward always, I had swallowed a tablet with my breakfast tea in Stromness. I had no sooner gone ashore in Sanday than a wave of drowsiness went over me. I begged leave to lie down for half an hour; and I slept two hours away.

But in those hours, the all-pewter sky had been scrapped, and there were patches of blue everywhere in the vast sweep over the island. Nowhere in the world, I suppose, is the sky so dominant as in this place. I would like very much to be in Sanday on a starry winter night.

The sky and the beaches. The tide ebbs far out, leaving immense tawny stretches of sand. The first Norsemen had no difficulty in giving Sanday a name. After the fiords and the deep seas around their homeland, they must have found Sanday an extraordinary place—first keels whispering in the shallows, left high and dry then in swift unexpected ebbs.

A sprawling lobster of an island—Sanday has been called that often enough. A multitude of 'nesses'. In the car we visited the flung claws of the island, one after another. North Ronaldsay—even flatter than Sanday, it's said—lay to the north like the rim of a gramophone record. In the east we drove almost to the tall striped guardian of ships, Start Point lighthouse. (In sailing ship times, Sanday was a graveyard for ships—the helmsman was on the rocks before he knew an island was there at all...)

It was all over, too soon. To savour any island fully, you must stay a week at least. I might next time. We finished the day with a dinner of delicious mouth-melting Sanday steaks. Just before I left I had the pleasure of meeting Kenny Foubister, the postmaster, and his wife; and had admired his large colour enlargement of Kettletoft in the days of its herring boom.

My kind hosts, James and Carlene Mair, have given me as much of Sanday as could be crammed into 24 hours.

In a freshening wind and a dancing glittering sea, the *Orcadia* left Kettletoft for Eday and Kirkwall.

Food and Drink

17.8.1978

One of the chief joys of August, whatever the weather, is the marvellous variety of food that descends on the palate; and is gone again, after a few weeks of gastronomic delight.

A friend arrives with a gift of a trout out of Harray or Swannay. The fragrance that rises from the frying pan is more than matched by the melting roseate flakes of that most tasty of fish in the mouth.

It is a time of year when you might arrive home to find a poke of new tatties at the door, crumbs of earth still clinging to them. It's no surprise to me that the pre-famine Irish flourished mightily on a diet of potatoes and milk. A simple meal of new tatties, with butter, is hard to beat.

Now, too, the tomatoes are at their best. Early in summer they arrive from distant places, gradually coming closer and always improving in flavour. At last the supreme consummation—'Birsay Tomatoes' appears on a placard in a shop window. For firmness and lusciousness (an exquisite blend of sweetness and tartness) they have no equal. Even to hold one in the fingers is a sensuous delight.

Peaches, too, are at their best; though they are exotic and expensive. I like to bite into one first thing in the morning, before breakfast. Mouth and throat and palate are cleansed in one sudden gush of freshness. 'The nectarine and curious peach' (wrote the 17th-century poet Marvell, celebrating all the marvellous things his garden yielded) 'into my hands themselves do reach...'

And the pears of August, too, yield and melt and are nectar almost before the teeth have closed on them.

But there are delights in the shore fields everywhere that cost not a penny. A walk on a summer evening beside the the loch can show, suddenly, two or three fine mushrooms beside a stone. You carry them home carefully for the frying pan next morning. Or on a clifftop, searching, you may come on a host and a multitude, where there was only grass the day before. Then and there they are gathered into baskets and bags and brought home to share at half a dozen doors. There are those who declare that wild mushrooms fried are richer on the palate than the best bacon.

Old islanders used to say that the ale brewed in March is best of all. In a Birsay house, last week, I sipped a glass made from corn-malt. It was certainly the most delectable ale I have tasted this year. I sipped, and swilled, and swallowed: and felt suddenly without a care in the marvellous rich beautiful world. I don't know whether it was March ale or not, but Mrs Matches the brewer was right when she said it would be worth coming from Stromness to experience. No brewery puts out such marvellous beer, believe me.

A Man Could Walk

24.8.1978

I think this is the first day this year I have been able to write 'Under Brinkie's Brae' in the open air.

For the second day running, sea and sky keep their intense different blues. (Except that today there are little wind-wisps in the high serene, and the harbour below me has a brave southeasterly ruffle to it. Yesterday the sun was a limpid burning flame.)

The tide has ebbed far out—on a grey day a matter of desolation and melancholy. The Inner Holm and the Outer Holm are one long green tongue of land. The shore under the breakwater is heaped and layered with seaweed. For an hour or so the piers of Hamnavoe have no reason to exist at all. A man could walk, if he wanted, all the way from the Navigation School to Ness.

Not long ago the *St Ola* went out, lines of tourists aloft. Those who arrived in the grey days will have little joy leaving all the swarming colours of Orkney on such a day. (But still we are an occupied town; there are at least twice as many tourists on the street as Stromnessians.)

The gulls in all their variety come and go on the pier these days. It seems impossible to understand what motivates them in their sudden upsurges and circlings and returns. Sometimes one stretches out his throat and gives vent, alone, to a single barbaric shriek, as if he was uttering a dirge or a warning. The others pay no attention. Throw out a few crusts of stale bread, and the air between pier edge and the sea is thronged with flashing clamorous wings... The two swans drifting nearby wonder, disdainfully, what all the plebeian fuss is about. They drift closer. The gulls veer away, they give those immaculate powerful birds plenty of room to manoeuvre in. A last crust is for the arrogant ones...

Yesterday, at the West Shore, we could watch the dramatic to-and-fro of Hoy Sound; how the fishing boats battled stickily in the ebb making for the harbour; then, an hour later, came swiftly in on the first brim of the flood.

Today, in this walled enclosure, I will only be able to tell, at first, the change from ebb to flood by the music the sea makes on the lowest pier stones. By 10 o'clock, under the full moon, the sea will be lipping the piers.

Erosions

31.8.1978

Slowly, Orkney gets eaten up by the sea.

A few years ago, there was that massive cliff-fall at Yesnaby, when thousands of tons suddenly collapsed. Now notice boards warn us to keep well back.

At Rackwick, earlier this summer, another cliff-fall was pointed out to me on the south side of the Bay—a vivid red patch among the gentler crag weatherings.

And, not so long ago, a large chunk near Rora Head slid down into the sea.

Daniell's print of the Old Man of Hoy, made a century and a half ago, shows a very different outline from today's stack. Then the Old Man stood on two legs, firmly 'based on the sea' (as the poet John Malcolm said of it). One day, suddenly, a century ago or thereby, one of the legs collapsed, and the most famous rockstack in the world stood poised on one leg like a heron. (It is certain that nobody ever saw this cataclysmic event—no sailor or fisherman or shepherd—otherwise we should have a record of it. Perhaps it happened at night. In the next dawn, Hoy was 'as much the less'...)

The other Sunday four of us took a picnic to Skibbigeo on the North Side of Birsay. It had been a typical day in this summer of '78—thin smirrs of rain, cold moving patches of sun. In Skibbigeo there was shelter; it is a marvellous natural cove much used in former times by the Birsaymen for their boats and fishing gear. We sat on the stones and enjoyed ham sandwiches and cheese sandwiches and apple juice. A rat came out of a fissure—not large enough to be called a cave—

and looked at us, and withdrew, and after a time ran, a swift dark silent shadow, up a ledge of the cliff and out of sight.

We noticed a heap of sharp-angled unweathered rocks near us. Up above, on the face, a new vivid scar. Not so long since, part of Skibbigeo must have come down in long thunders.

This erosion is happening all the time all along the west of Orkney, from Noup Head to Hoy.

But it'll be a long time till the battering-down is finished; and, for all I know, Orkney may be getting slowly built up on the other side—shelved and shored.

September the First

7.9.1978

Friday, September the first... I remember another Friday, September the first, 39 years ago. I think it was our English teacher who told us in the classroom some time that morning, that German forces had invaded Poland.

It was all very exciting for young people. It was like the re-enactment of the events of September 1938, when the confrontation was between Germany and Czechoslovakia. On that occasion our Prime Minister, Neville Chamberlain, had flown to Munich for a last desperate high-level talk with Hitler, and had flown home waving the famous piece of paper: 'Peace in our time'... He had been received like a hero in London.

We youngsters in the distant Orkneys were outraged. Czechoslovakia had been betrayed—we felt—in order that some kind of a ramshackle peace could be patched up—it was monstrous!...

Politically, we were very innocent and idealistic. A year or two before, in the first flush of political enthusiasm, we had been all for disarmament. Let us take the way of the dove, and all the rest of the world would follow. 'What?' we were challenged. 'Will we disarm even though Germany and France and Italy keep their guns and bombers?' ... 'Yes,' we serenely replied, 'even in such a case Britain ought to disarm.'... No more touching tribute could have been paid to innocent idealism.

What I can't quite remember is how we reconciled the dove and the hawk in us... That Friday, and the day following, we waited for Mr Chamberlain to declare war. The declaration did not come. 'What?' we asked each other in schoolboy rage. 'Is he trying to patch up another disgraceful peace with Hitler?' It seemed quite possible.

* * *

All that summer, exciting things had been happening in Orkney. We saw troops of our fellow-islanders in Territorial uniform, parading at Ness. A great, green slice had been lopped off the Golf Course to make Ness Battery. (Being very fond of golf that summer, we weren't pleased about that either. The beautiful sixth hole, that sloped down beside a cornfield to the banks above Hoy Sound, had been taken from us.) A company of Marines arrived suddenly, and camped at the Point of Ness. We had been issued with gas masks at the Temperance Hall. An innocent old ragged bearded man who sold trinkets at the doors and lived much of that summer in a tent at the Lookout was, it was rumoured, a spy.

The air crackled with excitement as summer shaded into autumn.

Finally, at 11am on the Sunday morning Chamberlain spoke on the wireless. We were at war. The elders, sitting around, looked very grave.

Stone Pages, Stone Books

14.9.1978

Wandering round the kirkyard at Warbeth, one can spend a pleasant afternoon. It's as if the whole social history of Stromness was there—the three kirkyards are books and the memorials are the stone pages.

But many of the pages are obliterated. Or have never been written on at all: they simply are not there.

Where, for instance, is Alexander Graham buried? There is no stone to mark the burial place of the most famous Stromnessian of them all. Can it be that the Grahams were so poor at the time of his death that there wasn't enough money even to pay mason and stone-carver? We know that Graham poured every penny into the prolonged litigation that secured for the 18th-century Stromness merchants freedom to trade, unhindered by the merchants of the royal burgh fifteen miles away. We know that not all his fellow-merchants in Stromness gave Graham their full backing. There was much jealousy, backbiting, craven talk down the piers of Hamnavoe and in the coffee-and-rum-and-tobacco-smelling merchants' doorways... Not everyone, it seems, raised his hat when Mr Graham passed along the street.

It required a man of extraordinary courage and tenacity to persevere in the fight.

The dust of the hero lies there, somewhere, between the green ridge of Innertown and the slow pulsings of Hoy Sound, in 'God's acre'... To our shame, we Stromnessians cannot seek out the spot and pause there for a minute in tribute to a great man.

* * *

And Bessie Millie, where do her ancient bones lie? Not every Stromnessian of the past is recorded on the stone pages at Monkerhoose. Only the comparatively affluent could get stonemason and carver to record their brief biographies for a century or two. For every one name on a tombstone, ten or a dozen lie in the earth nameless.

Bessie Millie was nearly 100 years old when Sir Walter Scott spoke to her in 1814. She cannot have lived very long after that date.

When they came to take her to the kirkyard in the 'mort-cloth', they might have found in a kist or a stocking under the bed a few last sixpences that the stormbound skippers had paid her, between jocularity and some primitive sea-dread; so that she could bespeak them a favourable wind.

But not enough sixpences, surely, for the mason to sharpen his chisel.

Death of a Poet

21.9.1978

There we were, all set for a bit of autumn excitement—a General Election—when Mr Callaghan appears on the box and says, genially, 'Oh, no—no General Election this winter...' It is merely a mild disappointment for us millions of voters—but think of the politicians who have had to scrap their carefully-laid schedules for the three following weeks, and now face a blank in time! Think of the army of journalists who have been sharpening their pens for the battle, all agog to spill millions of meaningless words. (Let them spend the three weeks with a good book, to see how words ought to be used.)

* * *

Yesterday (13 September) the poet Hugh MacDiarmid was buried, aged 86. No doubt he was one of the most flamboyant and colourful figures on the Scottish scene this century. No doubt he was a poet of genius. I think—like Wordsworth—he wrote his best work as a young man, the lyrics in Scots and the long poem 'A Drunk Man Looks at the Thistle', which is a patchwork of rare genius rather than a perfectly woven work.

He conducted a long one-sided 'flyting' with his contemporary Edwin Muir, because of a remark Muir let drop about the doubtful validity of Scots as a literary medium.

He endured neglect and extreme poverty in Whalsay, Shetland, in the thirties; and through the storms of that time he held fast to his beliefs in nationalism and socialism and the heroic destiny of mankind. In the end honours and fame—though not wealth—were heaped on him.

A very remarkable man has passed out of the life of Scotland—a kind of Moses who glimpsed independence from the mountaintop but was not to live to experience it.

* * *

The grey bleak summer of '78 has passed into the gales and tumultuous rains of September. There's a feeling of autumn in the air, a first delicious morning chill on fingers and cheeks. The shadows cluster, one after another, shuttling on towards the magical dark web of December. A few late tourists drift here and there, mostly young, waiting for the colleges to open. I know winter is on the way, because yesterday I bought a rib of beef and put on a first pot of broth since March. Farewell to the days of salads and fruit and tin-openers. The soup lay thick on the spoon, and tasted delicious.

Equinox

28.9.1978

The equinoctial gales came early this year. Last weekend under the full moon (and an eclipse) a southeaster tore up boats from moorings and flung them ashore; drove shoppers along the street like dry leaves or took them and half-choked them; poured turbulent dark cold seawater into Stromness kitchens and cellars.

Today, as I write this, is really the equinox. It has turned out a mild day, with rags of cloud and, between them from time to time, a bright blue patch. A mere ordinary day of the year, 21 September, with nothing much to mark it out from a hundred other days... To earlier Orcadians, much more sensitive than we are to the dance of the earth about the sun, the autumnal equinox (whatever the weather) was something to marvel at, something to make a catch in the breath.

For now, darkness and light hang perilously poised, each balancing the other. After tomorrow, the shadows begin to cluster ever thicker about the dark scale, taking us with it down to the dark boreal night, the winter solstice.

It is the dramatic behaviour of light and darkness that is perennially fascinating in the north. (Imagine living somewhere near the equator. where this marvellous dialogue of sun and night doesn't exist.)

It is only three months to the day when we sat on a hillside in Rackwick, Hoy, eating hot dogs and sipping red wine. That day the imperious sun had the whole blue sky to himself, and he poured out light and warmth without stint, a generous king. That midnight, from a window in Evie, we saw the sunset gradually become the dawn, with only a few shadows intervening. They mingled their fires on a sea horizon stained, alas, with rain clouds; that turned out to be harbingers of a dull cold summer.

* * *

In only three months, if the sky is clear, we might be setting out between the two darknesses of 21 December to see the cinder sun performing his most thrilling miracle—putting a spark of light on the farthest death-wall of Maeshowe. It is a sign that we, the children of the sun, are not to perish in an ultimate winter (bones under an increasing armour of ice); but that Spring will certainly come again: the whole round year being an exquisite dance of light and shade— an interweaving, a poise, a dapple.

Flitting

5.10.1978

A friend who keeps a diary tells me it is ten years this month that I moved from Well Park to Mayburn Court.

The prospect of a flitting is very daunting, to people of a certain temperament, like me. Suddenly to be uprooted from a place where one has lived for 34 years! Everything in the house—chairs, pictures, mirror, rugs, vases—seems to fit perfectly together: to be part of a pattern that ought not lightly to be broken.

Yet broken it must be, and that drastically, before the flitting can begin.

How will those old familiar friendly books and furnishings look in a new alien place? And then, the immense Herculean labour of transporting and rearranging everything!

Friends promised to help, of course. Weeks beforehand I began to stow books and crockery into tea chests (given by another kind friend).

I put on a brew that, on the flitting day, might give strength and urgency to the labourers.

The flitting day came—a Saturday morning. My helpers turned out with a lorry and a Land-Rover (another kind loan). Somehow I expected the uprooting to go on all morning. Nothing of the kind— in half an hour the lorry loaded with beds, chairs, sideboard, tables, chests, suites, washing machine, TV, and the Land-Rover crammed to the roof with lesser impedimenta, had come and gone, leaving 6 Well Park as bare as if a mighty hurricane had gone through it.

So far, all was well.

But what of the utter impossible chaos waiting at the other end, where the May Burn (that in better times had gone to the making of Old Orkney and Old Man of Hoy malt whisky) empties itself nowadays, barrenly, into the harbour?

There was no chaos whatever. I need not have grown a hundred grey hairs. The workers moved with a sweet rhythm and precision. It was almost like a ballet. Beds were screwed together, tables and rocking chair and bookcases and suite allocated their position in the empty virgin spaces of 3 Mayburn Court. An hour after the door of the new house had been thrown open, the interior was quite habitable. My friends departed.

It had been a small miracle of organisation (no credit to me).

In the middle of the afternoon Jimmy and I sat beside a table crowded with empty ale bottles, at peace with the world. We considered that enough had been done for one day.

Slowly, as the hours passed, the old furniture began to look at peace in the new house. All might yet be well before winter.

Outside, with brave bell-like clangings, the last section of railing was welded in place.

Winter Is a-Cumen in

12.10.1978

The rain has been bucketing down all morning. Ten thousand buckets must have fallen about the roofs and doorways of Mayburn Court.

Winter has come early. A few afternoons ago I was writing in the kitchen when a sudden immense grey fusillade of hailstones crashed against the window.

But the signs of winter's onset have been accumulating for weeks. It begins when the children, newly back at school, come knocking at the door for Guy Fawkes paper. This goes on for several evenings. (I wonder, how do they manage to keep all that newsprint and cardboard dry till November 5th?) The days narrow with disconcerting speed. Where are the sweet lingering evenings of only a month ago? Soon after tea, these nights, the curtains are drawn against encroaching night.

The old tried winter favourites are back on TV—*When the Boat Comes in*, *Mastermind*, *The Good Life*, *The Generation Game*, *All Creatures Great and Small*'... The mind is fed full with shadows.

The graph of temperature has dipped and found its first winter level. It is not yet time to change into winter clothes: that acknowledgement of the cold time is put off until the last possible moment—until you can almost feel the bony touch of pleurisy and pneumonia. But, these nights, the bed is chilly when first you climb into it; it takes a good five minutes for the quilt to lap you in its downy warmth. Last week, just in case the graph took a second downward dip, I bought a hot-water bottle...

And yet, winter keeps a few bits of magic for us. Without the dark season we could never know the full glory of moon and stars. The elusive sorcery of the silk-swirling Merry Dancers is always liable to happen. The first pure soft-fallen snow, too, is a thing to make a catch in the breath. There is the majesty and awe of a great winter storm; and the marvellous tranquillity that comes after.

There is the glow of heaped oranges in a crystal vase.

There are the cards and candles and charities and apple-bright cheeks of Christmas.

Let winter be true to itself and us, and there is a dark magic in everything around, even in bare twigs and the first-lit afternoon lamp.

A Seal at Nethertoon

19.10.1978

It must be 'the peedie summer'. We have had now six sun-filled days, almost in a row—a thing that did not happen in June, July, August, the traditional summer months. The big summer was as drab and sluttish a season as I ever remember. Her little late sister is all sweetness, mellowness, pale gold.

Nature, however we complain about it, is full of compensations.

'Nineteen twenty-three,' said a retired island farmer to me one day at the Pier Head. 'You have to go back to nineteen twenty-three to find a worse summer than this one...' A few days later, another retired farmer confirmed this. He told me of the toil they had to get the meagre battered harvest in that year. The harvesters spent more time hunting rabbits by lantern-light than setting up stooks, so impossible were the conditions.

(In 1923 I was of an age when weather neither adds nor subtracts from the sum of joy.)

* * *

Two afternoons ago, we walked up the grass verge of the covered May Burn. The ground, remembering the recent deluges of rain, squelched under our feet.

We took the Midgarth road down to Nethertoon. A tractor went past, with two farmworkers eager to salvage what they could of the rain-beaten harvest of 1978. Indeed, a field over towards the kirkyard had a brave well marshalled army of stooks, under the blue sweep of sky.

I had never seen Hoy Sound so still and bright—perhaps it was the few minutes of slack water in that turbulent sleeve. The sun flashed off a stretch of blue untroubled silk.

We sat for an hour on sun-warmed stones above Nethertoon noust. A solitary seal bobbed a bottle-bright head in the bay. Two fishing boats came in, quickly, on the rapids of the flood. The seal disappeared.

In the gap between the Ward and the Coolags, a fleece of cloud lay. Tufts and shreds began to detach from it and to wander idly into our immaculate blue. And when a little cloud did cover the sun, the air had a passing shiver.

Where was the Nethertoon seal? Perhaps, I said, he's come ashore and put on his clothes and gone off somewhere ('I am a man upon the land'). Sure enough, a man was walking towards Warbeth; only he had a dog at heel.

We humans thrust clumsy fingers into the delicate web of nature, thinking to fix it (to our financial advantage, mainly) one way or another.

You may be sure, in the matter of seals and fish and men, nature long ago achieved a near-perfect balance.

Nature is more wise in these matters than statisticians or statesmen. But we never learn. We plunder the sea, and blame the seals.

Diaries

26.10.1978

The keeping of a diary is a slight itch, to begin with, that becomes in the end a devouring compulsion.

If a day passes that hasn't been recorded, there is a vacancy, a sense of loss. It won't be repaired until that little white space in the little book has been filled.

It is, when you think about it, a very silly habit, especially if you lead a quiet life and hardly a thing of moment happens to you. 'Had bacon and toast and four cups of tea for breakfast...'

'Went for a walk along West Shore—tide out—a few spots of rain...'

'Read the *Sunday Times* till my eyes were dim and mind a blank...'

'On TV, a play about J.M.Barrie and the making of *Peter Pan*: view it through pints of home-brew...'

'Toss and turn till two or three in the morning...'

This is hardly compulsive reading, even to the person who wrote it. Sometimes you idly flick through the pages of a diary five or six years old: the utter inanity of existence could hardly be more starkly expressed.

Suppose something of enormous importance happened. Suppose you were to win £50,000 on the Premium Bonds, or a letter came saying you had won the Nobel Prize. (I choose examples from the extreme verge of improbability.) How could that little blank square in your diary contain such momentous events? You would have to go on pouring out your wonder and thankfulness and ecstasy for page after whirling page...

What is the point then, I frequently ask myself, in making notes of all the thistledown and motes of dust that is one's life? I really don't know. All I know is, once breakfast is over and the table cleared, I fall on that little book of white squares and record briefly and succinctly the boring events of yesterday—how I cut my lip shaving; how a letter came from a friend in Australia; how the first clapshot of winter, with just the right amount of pepper in it, was a joy...

Some writers say that even the most exciting life is, at bottom, a tissue of boredom. Others say that the most ordinary humdrum life is, on the contrary, a unique thing—a thing of unimaginable depth and mystery.

I fear, alas, that the many little scrawled-in diaries I have hoarded over the years will show no such thing.

November the Fifth

16.11.1978

Last Saturday morning, I was wakened by a mighty thumping and thundering on the door.

What could that imperious summons be? Something of vast importance, certainly. I threw myself into my clothes with all haste and stumbled downstairs.

There was nobody at the door.

But I was in time to see two children disappearing round the corner with their carved turnips—'pops'.

That was only the start of it. The children kept coming all day—sometimes singly, sometimes in groups. There was an endless variety of 'pop', from very primitive carvings to sculptures of some sophistication. Some were hollowed out, so that they could hold a lighted candle after dark. One very tiny child had a potato with a face on it.

It began to rain. That didn't deter the children of Stromness from their Fifth of November ritual. With sodden jackets and streaming faces and plastered hair they stood at the door. The ermine cheeks of many a 'pop' ran red, and their eyes were a watery black. It was not a good day to get settled down to any serious work. You have just put pieces of egg and toast into your mouth when—bang! crash!—there tremble the door panels again, and the sweet little turnip-bearing tyrants are outside, smiling, demanding tribute.

What is fair tribute-money in these inflationary times? In the 1920s we got a ha'penny (an old half-penny). Nowadays, everything is ten times as expensive, at least. Two pence seems an appropriate equivalent.

Fortunately, I had a little brass bowl overflowing with two-pence pieces. It ebbed, ringing, all through that rainy Saturday.

I'm glad to say that nowadays the children have, mostly, stopped saying the old ritual fiery words at the door. Instead they say, in their dewy voices, 'A penny for me pop.'

Ecumenism or ignorance or innocence, that demand makes a sweeter music in the door of winter.

Power Failure

23.11.1978

For the past fortnight I have been writing a sequence of short stories for children, about a mischievous boy called Jock who lived in an island in Orkney.

In the latest story, Jock runs away from home.

I was sitting writing away with great fluency on Tuesday afternoon. Outside, Orkney was being battered by a huge tempest. Once or twice, earlier, the table lamp had flickered and the fan heater hesitated.

(Everybody in the island has different opinions as to what has happened to the bad boy, Jock; from his stricken mother who thinks the blazing row she gave him has forced the poor lamb from home, to the two old island sybils who think the trows have taken him down to the place where he truly belongs...)

Suddenly the light went out, with a soundless black snap, as if to say, 'There, this is for good!'...

It was just the worst time, the first onset of darkness, the shadow cluster, the cloak of coldness.

I found a torch that gave more a glim than a light, the battery being two years old. Happily, I had bought some candles during the January blizzard. One was stuck in a wine bottle and one in a beer bottle. Living room and kitchen each had its star of light, mysterious and beautiful.

It was a serious matter, though. I had pies in the cupboard that I intended to have with a tin of spaghetti for dinner. Who could ever think of eating cold pie on a storm-black November evening?... Also, the heat was slowly draining out of the kitchen. As for the living room, it was as cold as the heart of an iceberg.

The South End of Stromness, when I went down to the little candle-splashed shop below, was as dark as the kirkyard. Car headlights blazed and dwindled on the Scorriedale road across the hay.

A dreich evening stretched ahead. I could go to bed, of course, and try to read by the little wavering splash a candle gives. I sat in the cold living room, with that thick Norwegian scarf wrapped twice round my neck. I felt spectral, a being between two ages.

Suddenly the room was drenched in a torrent of blond light. The bars of the electric fire began to buzz and spit and give out a fierce dry heat.

I felt like a man whom the 20th century has rescued from a half-frightening medieval enchantment.

I switched on the TV. The 5.40 News was just beginning. The 20th century, with all its strikes and bombs and glamour and hysteria poured in.

The menace and the magic had not lasted too long.

Robert Shaw, Novelist and Actor

10.11.1978

I watched last Sunday evening on TV a marvellous film called *The Royal Hunt of the Sun*. It was about the Spanish conquistador Pizarro and his soldiers, who captured a vast treasury of gold in the 16th century, in Peru, and finished their splurge by judicially murdering the great Inca himself. (How dreadful, incidentally, is the record of the European nations in their savage ransacking of the other 'inferior' continents! 'Cupiditas' was at the root of it, no matter what loftier and pious motives were urged at the time. Whole cultures and civilisations were uprooted—delicate and beautiful ways of life that could never he replaced. In Africa, Asia, Australia, the Americas, the pillage went on for centuries... Truly, the white nations have much to answer for; maybe we are beginning to be forced to answer for it now.)

But the real reason for writing about *The Royal Hunt of the Sun* is that the Spanish general Pizarro was played by Robert Shaw, and it was a marvellous performance. It is sad to think that such a brilliant actor will never make another film; he died, in his fifties, earlier this year.

It isn't true that Robert Shaw was a Stromnessian. In fact, he came to Stromness in the nineteen-thirties as a small boy, when his father was for some years a doctor in the Victoria Street practice—from which Dr Cromarty operated both before and afterwards.

I remember Robert Shaw as a boy quite well, doing all the things that small Stromness boys did in those days. There was a few years difference in our ages, and between boys of fourteen, say, and eleven, there is a great gulf fixed; there is simply no communication; you keep severely to your own age stratum; I never remember once speaking to Robert Shaw.

The mistake people make now is to think of him exclusively as an actor. In fact he was a man of many talents. He himself wished to be thought of as a novelist. How he managed to write between spells of intense studio work is a marvel in itself, but he did produce a handful of outstandingly good novels—*The Sun Doctor*, *The Flag*, etc. I have rarely read such a marvellous evocation of central Africa as one part of *The Sun Doctor*.

Robert Shaw did return to Orkney on holiday in 1963. In a TV programme about himself, some time later, he mentions Stromness as the most beautiful place he had ever seen.

It is sad, now, to think that Stromness will not see him again.

An Article in Hiding

14.12.1978

Over the weeks letters begin to pile up on the kitchen table where I eat breakfast and afterwards write for an hour or two, six days in the week.

Letters come nearly every day, sometimes one or two, sometimes a swarm. The pile grows between table and wall. 'Tomorrow,' I say, 'I'll sort them out'—that is, keep the ones worth keeping, and get rid of the ephemera.

And the days pass, and the pile grows higher; one or two letters brim over on to the butter and the toast.

I realised last week that December was here, the month of a thousand letters and cards. Something would have to be done, quickly, with that shaggy epistolatory haystack on the table. Grimly I set about separating the grain from the chaff. The 'letters worth keeping' were put in a little plastic bag and carried upstairs to join thousands of other 'letters worth keeping', a twelve years garnering. The rest were cast into oblivion.

After the job was done, how neat and shipshape it looked, the piece of Victorian plastic-covered furniture that is both kitchen-table and writing desk! It had been a tedious job, but it had been worth doing.

Then I looked for the manuscript of 'Under Brinkie's Brae', in order to read it over and make corrections and carry it on Monday afternoon to Wishart's shop, where the editor would uplift it on Tuesday morning.

'Under Brinkie's Brae'—that particular week a profound piece of sapience about Remembrance of Things Past—was nowhere to be seen. I searched high and low. I rifled the desk. I sifted through many papers. The tiny essay-in-manuscript had vanished like the butterfly.

I concluded that it had been swept away in the great winnowing of the letters.

It was certainly too late to write a substitute.

Yesterday morning I was sitting idly, after a late breakfast. Outside a grey storm was pounding on walls and windows.

A buff envelope lay in a corner of the desk, addressed to 'The Editor, The Orcadian'... It was the lost article[1]. Where had it been in the two or three days of its vanishing? The simple answer is that it had been there, on the table, all the time... Perhaps, to be safe, it had hid itself under the jar of paperclips or the sellotape tin until the great sifting of the letters was safely over.

1 The article finally appeared on 10 May, 1979.

Winter Long Ago

21.12.1978

The long golden days ended, blue water and silver fish in barrows, bare feet on warm flagstones. We were urged to the great gloomy building on the side of the hill, a bag with a thin book of pictures and words on our shoulders. The playground brimmed over with more children than the world could hold.

The days got colder. We sat on the classroom hot pipes. We lived in a world of numbers and words and strictness.

The nights got longer. On the dresser a tall paraffin lamp threw a circle of light. Inside the circle lay an open book and a sock with a hole in it and a card of wool.

If I put my face out into the night, the sky was thick with stars. The street lamp at the top of the pier washed the stones with magic; except when, on nights of full moon, houses and sea and islands were held in a more marvellous white enchantment still (on those nights the gas lamps along the street were not lit).

There were nights when the house was shaken with storm. How wonderful, to lie warm in bed while the wind soughed and moaned in the chimney!

The deepening winter brought battered trawlers to the piers— sometimes a dozen out of Grimsby and Aberdeen. Frightening men with strange accents roamed the streets.

There was a spell of stories beside the black flame-flowering range— King Haco and Largs, Willie drowned in Yarrow, the witch and the children and the gingerbread house. (Winter was the time for stories—songs and butterflies belonged to summer.)

What was summer? A half-forgotten dream. A boy lives in an eternal present. He lived now in ever deepening darkness and storm, pedantry and magic.

Suddenly, in the infant school, the children were all concerned with cutting up long strips of coloured paper and pasting them into chains. What a wonderful day when the classroom was festooned with that bunting!

And in the house too the penny decorations were hung across the rafters and a whispering paper bell depended from the centre, with a sprig of mistletoe cunningly concealed in it.

I wrote my first letters and sent them up the roaring chimney. Sometimes they fell down again, half scorched.

And Santa received the letters among his toy factories and orchards in Greenland. He read them to the last crudely-formed syllable.

There the gifts were, bulging the stocking at the end of the bed in the first cold light of morning—a game of Ludo (perhaps), and an apple, and a poke of sweeties.

New Year

28.12.1978

Small boys, we left at last the magic House of Christmas with its decorations and cards, mistletoe and apples and goose and chocolate. Kind old Santa, urging his reindeer through the brightest stars of the year, had gone home to Greenland

Ahead, seven days on, lay the dark House of Hogmanay. We had to pass through that too, but only the adults seemed to look forward to the experience.

When we were very young, we were put to bed early on Hogmanay; and woke up in the grey light of January the first to a table strewn with empty beer bottles and fragments of scotch bun.

Outside on the street, a few belated revellers lurched extravagantly home.

Always on New Year's Day there was roast beef for dinner. (It was generally goose or duck or a very fat hen on Christmas Day: but roast beef was the main item on the New Year menu).

The decorations still hung from the ceiling, until January 5th. The Christmas gifts lay, somewhat battered now, in their various boxes.

The mantelpiece was crowded still, with celluloid and gilt cards (which seemed to be the fashion in the 1920s). Looking back, these cards seemed like nothing so much as tiny replicas of tombstones—cards nowadays are much more gay and imaginative.

In the afternoon, there was the annual visit to the Museum, kept in those days by a lady called Mrs Lyon. Round the stone Buddhas and a carved wooden totem of some savage Pacific tribe, we drifted, open-mouthed. And out again, into the cold grey air.

If you happened to meet a school contemporary on the street, you went up to him and chanted quickly,

> 'A happy New Year,
> A bottle of beer,
> And a box on the ear.'

Then you tried to wallop him, but as often as not he was off and away, forewarned by the rhyme. His mocking laughter came from a distance of two closes.

The plates on the table were never empty of scotch bun and cherry cake. We young ones drank endless glasses of sweet spicy 'ginger wine'. Neighbours and friends came and went in the failing light.

On New Year's night, we were taken to the Town Hall to 'the pictures' for the one and only time in the year. The only thing I remember on that enchanted flickering screen was 'Felix the Cat', who was the great cartoon hero till Mickey Mouse dethroned him.

Late at night, guisers came round the houses—young folk dressed as Chinamen, bullfighters, gypsies, Red Indians... With them, the New Year was finally established.

Bridge of Snow

11.1.1979

The last day of 1978. Nobody seems to know the origin of the word Hogmanay—it is lost in some savage winter festival of pre-Celtic tribes. It still retains a slightly sinister aura, as if unmentionable on-goings were licensed and allowed at that time of the year, while storms raged around.

There was no storm on the last afternoon of 1978. Indeed it was one of the most beautiful days of the year. The tide was ebbing rapidly through Hoy Sound, slumbrous and pure and tranquil, as we walked along the west. The snow was firm under our feet. The sun hung poised, in a blue and gold sky, to set between Hoy's two largest hills.

It was so still we could hear a cow lowing in Graemsay.

Then round the West Lighthouse appeared a small boat, and turned into Hoy Sound. It appeared as though some of our friends who had been snowed up in Rackwick had been released in time...

Maybe about a dozen Stromness folk were on the coast road, on this peerless afternoon. Where were all the sixteen hundred others? Stuffing geese maybe. Or setting out bottles of ale on the sideboard.

We had a delicious Hogmanay lunch in a hospitable house, with wine and talk flowing...

In the evening we set out for another house. It seemed likely that the big ugly thaw was beginning. The snow on the street had the colour and consistency of brown sugar. There were soft dark drippings from spouts.

At five to twelve, I being dark-haired went out into the last ebb of the year. The snow, far from vanishing, was getting new vast reinforcements. There were darkling swirls past chimneys and windows.

A boat's siren went off at the pier. The hour had struck. I went in with my whisky and a piece of coal wrapped in kitchen paper. (This must be a very ancient ceremony too: for the fire in the hearth is a sign of life and well-being in a house. And the whisky: what is it but the earth's rich essence, a symbol of all fruit and corn and cheerfulness and kindling?...)

Thousands of tons of snow had fallen over Stromness in the first hours of 1979... The street at 2.30am was heaped in new immaculate whiteness, quiltings and bolsterings of fresh snow. Through it a few first-footers trudged, with kind words and offered bottles.

There were only a few lighted squares in the dark winter labyrinth of Hamnavoe.

Burns and the Web of Creation

18.1.1979

The season of Burns approaches, as I write. He will always be, for me, one of the great poets. It is a pleasure to pay a small tribute to him each year as January the 25th comes round.

I wonder where Burns would have stood in relation to the seal controversy that seemed to take up most of the autumn here in Orkney.

No doubt some of those in favour of 'culling' (and myxomatosis if it comes to that) will be pledging Burns in high good fellowship at this time of the year. I wonder if they have ever pondered perhaps the most famous of his poems, 'To a Mouse'. The pity he feels for the winter mouse evicted from its nest by his ploughshare is no fake concern. How will the poor creature fare, when the worst of winter falls about its unprotected head?

There has always been an important 'lobby' that argues that 'the lower animals' are hardly worth our concern, except in so far as they serve our purposes. Horses, dogs, cats, fall within the circle of man's necessity, and so a certain measure of affection may be accorded to them.

But creatures like gulls, mice, fish-eating selkies, badgers—to accord the same respect to them is, they argue, affectation and sentimentality.

To Burns it was nothing of the kind. What marks him out as a great spirit—apart from the triumphant affirmations of his art—was the vision that he brought to bear on all creation. Everything that lived was a part of an intricate and delicate web, 'nature's social union'. For men to interfere with it, wilfully, was to destroy something unique, and to contribute inevitably to the coarsening of the human spirit itself.

Yet there he was, on that November day two centuries ago, going about the main work of man, which is to raise food for the nourishment of himself and his children: so that the generations might not vanish... And then, with hoof and share, a creature that has an equal right to breathe is unhoused, and in all probability marked for a cold and wretched death. The ploughman can do nothing about it, but wonder and sorrow, and think about the hazards of his own life.

The difference between the scientist and the artist is that the scientist thinks he has a right and a duty, in the name of humanity, to adjust the delicate web of creation as he thinks fit.

The artist celebrates the beauty and uniqueness of it. Sometimes, involuntarily, his finger might blunder into the web. It trembles, and is more beautiful than before.

The January Hurricane

25.1.1979

The days lengthen, perceptibly. I am writing this at 4.45pm; I can see, still, the dregs of light through the kitchen window. A month ago, all would have been pitch black at this time of afternoon.

The second great snowfall has packed and gone. The last crumb of snow has melted from the garden outside. Will there be a third snowfall before January is out? I think of last January's sudden annihilating blizzard, and tremble.

No doubt about it, January can produce the wildest weather of the year.

* * *

Twenty-seven Januaries ago, I was at Newbattle Abbey, in the gentle Lothian countryside. I was reading a book, or writing an essay, when an English boy came up to me and said, 'Poor Orkney, it got a terrible storm-battering last night!' (He had been listening to the wireless.)

'Pooh,' said I, 'Orkney gets battered by storm ten times a winter... '
And, immersed in words, I promptly forgot about it.

But soon everyone in the college was talking about the hurricane that had swept over Orkney the night before—a terrifying onslaught that came from the west in the darkness of night when, fortunately, everyone was in bed.

Henhouses had been blown out to sea. Small arks, they rose and fell among great waves, with cocks carolling aloft. And chimneyheads had been blown down, and haystacks scattered, and windows shattered by that fierce black breath!...

It seemed that something unusual had happened, even making allowances for the lurid colouring given to such phenomena by journalists and radio reporters.

* * *

I think, away back in 1959, I would have quite enjoyed that night-time tempest. (Even though my mother told me, in a letter, that a piece of flying metal had smashed my bedroom window at home and fallen on the bed!) Now, in 1979, I no longer wish such sensational storms to happen. My imagination, grown morbid, dwells on disintegrating bricks and bare rafters.

* * *

But even the mild Lothians had had a storm that night: through which we all slept soundly.

The pride of the beautiful Italian Garden was a massive beech tree, hundreds of years old. It seemed that only a slow withering through future centuries could kill it.

There, in the hush of next morning, the venerable beech lay level with the ground. An outrider of the Orkney storm had transfixed it in passing.

Strawberry Flavoured Ham Broth

1.2.1979

A friend arrived from Kirkwall about noon yesterday, just as I was finishing my ham-and-tomato-and-egg, toast and tea.

He brought with him a New Year dram, though it was January 24 and Burns Eve. We talked about this and that—stamps and strikes and the wintry air outside—and he took a little strawberryade (a relic of last summer) in his whisky.

It was good to see him. After an hour or so he left again for Kirkwall.

And I put the bottle with a remnant of strawberryade in it on the kitchen draining board.

* * *

From the Library window, in mid-afternoon that day, I saw a sudden whirl of flakes; it lasted a good ten minutes.

The street, when I set out once more with my shopping basket, had a light covering of swansdown.

I thought—How good my dinner's going to be around 6 o'clock— thick ham broth, and afterwards ham and buttered tatties!

And so, indeed, it turned out. A simple feast to keep the most rib-raking airs of winter out.

* * *

When I make a pot of broth, I make enough to last three days. The beauty of it is, the broth improves with keeping. On the third evening, it must be like the thick potage that they supped in the long halls of Birsay and Orphir a thousand years ago.

At dishwashing time, between two TV programmes, I thought of some way to make the ham broth better than ever before. Seeing some ale in the heel of a bottle, I poured that in. Seeing on the draining-board what seemed like the remnants of more ale, I decanted that into the pot too.

Suddenly, my nostrils were assailed by a sweet summer scent. I realised, too late, that I had poured a third of a cupful of strawberryade into the brothpot!

* * *

The third snowfall of winter came on Wednesday night.

What better, in such conditions, than to imitate the bear and sleep out the darkness and the cold next morning in a cave of warm down?

Unfortunately, by so doing, one is liable to miss the best of the day, for the light still does not last long.

As it turned out, I was almost dragged away from my weekly stint of letter-writing. The sun was going down over the Coolags of Hoy. The flood, broad and tranquil, poured through the Sound. The wind had blown last night's snow into curious formations—steep high-crested ridges with shallow valleys between. Sometimes the rubber boots sank deep; sometimes we walked on bare frosted road.

The sun died marvellously on the Coolag ridge, in leaping gold fountains, that dwindled, and were quenched at last. But Brinkie's Brae, and Orphir, and the highest farm in Graemsay, were laved still in a last tranquil light.

* * *

I arrived home and set about the interrupted letter-writing.

Halfway through, an immense hunger assailed me, sharpened by the winter air along that west coast.

I thought to myself: 'You're about to dine off something possibly unique in the history of gastronomy—ham broth, with a dash of strawberryade!'

Some time I may tell you what it tastes like. At the moment—as you can see—I am finishing my writing; the broth pot has not yet been put on to boil.

The kitchen window is a black square with a star or two in it.

A Confusion of Loyalties

8.2.1979

All the Stromness children of my age grew up loving everything about Scotland and its history.

That long gallery of heroes and tragic figures that touched the heart—Wallace, Bruce, James IV, Mary Queen of Scots, Charles I, Bonnie Prince Charlie!... There was endless delight and fascination in contemplating the achievements and fate of these rare legendary people.

How our ten-year-old hearts thrilled to the heroic deeds that were done, for example, at Bannockburn: King Robert cleaving the skull of De Bohun the reckless English knight; the 'schiltrum' formation like porcupines, that broke the English horsemen (those, that is, that had escaped the carefully laid spiked pits); the camp followers streaming downhill at the end of the day, that put the last ice of defeat in the veins of the English host as the long Johnsmas of 1314 drew to its bloody close...

It was not all history, either. Scotland had its modern heroes—the footballers who did battle each April at Hampden or at Wembley. Names like John Thomson, Alan Morton, Alex Jackson, Hughie Gallacher, Alex James, Jimmy McGrory we recited like a marvellous litany.

Of course we were Scottish boys. A sound of the distant bagpipes was the sweetest music imaginable—full of unutterable pathos, heroism, courtesy. As for Flodden and Culloden and the rest—these defeats were touched with high tragedy. For us, in a way, they achieved a beauty above victory.

* * *

As we got older, our horizons widened a little. We pored over *The Orkney Book* at slack end-of-term periods. There was an essay by Storer Clouston with words to the affect that Orkney, now a minor Scottish county, had once been a great medieval Earldom.

We discovered, further, that the Earl of Orkney had been as powerful as the King of Scots. Also, when the earldom began to crumble at last and the Scots took over, the change was frequently cruel and corrupt. We read about Robert Stuart and Black Pat his son, and their hangers-on.

It seemed that the Scots, great fighters for liberty, were no angels of light—to put it mildly—when they had a chance to oppress and rob weaker neighbours. We began to be proud of our Norse inheritance. We thought of ourselves as 'sons of the Vikings', which was true to a very limited extent, if at all.

We began to read, fascinated, the fragments of Dasent's translation of *The Orkneyinga Saga* from that same *Orkney Book* of 1909.

* * *

There was a great confusion of loyalties.

We had graduated to the study of British history in our school. The growth of the British Empire in two centuries was something that made us enormously proud. There, on the classroom wall, hung a map of the world. All the red patches—a quarter of the land surface—belonged to Britain. Each of us youngsters felt he was personally involved; one of the world's ruling elect, however poor and lowly.

* * *

Later, with adolescent eyes, seeing the poverty and unemployment everywhere in our great nation, many of us eagerly latched on to the idea of socialism—the vision of a worldwide brotherhood of free men, untouched ever again by war or material distress.

It was an innocent dream, but sincere.

* * *

With such a curious mixture of loyalties, how is a person in my situation—brought up between the two wars—to put his cross on March the first?[1]

---

1 The date of the first referendum on Scottish Devolution.

Tea by Daylight

15.2.1979

I am ashamed to say, I have never seen a sunrise for years until this morning. At about 8am, there in the sky between the two hills of Orphir, lay a reef of ore. The light flashed off a windless sea. The *Pole Star* was just leaving the harbour. Gulls planed and flashed past the window. The radiance grew in the east. Then, as often after dawn, the wind freshened and flawed the harbour water into stipplings and dapplings. Stromness, it seemed, had lost all its snow, except for a grey tatter here and there. But Orphir across the bay still wore a thin white mantle: lying supine, like the princess who slept so many years out in the fairy tale.

* * *

Who says February is a wretched month? It has that reputation: a trollop and filthy and the sooner gone the better.

But February has given us at least one peerless morning like this one.

And last night, in window boxes where I was visiting, the daffodils were thrusting up first green spears through an armour of month-old ice.

Outside, it is bitterly cold still. General Winter still has squadrons and battalions intact, but slowly they are being pushed back.

* * *

The other afternoon, too, as I was returning home with a loaded and highly expensive shopping basket, a lady said in passing: 'We're going to have tea by daylight tonight' ...

The light is growing rapidly. Whereas, six weeks ago, the sun set right between the Coolags and the Ward Hill of Hoy, these afternoons he trundles his golden chariot-wheel quite a distance along the line of the Coolags before sinking.

A few weeks more, and he will clear the Kame of Hoy and drop, muffling crimson and dark clouds about him, right into the sea.

February is not a grudging bitter little spinster at all—today she is a girl full of sweetness and promise...

I remember, like the lady on the street, how February half a century ago lit the paraffin lamp on the tea table: the frail soft circle of light fell over the scones and the bere bannocks, the oatcakes and butter and rhubarb jam—an ordinary family winter meal.

Then one afternoon/evening, at 5 o'clock—the statutory tea time in prewar days—February brought no lamp to the table.

The sense of delight, that the wheel of the year was bringing us among larks and lilies, was vivid even then.

The bread tasted of summer: no honey was ever so sweet as the rhubarb jam that had lain in a dark cupboard since the start of winter.

First Sight of Kirkwall

22.2.1979

Orkney children go to Norway and Italy and France nowadays, as if it was the most natural thing in the world. A generation ago, when we were boys, Kirkwall was as far as we dared hope for, once a year, in Couper's or Nicolson's bus.

Stromness being a sea-thirled place, it was easier to get to Hoy than to Kirkwall; for fishermen went back and fore every day, and other townsmen with boats.

* * *

I must have been about eight when my father said: 'We're going to Kirkwall tomorrow in the bus'... What excitement—it was as if he had said Cathay or Xanadu!—it was our first trip to Kirkwall.

My brother and I were dressed in Sunday suits next morning. Our pockets rang with pennies.

As Couper's bus rattled off from the Pier Head, no astronauts from Cape Kennedy could have been more tense and enthralled.

The fifteen-mile journey was pure rapture. Suddenly my father said, 'There's Kirkwall.' Our hearts turned over with joy and surprise. Perhaps we expected a bigger version of Stromness; not that sprawl of houses in the hollow about the Cathedral.

* * *

The first face we met almost, when we came entranced out of the bus, was a Kirkwall boy who used to spend part of his holidays in his grandparents' house in Melvin Place.

My brother and I gave him pennies out of our copper hoard. He came out of a peedie shop at the waterfront with a slice of melon as bright as a Negro's smile.

My father took us to visit the proprietor of the St Ola Hotel, a Stromness man called Andrew Johnston, an old friend of his. Munificence was everything that day. Andrew Johnston expressed his wonderment at seeing two small boys he had probably never clapped eyes on before; then he dug deep in his pocket and gave us twopence each!

* * *

The rest of that wonderful day I only vaguely remember. It must, I suspect, have been a confusion of sweets, ice cream, lemonade. The Kirkwall 'goodies' seemed, because of the novelty, infinitely tastier and more mysterious than what the Stromness shops sold.

All I really remember is a group of teenage boys conversing round a window in Albert Street, near the *Orkney Herald* shop. Their accents seemed strange to us. (Of course it is true that there is no single Orkney accent—each island and parish has its own peculiar utterance. It is easy enough, still, to tell a Kirkwall voice from the rest of Orkney.)

* * *

And I don't remember coming home Heavy with sweetmeats and wonderment, I wouldn't be surprised if we slept most of the way in the bus.

A Mutinous Brew

1.3.1979

Early in January, I discovered that my 'cellar' of home-brew was down to a last few bottles.

That would never do! Into the faithful old blue plastic bin went another dollop of malt, and a syrup compounded of boiled brown and white sugar. The yeast was sprinkled on. The mysterious whispering began. Next morning the brew had the noble mane of a lion.

The situation was saved, but only just.

I decided that there must never be such a low ebb again. The flood— so to speak—must be seeking into Hoy Sound even as the ebb uncovers the lowest of the harbour stones.

Two or three weeks ago I put down another brew. It seemed ordinary enough; except that perhaps I hadn't put in as much water as usual.

In such a winter as we've had, of course, a brew takes longer to ferment. It seemed that this one, after flaunting the tawny mane of a young lion on the first day, was not quickly going to assume the delicate Victorian lacework that is the secret signal—'Time to bottle'... There it lay, day after day, a spumy tarn, for a fortnight and more.

But at last it bore on its exquisite surface all the symptoms of good ale, ready to pass from bin to bottles.

Bottling is a rather tedious business; but one goads oneself on with thoughts of the relish and the rapture to come... At last the full bottles, all 25 of them, lay ranged in the cupboard, like soldiers new enlisted.

I saw, next day, that one or two of the bottles, held up to the light, were not 'clearing' as fast as they usually do. Perhaps the rubber bands on the stoppers had perished; in which case tighter stoppers would have to be used. The beer seemed cloudy and sluggish.

On opening two sample bottles in the sink, up came tawny fountains, with gouts of unworked yeast in them! They welled and welled, and a measure of the precious liquor was lost.

Of course the brew *WAS* very strong, and the frost was *VERY* cruel. Anything can happen in such circumstances.

Later I had, in order to save a major disaster, to open all the quarter hundred bottles. There they stand, uncorked, like disgraced soldiers waiting for the last mutinous ferment to work itself out. After which, they will be a brave and loyal little company, I hope.

Rats

8.3.1979

One day, soon after New Year, as I was writing at the kitchen table, I heard a sudden rustling from the direction of the sink.

What on earth could it be? I had never heard anything like that in my kitchen before. The rustling was swallowed up in silence. I concluded that some ball of rolled-up waste paper had opened in the warm breath of the fan heater, like a dry flower.

But no: next day the scraping was there again, and it was more insistent; and it was not the work of any discarded paper.

I had to face the possibility that there was a mouse loose in my kitchen somewhere. ('Not a rat!' I fervently prayed.)

The scratching and the scraping went on, intermittently. Bars of soap in the under-sink cupboard were scarred with nibblings.

One evening, late, I entered the kitchen, switched on the light, and two rodents scuttled behind the sink.

I ought to have known: those two shapes were more alert and sinister than mice...

My friend Stan arrived from Kirkwall one morning with a mousetrap. He baited it. We retired to the living room to give the intruders a chance... In five minutes or so the trap went off. Stan rushed into the kitchen. He called to me to bring a poker. 'It's a rat!' he said. The mousetrap had only dazed it. It retired, wounded and squealing, behind the sink.

I must have been grey in the face with dread.

Within an hour I had reported this invasion at the Town House. There I was given a poke of poison granules, which has, it seems, the effect of rendering the rats haemophilic; so that at the least knock or scratch they bleed to death. Also a proper rat-trap was provided—as wicked-looking a cage as ever I saw.

I could write many pages about these rats. How, for example, did they get into a new council house, and one which isn't even on the ground floor?...

I set two heaped ashtrays of poison, one in the cleaning cupboard under the sink, and one in the cupboard where I keep pots. They began to gorge themselves in secret from the first plate; they ignored the second. They must have had two immense meals a day for two days. I could hear them crunching with relish.

Thereafter the scratching and scuttling at the back of the sink gradually diminished. There was one last little scamper one afternoon as I sat writing. Thereafter, silence.

I have not heard them for many days.

This week a joiner has come and blocked in the open back of the kitchen unit, and the little orifice through which they had got into the kitchen, and some other place up in the attic. And my neighbours have been given the same security.

I hope we will not have another such visitation.

A Deluge of Books

15.3.1979

At last it had become positively dangerous, the mountain of unshelved books lying on top of the full bookcases in my living room.

They had gradually got piled up there over the years, without order or system (since I had long run out of shelf space). Higher and higher the precipice of books climbed up the wall, until they had begun to usurp the space of the pictures—G.S.Robertson's 'The Storm', Ian MacInnes' drawing of Robert Rendall, Rowena Murray's 'Maeshowe Runes'.

It had come to the stage that, if I was to attempt to select a book out of that lot, the whole tottering edifice might collapse in an avalanche. I used to say to visitors who marvelled at that high-piled chaos, that a few centuries on, diggers into the archaeology of Mayburn would discover a skeleton—me—under a heap of mouldy paper and the dust of words.

So I decided to do something about it before 1978 was out. It took the whole of one afternoon to pile into black bags the scores of books I knew I would not want to read again.

At the end of the task, the bookshelves looked neat and trim again.

I began to think about those I had kept: books given by friends, signed copies from authors, books that I loved dearly and others that once I had had a fleeting affection for.

Were some of them really so important? How often, in the course of the next decade (say) would they ever be opened and pored on, with amazement or delight? The answer is, sadly, hardly at all.

One of the sad things that time brings (as Wordsworth knew) is the gradual deadening of this nerve of wonder and joy that every child has for a few years, 'trailing clouds of glory'...

I remember the delight I once had in books—the very feel and smell of the pages were an excitement. All that has long since vanished. Occasionally, three or four times a year, some new book communicates a tepid warmth.

So, all the thousand books in my house could go, without any lasting regret on my part. I would, however, insist on keeping the works of Thomas Mann, E.M.Forster, A.E.Housman, Evelyn Waugh, Bertolt Brecht, J.L.Borges; plus a thousand or so poems, plays, ballads, translations, songs.

The Full Moon and the Town

22.3.1979

I was sitting up late, going over some manuscripts, early last Tuesday morning, when the Anglepoise light went out; and also, of course, the electric fire. The only thing to do was to light a candle stuck in a wine bottle, and stumble up to bed without a hot water bottle.

* * *

I have just been reading in the Stromness column of *The Orcadian* about how beautiful the town looked under the full moon that morning, without the electric street lamps.

This was an enchantment granted to us half a century ago for a few nights every month. It was not, I think, that the Town Council was moved by any aesthetic considerations; saving a penny or two on the rates was what mattered.

In those days the lamplighter went through the street in the gathering dusk, putting his long pole with the bead of light at the end of it into the gas lamps, one after the other. With a soft hiss the lamps threw out their spheres of light, and the dwindled circles intersected all the way along the street, from Ness Road to Hillside Road.

But Stromness Town Council saw to it that the light of the moon was not wasted. For two or three nights, while the moon was at the full, the lamplighter had a brief respite. The moon did his work for him.

What poetry went into that work! It was as if the full moon and the town were made for each other. The moon spread its silver and blue web over the piers and closes, and it was a masque of sheer enchantment. In return the harbour held its mirror up to the moon, and the water-image was, if anything, even more beautiful than the 'queen and huntress' of the night.

To walk about in Stromness on those nights of full moon was a lovely experience. The people moved in a hushed spell. Voices sounded pure in the silver and blue dapple. Cats seemed even more at home than people; but then there has always been an ancient bond between cats and the moon.

So, I wish I could have walked about in Stromness the other night, to experience once more one of the lost delights of being a Stromnessian. If only I had remembered that the moon was full!

Perhaps the Hydro-Electric might consider letting the street lamps alone once every twenty-eight nights.

Two Centuries on

29.3.1979

Imagine some compiler of a gazetteer writing about Orkney places some time in the 22nd century.

He comes to the letter S: Sanday, Sandwick, Shapinsay, Stenness, Stroma, Stromness.

There are a few statistics and notes to be written about all these places, except the last, which is completely derelict and uninhabited.

Still, he reasons, it was a valid, vivid, and viable place at one time; so a little description might be in order.

He writes as follows:

'At the beginning, there must have been only a few fishermen's huts along the west shore of Hamnavoe. There was a little monastery, further up the coast. The laird sat in his castle at Cairston; he drew his rents, and complained about the exactions of bishop or earl, and kept a watchful eye on the sea (from which danger invariably came).

'A man called William Clark built an inn at the end of the long blue tongue of sea. There were bigger and bigger ships anchoring and provisioning in the harbour now, from all the ports of Europe.

'A village began to grow. The Stromness merchants had their own ships and piers and cargoes at last. They ventured eastwards to Norway and Holland.

'In the 15th century they produced the pirate Gow and the hero Graham and the sea-witch Bessie Millie.

'The young men of Orkney went west from Stromness to the trading posts of Canada and to the whales of the Arctic. World-famous ships, Cook's and Franklin's, drew water from Stromness wells. The Stromness water had always had a special sweetness and purity.

'The village grew into a little town: the builders built functionally, without any aesthetic considerations. Here is a mystery; utility and beauty went hand in hand through the growing town. Nowhere in the world was there such an untidy sweet sea-loving salt steep place.

'The people born and bred in Stromness never forgot the place of their origin, no matter where they put their roots in later life. The generations returned, again and again...

'But it came to a sudden end. Now the only inhabitants are the guide and the few summer tourists who make the melancholy pilgrimage among the ruins of crumbling piers and choked closes.

'One might ask, if Alexander Graham had lived in the 1970s, could this thing have happened?'

'The Cleansing of the Knife'

5.4.1979

I am rarely excited by the fairly large number of books of modern verse that I read. (I say verse, advisedly, rather than poetry.) So much of it seems to be explorations of the ego. That could of course be interesting, if the ego itself was interesting; but in many cases it does not seem to be, particularly.

Furthermore, the standard of workmanship in verse is not what it used to be. In the old days, at least, the versifier had to rhyme, and use some kind of patterned metre. But now anything goes. Words are tumbled out on the page, and called 'poetry'. There is a delight in watching a real craftsman at work, whether in wood, metal, clay, pigment, or words.

I think of Robert Rendall. He wrote maybe a dozen or a score of great lyrics; which is enough for any poet to have done. But even in his less successful poems he was always a fine craftsman, so that it is a constant joy to see how well his sonnets and other poems are put together.

The 19th-century American poet Walt Whitman has much to answer for. It was Walt Whitman who inaugurated 'free verse', as if verse up to then had been in chains. Walt Whitman opened the door; three or four generations of versifiers have rushed through, and made unbelievable messes of our beautiful language.

To write this 'free verse', the poet must have an impeccable ear and an unerring sense of rhythm. Whitman himself had it; so did such 'free verse' writers as D.H.Lawrence and (to a lesser extent) Ezra Pound. Lacking this flawless sense of how language sounds and moves, a writer founders in words and is lost.

To write excellently in 'free verse' is more difficult by far than to proceed by the old strict means of rhyme and stanza-form.

* * *

Technical matters have carried me far away from what I set out to write; which is, that the only book of poetry to excite me lately has been published by a poet in her 82nd year.

Naomi Mitchison is no stranger to Orkney. She has attended the first two St Magnus Festivals, and is coming again in June. I hope she can be prevailed on to read parts of *The Clearsing of the Knife*.

That is the name of her book. There are two major large poems in it—the title poem and another superb piece about a night at the herring fishing off the west coast of Scotland.

This is poetry as it, I feel, ought to be—a clean wind that takes the dust and the cobwebs from the soul's nooks—an outpouring of light and joy. In old age a good poet is still young at heart.

The workmanship is of the highest quality, too.

I think Orcadian readers of poetry will be delighted by this volume; for the land's and the sea's essences are in it.

Air and Light

12.4.1979

The beginning of April. Surely April will give us some of the sweets of Spring, after the drab Summer of '78, the grim Winter, the reluctant early Spring...

The morning did not seem to know how it was going to behave. The early afternoon faltered into sunshine. But great grey clouds moved, with cargoes of rain on them.

Four of us drove in Dave Brock's car, by Heddle and Germiston and Scapa, across the Barriers to South Ronaldsay. We took the South Cara road that looks down on the red lingering wreck of the *Irene*: then turned off down a steep road that seems for a second or two as if it is going to plunge straight into the sea. But no, it ends between a little cottage and a farm steading.

Inured to cold, I was surprised at the first kindling sun-warmth when we got out of the car.

We walked along the sea banks towards the manse where the great 19th-century eccentric, Rev John Gerard, lived. It is a lovely gracious house, still.

But below, where two summers ago was a little curving beach of immaculate white sand, today there were only rocks and stones. That's how sand behaves. An easterly gale will give the beach back its billions of grainings.

Another foretaste of summer: Dave plunged into that cold water for the first dip of the year.

We drove westwards in mid-evening. I should not attempt to describe the marvellous changing sky of that day. It would take an air-and-light poet like Shelley to do it justice.

Hoy and the west were curtained with a long dark cloud, fringes of rain falling from it. Stromness might well be surging and throbbing with wetness.

Then the rain-curtain over Hoy was suffused with a pool of light, as if the sun had bored a golden finger into it.

Rain and sun were putting on a breathtaking ballet. In Orphir, silver raindrops spattered the car windows. Then, on the moor, a perfect rainbow stood, and glowed, and faded.

And then the western sky cleared. The sun had the sky to itself for its setting. The magnificent clouds had shifted into the south a little.

Somebody in the car mentioned Turner. And, indeed, if it required a Shelley to celebrate the first sky of April in words, Turner would have been the man to paint that shifting gold and black evanescent glory.

Life on Earth

19.4.1979

So there they were, our ape-cousins, some time on December 31 according to the vast timescale of life on earth—there they were on the grass plains of Africa, picking seeds and insects and berries. And one would rear himself up on his hind legs from time to time, and scan the horizon for lions or elephants.

They were so bright, they thought of tools and weapons. Hunting in groups with their clubs, they could bring down bison or antelope. They could tear the hide away with sharp stones; they could cut the meat into slices.

Their faces could express, as no other animals, the many emotions that surged through them—an eloquent play of eyebrow and mouth. Their lips could utter a far greater scale of sound than any other creature. (Words and language were just around the corner.) They scratched symbols on the rocks that were understood by all; the first writing. In the dark caves they drew pictures of the hunt—the beast with the pointed sticks in its flank, the hunters all around in a dance. Out of this kind of sympathetic magic—man imagining the successful outcome of the hunt before the event—came at last Leonardo and Rembrandt and Picasso.

Thereafter—given those simple beginnings—man's technology accelerated with frightening speed; and the acceleration is still going on, faster and faster. And who knows what the end of this creature will be?

We live in a time when the possibilities are endless and awesome.

* * *

I am referring above to that marvellous TV series, *Life on Earth*. We watched the last episode the other evening, in the Braes Hotel, while all around local ladies were engaged in a darts tournament.

The reception on BBC2 was poor everywhere that night, on account of weather conditions. The picture was there all right, but sometimes it disintegrated into a whirl of coloured dots. But we watched and listened, quite enthralled; and occasionally took a sip of beer.

Thereafter, the politicians on the election hustings provided thin fare.

We went out into a dreary wet cold night.

What group of 'homo sapiens' in a skin and wattle boat first had the courage to set foot on the bleak, black Orkneys, on such a night as this?

A Sea Anthology

26.4.1979

I am going to try, in the next week or two, to put together an anthology about Orkney and the sea, for speaking aloud[1].

It is of course such a rich subject that the difficulty will be just what to leave out.

There are the famous passages from the *Orkneyinga Saga*—St Magnus' last voyage to Egilsay—the Viking crusade from 1151 to 1154—one of Sweyn Asleifson's piratical cruises.

1 Verse and Prose for the 'Johnsmas Foy' (Midsummer Festival), St Magnus Festival, 1979.

There is the sad and touching story of the death of the little Queen of Scotland, Margaret, on passage from Norway.

There's Bessie Millie, the Stromness woman who sold favourable winds to sailors, and Sir Walter Scott's visit to her in 1814.

There is the tragic wealth of wrecks; one of which landed on Westray a little nameless Russian boy, to whom the islanders gave the name 'Angel'. There is that graphic description, on BBC tape, of the wreck of the *Shakespeare* at Breckness, by the late Tom Wishart, then a young member of the lifeboat crew.

There are the two Johns from Stromness: (1) John Gow the pirate, hanged in 1726, (2) John Renton, shanghaied in San Francisco, who later lived among cannibals in the Solomon Islands, and returned to die in those dangerous waters.

Then there are many fine imaginative sea pieces. I think of Eric Linklater's description of a regatta in the 1930s, and his tempest scene from *The Men of Ness*. There is Edwin Muir's long poem 'The Voyage', which is shot through with magnificent passages. And what about the piece from Muir's *Autobiography* in which the young Deerness girl (his mother, I think) was sitting at home alone when the room slowly filled with foreign sailors streaming with salt water...

In quieter mood, there is Robert Rendall's *Orkney Shore*.

One will have to choose carefully among a multitude of selkie stories.

I remember, too, what pleasure I got from some of the shore essays in *The Orkney Book* of 1909.

* * *

The trouble will be to choose right, where there is so much to choose from; so that an audience of miscellaneous tourists and Orcadians will not become bored, in June.

The Great Times

10.5.1979

We used, as boys, to delight in the slow chorus of the old men as they sat smoking in the tailor shop, or the saddler's; or in summer on a sun-warmed wall.

It was like a litany for a vanished Golden Age, which they had known in their youth. But alas! They had fallen at the last on shoddy degenerate days.

Nothing was the same as it had been—nothing.

'You don't get a smoke out of a wooden pipe like you did from the old clay pipe. There was a jar of clay pipes on the pub counter. You could pick one up for nothing...'

'Winter—I mind the real winters, when the snow was up to the eaves. The farmers could drive their carts across the Loch of Stenness...'

'Whisky, twelve-and-six a bottle! A disgrace. In Maggie Marwick's in "The White Horse", a bottle cost two-and-six, and you got a full glass of whisky along with it, lippan full, free...'

'Oh, them long ago summers! Sun shining for three months on end. Bare feet on the warm flagstones. Poor grey trashy things of summers nowadays!'

That's the kind of thing they used to say, to impress us boys. The Lammas Market, that we thought so magical in early September—it was, it seemed, a poor tattered remnant of a once mighty Fair.

So it went on and on. Everything had been better half a century back. The stars shone brighter, a westerly gale was more frightening and heroic by far, bread and beer were sweeter and more wholesome in the mouth, the people one and all were real characters; life was altogether a richer thing...

* * *

So, we boys were left marvelling. It seemed we had missed the great times. How wonderful it must have been to live in the year 1890! And yet, in 1930, life was still enjoyable enough, if you were young.

I think some of the world's great literature has come out of this 'remembrance of things past'—*The Iliad* and *The Odyssey*, Shakespeare's historical plays, Wordsworth's and Edwin Muir's poetry, and a host of other immortal works.

It is not that old men and poets are liars. They are sifters of the grain from the chaff—the pure gold from the dirt. They celebrate what is worth remembering; and, themselves growing old and feeble, they feel the grey draughts sieving in through every chink, and conclude that life is not at all what it used to be, or what it ought to be.

That is why, when I feel angry or outraged about the materialism and violence and utter superficiality of the times—and think then of the simple, humorous, poor, uncomplaining, hardworking folk of the 1930s, I think it best to hold my tongue.

For it must be that this decade has qualities and virtues that I am blind to.

Two Kinds of Pirate

17.5.1979

It is a morning of hard, brilliant sunshine as I sit writing this at the kitchen table, having cleared away the breakfast dishes and thrown the empty eggshell into the bin.

We are so starved of sunlight that I long to be out on the street, or down some pier, or sitting in a garden. But there is a cold south-easterly blowing, and to linger anywhere would chill you to the bone.

We have become acquainted with cold for almost a twelvemonth now. We yearn, as rarely before, for warmth and light. The light is here today, a great outpouring well of brightness; but, except in a sheltered corner here and there, the air is like a whetted knife.

For the first time, ever, I think longingly of Spain and Greece. But I will have to settle for less farflung places, a Perthshire lochside and the wynds and classical squares of Edinburgh.

* * *

Going through this growing collection of Orkney poems and prose-pieces about the sea and sailors, one or two things perhaps call for comment.

It is surprising, for example, to discover how little Edwin Muir wrote about the sea in his poetry. His is the writing of an earth worker, a peasant, with the ancient wisdom of the soil grained into it. The single exception, almost, is 'The Voyage'.

And I was delighted to rediscover some Robert Rendall pieces I had quite forgotten. One cannot drag 'The Fisherman' and 'Cragman's Widow' into every recital. There, in his penultimate volume, *Shore Poems*, are at least two equally good, the sonnet 'The Beachcomber', and an eight-liner, 'Angle of Vision'.

One can hardly keep Gow out of such a programme. He was, to put him in as good light as possible, an ill-starred young man. He was also as blackhearted a villain as ever sailed the oceans. There is little likelihood that any future Stromness housing scheme will be called Gow Terrace. And yet we honour and laud men like Sweyn Asleifson and Sir Francis Drake, whose piratical acts were every bit as shameless as Gow's. Sweyn killed men with as little compunction as Gow. The difference is, Sweyn (and Drake, too) had a going relationship with the powers that be, the establishment; whereas Gow operated, so to speak, in the sewers, where the air is always more dangerous.

The moral is, perhaps: if you want to behave badly, and yet be honoured in centuries to come, see first that you have important friends.

* * *

The wells of light brim and brim. There's hardly a cloud in the brilliant blue dome. East wind or no, I must get up and out.

Boat and Train

24.5.1979

The modern ego demands its holiday at least once a year; otherwise it will go to seed, in some way or another.

Since I hadn't really been out of Orkney for more than two years, it seemed that some deterioration might take place if I didn't get away fairly soon. (And yet most of the world's population in the past—apart from soldiers, sailors, and gypsies—had to spend all their lives rooted in one place. The other side of the hill, the other shore of the Sound, were alien territory.)

But, increasingly over the last century, we must suffer ourselves to be shifted here and there over the earth's surface; otherwise we are thought to be droll, or akin to vegetables.

* * *

In order not to be thought droll, one recent Monday morning I found myself on the *Ola*. We left the pier and the quiet harbour water. Midway through Hoy Sound, the *Ola* acknowledged the open Atlantic with a nod and a curtsy; the first of many.

There was a fair number of passengers, known and unknown. The morning was grey, but there was elusive ore in the southern sky. We might be moving into sunshine. (The day before, Sunday, spring had come suddenly; hours of unexpected warmth and radiance after the long austerities of early spring. Today, even on the sea, there was a new warmth in the air.)

With rolls and heaves, a few of them quite thrilling, the *Ola* brought us past the magnificence of Hoy to the sheltered waters of Caithness.

* * *

From Thurso, it was the long train journey to central Perthshire; through the austere moorland of Caithness and then among the snow-patched mountains of Sutherland, Inverness-shire, Perthshire.

The scenery becomes ever more beautiful as the train seeks into the heart of Scotland. Always the tendency is upwards, until the patches of snow are just across the scree-strewn hollows. A little solitary farm or cottage appears; and one thinks, 'In no part of Orkney is there a lonelier dwelling than that!'

At Pitlochry Station, at 7pm, our friends were waiting with their car, which brought us along the south shore of Loch Tummel to our destination, Frenich, bright with hundreds of daffodils.

Under Schiehallion

31.5.1979

Mungo, the great grey deerhound, died a few months ago, aged ten. (That, it seems, is a fair age for such pureblooded creatures, who are delicate in spite of their great power.) No longer will Mungo come up from the burn on the trees and thud across the library floor and ease his exquisite bulk down in front of the log fire at Frenich.

Mungo lies buried at Loch Tummel, beside the two shy Abyssinian cats who predeceased him, Tobias and Clinker, under a willow tree.

But now Mungo has a successor, a young dog of the same breed, still under half a year old. Appin is his name. Being young, he is as full of energy as if a spring wind is blowing through him all the time. Appin is enormously friendly to everyone, known and stranger. His favourite greeting is to seize your fingers, all five of them, in his powerful jaws; but gently, as though he is kissing butterflies.

* * *

The cold wind has blown all through the month of May; sometimes crested with a grey rain, sometimes giving the fugitive sun an extra burnish.

On an afternoon of sun and wind we had a picnic beside the rushing mountain waters of the River Tummel, under trees wearing the first delicate tracery of this tardy spring. Pâté and bran rolls and cans of beer: all had an extra relish in that cold high air.

Coming back, we made a wide circuit of hills and waters. Then, through a gap, we saw the long blue gleam of Loch Tummel. We dropped down, to the beautiful house adrift in its sea of daffodils; and Appin's welcome, delicate jaws folding the fingers.

Everywhere, we were guarded by the magnificent mountain, Schiehallion.

* * *

Not many hours later, in torrential rain, our new friend Andrew drove us from Perthshire to Edinburgh, just when the shops and offices were closing, and the streets were choked with cars... Through a high window, Arthur's Seat and Holyrood and Salisbury Crags; and the marquees going up for a royal garden party in General Assembly week.

Under Arthur's Seat

7.6.1979

After a long interval, one forgets how beautiful Edinburgh can be at this time of year.

Returning to Edinburgh University from Orkney twenty years ago, for the summer term, the new delicate green on the trees, the first blossoms in a hundred gardens, made us northerners pause in wonder.

And the people too, after the snow of winter and the austerities of spring, seemed like new free creatures as they moved through the streets and the Meadows.

* * *

So it was again, this May: except that one did not have the burden of textbooks and exams on one's mind. The greatest joy of all was to meet, at unexpected corners, old half-forgotten friends. After the mutual shock of grey hairs and extra wrinkles, laughter and old memories washed away two decades of time's subtle and secret workings... Then a drink or two rekindled old fires.

* * *

But the endless walking on hard stone streets—the sudden hesitations and spurts to negotiate the endless flow of traffic on busy crossroads!—These are wearing to the body and the spirit... One drops into a picture gallery or coffee-house to rest one's back. Then out again to the hurly-burly, the helter-skelter, the crowds and the exhaust fumes.

But all around, the fountains of early summer are rising, green and delicate.

* * *

The weather pattern has remained the same, day after day: broad patches of blue sky, among high remote dove-grey clouds, rounded and heraldic like thunderheads. There were long periods of sun. Sporadically, a few drops of rain fell. One afternoon there were rollings and mutterings of thunder.

* * *

I have not seen TV or heard a radio for a fortnight, and I haven't missed them at all. Yesterday (Saturday), at home in Orkney I would have been watching eagerly the England–Scotland football match. Instead I sat in a garden under the Braid Hills idly turning pages of a manuscript.

In the evening we drove to Cramond Village, with its white houses. The tide was far out, a sea-haar moved in from the east. The shrunken River Almond kept its river-smells... Driving home, Edinburgh showed us all its classical splendours in the last of the sun.

A Quiet Crossing

14.6.1979

Waking up in the hotel in Helmsdale on the Thursday morning, it looked ominous. After the sun-splashed Wednesday, a cold grey light seeped through the bedroom window, and occasionally rain lashed the roof. Great trucks and lorries went past, water zipping from their tyres.

I don't like a large breakfast, usually; but on holiday the stomach can take an unwanted amount, and enjoy it. (Besides, no one dares the Pentland Firth on an empty stomach.)

It is a most beautiful road that goes from Sutherland into Caithness: Berriedale. On a clear day, there are those breathtaking valleys and eastward seascapes, and the road wanders perilously up and down among grand houses and little hamlets.

But today the upper landscape was scarfed in mist, and the sea was blotted out. The cars and lorries we met had yellow eyes to pierce the fog. And yet this haar invests everything in mystery; one realises how the Celtic tales came into being, with their magic of giants and small folk and ghosts. Quite suddenly, that mountain road becomes a moor road. Through the flatlands of Caithness we sped towards Thurso and Scrabster.

There the *Ola* was, fast at her pier. A thin cold smirr moved everywhere. I cast a worried look at the choppy inner harbour. If there were waves in this haven, what might we not expect in the open Pentland?

It so happened that it was perhaps the smoothest passage I ever had. We moved, it seemed, through a vast grey quiet seacloud. Once I looked out: darkness lay ahead. I thought, another ten minutes and rain will take over from haar... Then I realised that it was Hoy looming up, and suddenly the Old Man was there, cold tatters about him; as if to say, 'Welcome back'...

A young Australian photographer said, 'I have to take pictures of the wildlife of Orkney in the next two days—I hope the weather's going to improve!' Fortunately for him, and for all of us, the next day was as bright and warm as anything we are likely to see in this beginning summer of 1979. (I had comforted the photographer that in Orkney we are subject to bewildering variations in the weather, from hour to hour.)

I found a scattering of letters behind the front door, a 2½ weeks' accumulation, that kept me reading late into the afternoon.

'Solstice of Light'

28.6.1979

What a shame!—here I sit on the afternoon of the longest day; and outside the rain is bucketing down. It has bucketed down since I got up, and it looks like bucketing down for the next twelve hours or so... The sky is an unrelieved wash of grey, with not a thread or fissure of silver anywhere.

Not much point in climbing up Brinkie's Brae tonight, to see the over-brimming of the year's well of light. (No, actually the over-brimming takes place at noon: at midnight, in the north, comes the magical joining of the fires of sunset and dawn.)

Today there will be nothing doing: greyness at noon, a darker grey at midnight. This, it seems, is not going to be a memorable solstice.

Yet one hopes. There is some sort of dispute as to whether 21st June or 22nd June actually has the most light in it; a couple of lustrous drops more or less in the well.

So, tomorrow the huge rain cloud might have vanished across the North Sea, and the green and blue and gold be everywhere; and we will, after all, be able to welcome the Solstice with joy.

* * *

But if that isn't possible, at least art triumphs over the churlishness of weather.

On a few mornings last July, I happily threw together a few lines and rhythms and images that I thought might go well with music, and sent them to my friend Peter Maxwell Davies in Rackwick. I was so uncertain of the words that I couldn't even think of a title for the sequence. In no long time, Maxwell Davies replied by letter that he would indeed like to set the words for the 1979 St Magnus Festival. And some time later he suggested a title, 'Solstice of Light'.

The result I heard for the first time in St Magnus on Tuesday evening. I have rarely been more deeply moved. The words were transfigured by the music and the music-makers. The midsummer of 1979 had been given a beauty that had not existed in Orkney before.

* * *

So, whatever the weather today or tomorrow, art has triumphed.

Another first performance at the Festival—which, alas, I could not hear—was Judith Weir's 'King Harald Sails to Byzantium'. It was just those triumphs of art and artifice—the golden domes and the mosaics—that must have astonished the men from the bleak cold cultureless north... The poet W.B.Yeats, bending under the first grey winds of time, realised that he could be sure only of the things made by craft and imagination. 'Therefore' (he sang), 'I have sailed the seas and come / To the holy city of Byzantium'.

Kirkwall, for a brief hour, was Byzantium last Tuesday evening.

PS—The rain took off, after all, on the 21st. But, after a spell of sunlight, it was towards a huge blue-black reef of clouds that we drove near midnight, with one long fissure of gold in the north-west, beyond Brodgar.

Place Names

5.7.1979

There is a constant fascination in place names.

I was sitting idly in the sun the other afternoon when, seemingly out of the blue, the words 'Orkney Islands' came into my mind. A waste of syllables, really; since Orkney itself means Orc islands. The fault is what is called, I think, tautology. (Whether 'Orc' means whale, or seal, or boar, I leave to the experts to decide.)

That's not the only tautology in our list of place names. 'Houton Head'—the Hout part itself signifies headland (like Howth promontory outside Dublin).

Another misnomer is Brough of Birsay. Possibly the whole parish derives its name from the tidal island where there was originally a keep or fortification of some kind.

The very south end of Stromness is called the Point of Ness; which is to say, 'the point of the point', Ness meaning a piece of land thrusting into the sea: in this case, into the tiderace of Hoy Sound. That is why Stromness is called what it is. Living in the town itself, this is not so obvious. But coming down the Scorradale road into Orphir, there it lies, a thrust of hard land into the wide strong waters. (Maybe the Norseman who gave Stromness its name was looking west one day from the Orphir foothills.)

* * *

Then there are the unfortunate misnomers. Papa Westray is called by the folk of the north isles Papey (isle of Celtic priests) to this day. This is a case where popular usage preserves an original purity.

When did Rinansay become North Ronaldsay? Here the popular usage faltered, somewhere back in time. A beautiful name was lost.

There is the mystery of the islands called after forgotten great men. Who was the Rognvald of Ronaldsay? Who was the Garek of Gairsay? Who was the Grim of Graemsay? Who was the Rolf of Rousay?

'They have all gone into the dark,' as T.S.Eliot said. It took an obscure Irish soldier, a Peninsular veteran, to impress his name on a new place, Finstown—and none of the lairds or commissioners or ministers could do anything about it.

Another lost name: 'Hrossey', the island of the horse. This was originally the name of our largest island which we call now, insipidly, 'Mainland'.

* * *

Another hundred years, perhaps, and our grandchildren will have replaced all the names with numbers.

Where Are the Suns of Yesteryear

12.7.1979

It's no use getting angry. Anger will get us nowhere. I admit that one or two mornings, when I got up to see bleakness and rain outside, I shouted 'Scum!' at the elements. The elements are neither shamed nor encouraged by any attitudes we strike.

I am referring to the summer, into whose kingdom we have wandered once more, with feelings of dejection and disappointment. It looks, with every precious day that passes, as though we might be in for another poor season.

Those in the know agree with our apprehensions. I read in a newspaper the other day a gloomy prediction for the rest of the summer. The icecaps, it seems, are growing. Therefore the cold boreal winds are being squeezed southwards; and the British Isles lie directly in the path of the grey air streams.

The children seem to take the cold summer days quite cheerfully; young flesh can accommodate itself to almost anything the weather can bestow. The snow of winter, the sun of summer, are poised and equal and opposite delights. Even this patchwork weather is acceptable to them.

It's only we old ones who go about the draughty street complaining: 'Oh, we didn't have weather like this when we were young!'... And we never tire of evoking the Eden-like image of us roaming here and there, from hill to beach, with bare feet, summer-long...

Maybe the weather pattern is changing, rapidly and drastically, for the worse. In which case, we will have to hoard every sunny day like a miser hoarding gold coins in his purse. Every wild flower and every birdsong will be emblems against oblivion. (In days of shortages and rationing, people in many ways show a side to their character which affluence has coarsened and atrophied.)

But winter: what of that? Last winter was a drab, miserable affair. Is that to be the pattern for the next decade of winters?

Meantime the world's oil reserves are running out. In spite of what Orcadians may think, 'uranium' and 'nuclear power' are words increasingly used in high places. 'Forward though we canna see, we guess and fear,' like Burns contemplating the ruin of the mouse's cell.

Forgive the above gloomy sentences. Forgive them especially if today is beautiful, after a warm yesterday and the probability of a blue-and-yellow tomorrow... We are only on the threshold of summer and it may yet be full of treasures and delights.

The Pier Arts Centre

19.7.1979

We had seen it taking shape gradually for years—the Pier Arts Centre—and we could guess what a beautiful place it would be; and what an asset to the town and the islands.

First of all it was a merchant's store, built long-wise down the pier, with—at right angles to it—a street-facing house. The old Stromness merchant family of Shearers owned the premises. In the town's heyday, they dealt in many lines of business, and they had their own sailing ships for importing and exporting.

Worthy old buildings in the local tradition. Nothing much more would have been claimed for them.

But then the imagination got to work on them. First Sylvia Wishart the artist turned the store into a beautiful house and studio. The ground floor was a private hostel; summer hostellers can hardly have had a more charming place to wake up and cook their breakfast in, or to return to at the end of a long day among the hills and islands.

The imagination went further still. Margaret Gardiner could see, in this little complex, a unique place to house her collection of paintings and sculpture, which she was determined to donate to the islands in which she had lived so long. Her architects rose splendidly to the occasion.

* * *

On Saturday afternoon the dream was realised. It turned out to be a lovely day—in spite of the TV weather forecast. It was almost as if the elements were putting their seal on the exploit. The sun lay bright and warm on the pier where the scores of guests were assembled. There was traditional Orkney music. The chief guests arrived by sea: how other, since in an important sense the harbour is the real thoroughfare of Stromness, especially to people harassed and bullied, deafened and half-stifled, by contending streams of cars...

The wine and savouries in the Stromness Hotel, during the opening speeches, were delightful; and filled my evening at home with a slow languor.

There is no doubt that works of art will look beautiful in those small exquisite chambers, with the sea-lights playing over them. Works conceived and wrought in Cornwall will be quite at home in this setting. I remember how Naomi Mitchison's poetry-reading a few weeks back was enhanced by the gentle sea-sounds all around. And Saturday's music was touched with the sea magic also.

The Pier Arts Centre could be a fit dwelling for all the muses.

Also by George Mackay Brown from Steve Savage Publishers

Letters from Hamnavoe

A paperback edition of the first collection of George Mackay Brown's articles in *The Orcadian*.

'*Letters from Hamnavoe* was first published in 1975, but time has not diminished its pleasure ... There is humour, wit, a playful—sometimes self-mocking—irony in many of these letters ... There is also pure poetry.'

—Margery Palmer McCulloch, *Times Literary Supplement*

ISBN 1-904246-01-X

Paperback. RRP £7.50.

Rockpools and Daffodils

(a Gordon Wright title)

Published in 1992, *Rockpools and Daffodils* is the third collection drawn from George Mackay Brown's weekly column in *The Orcadian*.

'Each essay is coloured by the "sounds and delicate pulsating of nature", the "astonishing weather", the "horizon hazy with haar", the autumn on a "wild raging slut of a day". Read this book and discover the poet, his sources and his muse. You won't be disappointed.'

—*The Scots Magazine*

ISBN 0-903065-76-2

Hardcover. 28 colour photographs. RRP £14.95.

Available from bookshops or directly from the publisher.

For information on mail order terms, see our website (www.savagepublishers.com) or write to: Mail Order Dept., Steve Savage Publishers Ltd., The Old Truman Brewery, 91 Brick Lane, LONDON, E1 6QL.